The Rt Hon. Lord Hurd o[...]
tinguished career in gove[...]
was educated at Eton and Trinity College, Cambridge, where
he obtained a first-class degree in history. After joining the
Diplomatic Service, he went on to serve at the Foreign Office
before running Edward Heath's private office from 1968 to
1970 and acting as his Political Secretary at 10 Downing Street
from 1970 to 1974. Following terms as Minister of State in the
Foreign Office and the Home Office, he became Secretary of
State for Northern Ireland, then Home Secretary before his
appointment as Foreign Secretary in 1989. He was MP for
Mid-Oxfordshire (later Witney) from 1974 until 1997. He is
now Chairman of the Prison Reform Trust charity.

Douglas Hurd, who is the author of ten books, lives in
Oxfordshire with his wife Judy and their son and daughter.
He has three grown-up sons.

# VOTE
# TO KILL

## Douglas Hurd

**WARNER BOOKS**

A *Warner* Book

First published in Great Britain in 1975 by
William Collins Sons & Co Ltd
This edition published by Warner Books in 1999

Copyright © Douglas Hurd 1975

The moral right of the author has been asserted.

The author gratefully acknowledges permission to quote
from *High Windows* by Philip Larkin. Copyright © Philip
Larkin. Reprinted by permission of Faber and Faber Ltd.

*All characters in this publication are fictitious and any resemblance
to real persons, living or dead, is purely coincidental.*

All rights reserved.
No part of this publication may be reproduced, stored in a
retrieval system, or transmitted, in any form or by any means,
without the prior permission in writing of the publisher, nor
be otherwise circulated in any form of binding or cover other
than that in which it is published and without a similar
condition including this condition being imposed on the
subsequent purchaser.

A CIP catalogue record for this book
is available from the British Library.

ISBN 0 7515 2661 4

Printed and bound in Great Britain by
Clays Ltd, St Ives plc


Warner Books
A Division of
Little, Brown and Company (UK)
Brettenham House
Lancaster Place
London WC2E 7EN

To
Ted Heath

from whom I have
learned much

Next year we are to bring the soldiers home
For lack of money, and it is all right.
Places they guarded, or kept orderly,
Must guard themselves, and keep themselves orderly.
We want the money for ourselves at home
Instead of working. And this is all right.

Next year we shall be living in a country
That brought its soldiers home for lack of money.
the statues will be standing in the same
Tree-muffled squares, and look nearly the same.
Our children will not know it's a different country.
All we can hope to leave them now is money.

From HIGH WINDOWS by Philip Larkin.

# FOREWORD

It is a quarter of a century since I worked for Ted Heath at 10 Downing Street. Out of those four years came a serious work still occasionally quoted by academics – and this novel. It is the novel rather than the academic work that is being re-issued; this perhaps says something about the best medium for a political portrait or a political message.

Of course much has changed since 1975. There has been an agreement on Northern Ireland (the word agreement is perhaps more accurate than settlement, since the Irish question is like a Grand National without a finishing post). Hong Kong has passed to China. The Soviet Union has disintegrated.

In Number Ten itself four Prime Ministers have come and gone; the photographs on the main staircase have been duly shunted upwards. One Prime Minister worked in the study on the first floor, the next preferred the Cabinet Room itself, the next worked next door in the room formerly sacred to the senior Private Secretaries. The decorators have more than once been at work. The pictures have been hung and re-hung, as each Prime Minister tut-tutted over the taste of the one before. The upstairs flat is now occupied by the Chancellor of the Exchequer.

I considered whether to try to update *Vote to Kill* to accommodate these and other changes, but decided against. It is a creature of its time. Re-reading it I find embedded anecdotes from my own past. I did find a finger of Polish vodka in a sticky bottle and a dirty glass when I moved into my office at Number Ten the day after Mr Heath's victory in 1970. There was a small commotion about the food to be served to the new Prime Minister and his colleagues that evening, a matter better handled in the novel than in reality. We did have to tell Ted Heath more or less in public of the last and desperately unfavourable opinion poll before the polling day which ended in his triumph. There is more of myself in John

Cruickshank, the dim hero of the novel, than I remember acknowledging at the time.

Much has changed, but much remains. *Vote to Kill*, like its successor *The Shape of Ice*, tries to tackle the tension between private and public emotion. This is more evident in politics than in other professions, because politics as a career are more pervasive, even obsessive. In *Vote to Kill* I also tried to tackle a different question; what happens when a demagogue is let loose on the scene, a man attractive in himself and armed with an attractive cry? It surprised me that in all the years since the latest Irish troubles began in 1969 no politician tried to rouse the English against the bloodshed and expense involved in honouring our commitment to the Union. 'Troops out' was a tired cry this side of the water, an occasional handful of banners on a street corner, with no resonance or power. It might have been otherwise, as the novel suggests.

I was influenced by a recent example of an avalanche of popular emotion with an eloquent politician at its head threatening to sweep away a consensus on policy between the parties. This was the effort of Enoch Powell between 1968 and 1970 to bring an end to coloured immigration. Enoch Powell was, I hasten to add, different from the demagogue in the novel, not least because he did not deliberately set himself at the head of a crusade and would have scorned the tricks and manoeuvres here described.

*Vote to Kill* ends with a melodramatic twist which enables good sense to reassert itself. I am not sure that I would venture on that melodrama if I were writing today. But nothing in the last twenty-five years, despite the damp criticism of outsiders, has obliterated the excitement of a British general election campaign for those who take part. A general election in real life, as in fiction, represents the climax and the justification of any career in politics. It may be disastrous, but it cannot be dull for the practitioners. It would be a great pity if it became dull for the public.

# CHAPTER ONE

'Surely we could ring up the Palace now?' said Antony.

It was past midday, and the chilly sun was full on the daffodils in the window box of No. 16 Trevor Square. There were three other men in Sir James Percival's first-floor drawing-room, all of them in different ways his dependants. His wife had bustled efficiently in and out most of the morning with trays of coffee and ginger biscuits. Her latest tray carried two bottles of champagne with glasses, and it was this which prompted Antony Percival's question to his father. Spring sunshine, champagne, victory, the Queen . . . it was clear enough by now. It was no good being Leader of the Conservative Party if you did not enjoy success.

They all looked again at the television set, which had done most of the talking that morning.

'The results are slowing down now, only thirty or forty to come in – here's another, yes, the Tories have held on to Norfolk South. Well, that was predictable, there's a recount I gather in the Isle of Wight, that's one the Tories might expect to win back the way things are going, though of course local factors . . .'

On the BBC they had found a fat don and then they had found a thin don. The dons had been up all night, but both were on top of their form. For four years they had trained for this moment. They were sweating, but in fact the election had gone smoothly. For once, the people had behaved according to the mathematical patterns approved by the experts at Oxford and various Scottish universities. A uniform swing to the Tories across the country, not big enough to upset the swingometer, but definitely big enough to edge out the ageing Labour Government which had held power for seven years. No nasty regional variations, no inexplicable crosswinds of opinion. The two television dons glowed with virtuous satisfaction above their bow ties, past

1

confusions forgotten, their love affair with the electorate at last rewarded.

On the screen a car turned into Downing Street. The movement of the wheels seemed as weary as the blurred white faces in the back seat.

'There is the Prime Minister and Mrs Wellcome. They've driven down this morning from his Manchester constituency. A sad home-coming for Mrs Wellcome, perhaps she's thinking already of all those suitcases that will almost certainly have to be packed. The Prime Minister looks tired, as well he might . . .'

Tired – they were all tired, thought Antony looking round his father's drawing-room, all tired inside except himself. But that morning it was only the losers who already felt tired. The winners had found success, a new drug which would keep them going for a few days longer.

His father for example, who for three hours had hardly moved from the only armchair in the room. It was not long since his father had physically filled that chair. His burly but self-disciplined body had seemed for many years too young for his lined sallow face and silver hair. Now it was the other way round. Sir James's shrewd eyes followed each nuance of the Election results alertly, as if he had not just finished a gruelling Election campaign. But his body no longer did justice to the dark green leather recesses of the chair; it seemed smaller and less controlled than even a few months ago. Oddly, his moustache was still black. On his knee he held a small white pad on which he occasionally jotted a note. Antony guessed he was sorting out in his mind the names of the Government which he would have to form within the next twenty-four hours.

'I am sure the Queen's Private Secretary will telephone to you when the time comes,' said the Opposition Chief Whip. Antony could see that Paul Bernays was irritated with him for butting in. His plump red face swelled with strain and exhaustion. It was understandable enough. After all, Antony's only contribution to the campaign had been disastrous. He had been photographed in a white tie outside the Cabal nightclub in the small hours of one morning, pulling his trouser pockets inside out to show the taxi driver that he had no money for his fare. The picture had appeared on the front page of the *Daily Mirror* alongside a report of one of his father's speeches: 'As Conservatives we believe that those among us who lack the resources to face the cruel hardships of life should have the first claim on our social policy.' Bernays, whom Antony hardly knew, had rung him up the next morning and offered him the loan of a villa in Tuscany provided he kept out of the country for the rest of the campaign. Antony had taken his girl Trisha there for a couple of days but had drifted back well before polling day. It had rained, and Trisha came out in spots.

'So at 12.15 with twenty-five results still to come, the state of the parties is: Conservatives 296, Labour 254, Liberal 12, Ulster Unionist 8, Scottish Nationalist 7, others 4.'

Helena Percival came into the room with a batch of telegrams, most of them in glossy greetings envelopes. The green silk dress was expensive and went well with the red hair piled on her head. Antony knew that his stepmother, an intelligent woman, realized that she was hard and that she looked hard; but despite much care with her voice and appearance she never quite managed to conceal the fact. He had watched her carefully for several years now, and could see that today beneath the self-control she was excited. He appealed for her support.

'Helena, don't you think we should ring up the Palace?'

'Yes, of course, we can't sit here all day goggling at the box. Wellcome is quite capable of sitting tight just to spite us till the very last result is in. He ought to have resigned already. If he doesn't soon the Queen should tell some courtier to stir him up.' But she would make Antony pay for her support. 'Why the hell aren't you opening the champagne? You may drink it warm at the Cabal, but this is a respectable house.'

As he untwisted the wire on the first bottle Antony watched his father. If Sir James disliked the absolute way in which his wife laid down the law he never showed it. But her advice weighed no heavier than anyone else's. Sprawled untidily in the armchair he was making up his own mind. He spoke to the fourth man in the room.

'John, if you don't mind, I think it would now be right to ring Sir Robert Lorne at the Palace. Use the telephone in the study. You can say that I am of course at the Queen's disposal whenever she pleases, but it would be useful to have some idea of the timing she has in mind.'

3

'Of course,' said the young man, getting up from a hard chair.

John Cruickshank had run the Leader of the Opposition's office for three years now, first under old Mr Topping and for the last twelve months under Sir James Percival. Everyone liked him, nobody knew him well. He was tall and pale with a dull face except for the brush of stiff fair hair twisting untidily across his forehead. Antony knew that he was twenty-eight because they had known each other quite well at Oxford. Then they had drifted apart. John Cruickshank worked late, was polite to everyone, and never got his name in the gossip columns. He listened a great deal more than he talked. This above all had been the secret of his modest success so far.

When John had left the room Antony poured out the wine and handed it round. Bernays raised his glass.

'To the new Prime Minister, and may your reign be long and prosperous. And above all, well done.'

Antony was surprised at the warmth in Bernay's voice. But that was because Antony did not yet really understand politics. He knew the gossip all right. He knew that Bernays who was short, stout and only forty-five had hoped to be elected Leader of the Party himself. That was twelve months ago and when it failed, he had ranged himself with those who tried to persuade old Topping to stay on and fight another Election rather than stand down for Percival. There was no obvious young candidate yet, Bernays had argued, and it would be a mistake to replace Topping, a seventy-year-old whom everyone respected, by Percival, a sixty-year-old whose merits were at that time known only within the Conservative Party machine. But having lost the argument Bernays had agreed to take on the job of Chief Whip under Sir James. The Election campaign just over had cemented a surprising comradeship between them.

'There are one or two things we ought to discuss today,' he said, pulling a list of names out of his pocket, and glancing round at Helena and Antony. But Sir James showed no sign of wishing his wife and son away.

'The first thing is whether you want Jeremy Cornwall in the Cabinet.'

It always amazed Antony that so much in politics was

left to the last minute. After all, the Conservatives had expected to win, his father and Bernays and the others had had plenty of time to decide whether Cornwall should be in or out. Yet it sounded from his neutral tone as if Bernays was raising the matter for the first time.

'You can't possibly have him in.' Helena was genuinely indignant. 'He's disloyal and a demagogue. Topping was weak and stupid to put him in charge of the Young Conservatives. And his wife's worse than he is, a poisonous little girl. All eyes and no mind.'

Sir James answered Bernays as though Helena had not spoken.

'It needs a lot of thought. A nuisance in and a nuisance out. He might turn out a good administrator, but it's a gamble. After all, he was never in the Shadow Cabinet. The colleagues won't work easily with him.'

'He'll be riding high after that party political broadcast. Central Office have got the research, and it went very well indeed, damn it. I wonder about Ireland?'

'It'd get him out of the way. But the risk . . . and I have another thought about Ireland.'

Antony recalled Jeremy Cornwall as he had seen him a few hours earlier at Conservative Central Office. It had been a jostling noisy party, made up of anyone who had felt inclined to drop in at Smith Square to watch the results come in. On the whole they were not the people who had worked hardest in the campaign, but they behaved as if they had done it all. Antony had gone there just after midnight, and Helena had snapped at him for wearing a dinner jacket and for bringing Trisha. There had been a group of wellwishers round his father, and an almost equal group of much younger people round Cornwall at the other end of the bleak conference room on the ground floor. Cornwall had been sweating with fatigue and excitement, looking for once more than thirty years old. His deep eyes had glistened beneath the sweep of black hair which the cartoonists loved. But he was keeping himself back, insisting on plenty of water in his whiskies, and saying over and over 'Well, we shall see, we shall see' to the cronies who egged him on.

'Go and tell old Percival it's the Treasury or nothing for you.'

'We shall see, we shall see.'

Antony had not liked the sight of so much energy still held in reserve. But he knew better than to interrupt Bernays and his father. So did Helena, who stood by the window watching a small army of television crews assembling on the pavement below.

'On the whole I'd have him in,' said Bernays. 'Perhaps not Ireland, perhaps Trade and Industry, something with plenty of detail to keep him bogged down. He ran twelve betting shops in Islington before he was twenty-five, bound to have some sort of a head for figures.'

'Maybe, maybe, I'll think about it.' Like most political conversations, this one petered out before the point of decision. John Cruickshank was back in the room. The seat of his trousers was shiny and he had not cleaned his shoes that morning. He brushed the hair from his forehead, the nearest he ever came to a gesture of excitement.

'Sir Robert Lorne said that Wellcome had just rung through to say he's going to resign. He'll be at the Palace at 3, and Sir Robert thought the coast would be clear by 3.30. To be on the safe side he suggests you come at 4.'

And so three weeks of noise and effort ended in certainty. News on television came through a filter; the Queen's summons was real. It was less than thirty-six hours since the people of Britain had been safely tucked up in bed, floaters, grumblers, enemies, supporters, all asleep. Then twelve and a half million had gone out and put their cross in one place, and twelve million in another, producing within hours this convulsion for better or for worse in the government of the nation and several hundred private lives. Antony was not interested in political issues. He thought of flamboyant Mrs Wellcome with her collection of china shepherdesses. They wouldn't fit happily into the Essex cottage which was all the home the Wellcomes would have by tonight.

After his passive morning, Sir James Percival began to stir.

'Paul, thank you very much for all your help. Could you come round to No. 10 tonight, say around 7, and we'll complete the first list of senior colleagues? We should aim to announce the names of the Cabinet by about noon tomorrow, and I'll need help with the telephoning.'

'You can eat the first meal I shall cook as First Housekeeper of the Land,' said Helena.

'I know it will be delicious.' Paul Bernays nursed a secret diet, and knew Helena's cooking was rich. His pink face already wore the sheen of an expensive life. 'I'll go over to the Carlton Club now and count how many people will offer me a drink. A damn sight more than last week, that's for sure.'

'I suspect many of our colleagues will already be hunched over their telephones,' said Sir James. 'They say old Priestman once lost the Exchequer through choosing just the wrong half hour to take his mistress to tea at the Ritz.' Antony had often seen his father come alive like this in the middle of the day. All morning he would move, speak and look like an exhausted old man; then suddenly he would spring back into his forties.

Sir James rose to see Bernays out, and Antony too made to go. He was only a voyeur in this political world and the last thing he wanted at this particular moment was a talk with his father about his own affairs. John Cruickshank too was on his feet. Sir James continued to make his dispositions.

'John, you'd better get on to No. 10 straight away. Say that I've asked you as my political secretary to move in as soon as Wellcome leaves. You'd better check that he won't be coming back to No. 10 after he's been to the Palace. I don't imagine he will. Ask them to let him know that he's free to use Chequers for a week or so if that fits in with his plans. You've met Pershore, the top Civil Service private secretary at No. 10, he's the man to talk to . . . William, I think his name is. Make sure you get the office on the left of the main corridor with the door into the Cabinet Room. Tell them I'll come straight there from the Palace, that means about 5, I suppose. They'd better lay on plenty of whisky and sandwiches, it'll be a long night. Ask them to warn the Chief of Defence Staff I'll want to see him later about the security side of Northern Ireland.'

John Cruickshank jotted down the points on a stiff white card which slotted into a black leather holder with gold corners.

'What about television?'

'Yes, quite right. But there won't be anything substantial to say tonight. You'd better warn both channels I'll say a few

7

words impromptu on the steps when I go in, and that'll be it for today.'

'Won't that be for the No. 10 Press Secretary to handle?'

'Filton? No, I don't want him to handle anything, he's Wellcome's man, it isn't safe. He'll have to go as soon as I've got someone else. The rest of the private office can stay of course, but you'll have to do the Press and television work for a day or two. Anything else?'

'No, that seems clear enough.' John looked down his list, and put it in his pocket. 'Can I ring No. 10 from the study?'

'Yes, of course.' Sir James turned to his wife. 'Helena, you'd better stay here, hadn't you? I'll come back late tonight. There's no hurry about moving in, we can sleep here for two or three weeks. Why not come over to No. 10 tomorrow and look at the upstairs flat? You'll want things done to it as soon as the Wellcomes' furniture is out.'

'You mean you want me out of the way?' Helena had got used to being in the way when her husband's political decisions were made. Antony could see that she would find it hard to take the back seat, which was all that the British Constitution provided for a Prime Minister's wife.

'Well, you wouldn't expect to help me choose the Ministers, would you?'

That was exactly what Helena did expect. Her mouth worked nervously at the edges, then she made the best of it.

'You're going to have sandwiches tonight, and you've had nothing but sandwiches for weeks now. You'd better have something healthier for lunch. There's ham and salad and some of the walnut cheese you like on the side in the dining-room. There's enough for John too if he wants to stay.' Helena had always liked John because he served her husband well without trespassing into her domain.

'Well, there's obviously not enough ham for me,' said Antony, 'and that cheese is insipid. So I'll say good afternoon.'

'No, wait, I want to talk to you.' Helena made no attempt to sound conciliatory. She had no right to order him around, and Antony hesitated. But he found it less embarrassing to deal with Helena than with his father direct. So he waited till Sir James had ambled out of the room in search of lunch.

# CHAPTER TWO

'Sit down.' Antony sprawled himself on the hard shiny black sofa, pushing his long legs out in a way which he thought his stepmother would dislike. She stood in front of him, and he could see she was trying to control her temper. He wondered if she found him sexually attractive. She was only ten years his senior, and certainly he had never worked out a coherent way of handling their relationship.

'Well, what are your plans? I've hardly seen you in the last month.'

'I don't know that they've changed much in that time.'

'Well, they've got to change now.' Helena deliberately softened her voice. 'You must see you can't go on living with that girl any more.'

'I don't see why not.' Antony swung his legs round on to the sofa. He was relieved. If this was all, he could manage. Trisha was a dull girl, pretty when she had her make-up on, but after six months that was not enough. Tuscany had been a turning point. He had an excuse now for leaving her.

'Of course you can't. The Press will be on to you at once. All that stuff during the Election was bad enough. Now you're the Prime Minister's son the other papers won't hold back any longer.'

'Perhaps I'll marry her. She's keen enough.' He thought this would produce an explosion. But he was wrong.

'Don't be such a bloody fool.' She almost grinned at him. Antony had too high an opinion of himself to marry a sleazy little deb with a feather brain, and Helena knew it.

'Or I could take her off somewhere, and live quite separately from you all. The Press would soon forget about me.'

'Now, let's get this straight.' She lifted his ankles, and pulled him forward so that she could sit on the sofa beside him. 'So far as I'm concerned you're a pain in the neck, but let that pass. You can't talk to your father, and he can't talk to you, but he's fond of you and I don't want him to lose you. What's more, you're just about the only person he knows who takes not the blindest interest in politics, and that's going to be a big asset from now on. So you've got to stay around. You can have as many girls as you like, but not openly like Trisha. And, next and even more important, you mustn't get so deep into debt that people talk.'

Antony stared in front of him. Helena's voice grated like a dentist's drill. She was on to the nerve now.

'You're shacked up in Trisha's house, rent free, I suppose, but you've had no job for nearly a year, you live high. How much do you owe?'

'About three thousand. And I got Trisha to take out a second mortgage. That's another five, and it's almost gone.' He could not imagine why he was telling Helena the truth – to shock her, he supposed. Her arm stretched along the back of the sofa to within an inch or two of his shoulder. He had never disliked a woman more.

'So that's eight thousand. Worse than I expected. You know Lord Cloyne?'

'I've met him.'

'He's as mean as anyone I know. I had him to dinner last week. Your father doesn't know, he was in Sheffield that night. Jacky Cloyne will lend you anything up to ten thousand pounds interest free, and give you a job at the Hesperian Bank. The condition is, you break with Trisha. If you stay at the bank for two years and generally behave yourself the loan becomes a gift.'

Even Antony was impressed.

'Why should he do all that? I hardly know him.'

'That's why. I was able to tell quite a touching tale. You had been neglected, led astray, that sort of thing. And it was a good dinner.'

'Did you promise him anything?' This was an important question. Helena laughed.

'What could I promise him that he hasn't got? You don't understand rich men. If I had been after money for Oxfam or Shelter I could have fed Lord Cloyne, flattered Lord Cloyne and made love to Lord Cloyne till daylight, and I wouldn't have coaxed a penny out of him. But because it was

10

an odd disreputable pitch, it tickled his palate. I had no trouble at all.' She stood up, pleased with her cleverness. 'Will you take it?'

For the first time their eyes met. He saw that she was making as genuine an appeal as lay in her nature. He felt uncertain and confused. If she was his dentist, was the tooth out after all?

'I'll think about it.'

She nearly started again, but thought better of it.

'Think hard,' she said, and left to give Sir James his coffee.

As he shut the front door of 16 Trevor Square behind him, Antony was besieged by reporters. He backed against the door and raised his hand.

'I have an important announcement to make.'

'When's your father going to the Palace?'

'That is of secondary importance. The news is that my stepmother Lady Percival has accepted the position of Lord President of the Council with special responsibilty as censor of the Press and dictator of private morals.'

# CHAPTER THREE

Big Ben struck four, and John Cruickshank cleared his throat. He was not normally a nervous person, but there were several hundred people penned on to the pavement behind him, and a small regiment of photographers and journalists grouped in a semicircle immediately at his back. The policeman, polite but cautious, leaned forward to catch his words.

'My name is John Cruickshank, I am the new Prime Minister's Political Secretary. I think I'm expected.'

It was not absolutely accurate. Sir James was still at the Palace, still three minutes away from kissing hands as Prime Minister. But it served. The policeman banged the knocker on the door, an attendant in a frockcoat opened it, there was a muttered exchange, and John for the first time in his life entered No. 10 Downing street.

The house was bigger than it looked. He was in a wide hall, out of which led a corridor papered with a rich grey and white flock. On his right was an upright porter's chair with a thick hood above it to defy the eighteenth-century cold, and beyond that a little waiting-room in which he could see the flicker of football on television. To the left a door opened into another hallway, which he knew must be No. 11, the house of the Chancellor of the Exchequer.

No one was to be seen except the messenger who had let him in. The contrast between this silence and the excited bustle of the street outside was formidable. This was power, thought John, the possibility of quiet in a world of noise. Then he saw William Pershore coming quickly down the corridor towards him.

Pershore, who a few minutes before had been Mr Wellcome's Principal Private Secretary, now by virtue of the kissing of hands in the Palace half a mile away held the same position under Sir James Percival, without a word spoken or a document signed. It was an automatic transfer of loyalty under the British Constitution, and no one understood the nuances and ironies of the British Constitution better than William Pershore. He was grey all over, but the shining grey of a well-groomed thoroughbred, not the dull defensive grey which characterized much of Whitehall. About forty-five, plenty of smooth grey hair falling carefully across his forehead, a light grey suit cut rather young for his years, a large jade ring on one hand.

'Welcome to Downing Street,' he said, holding out his hand to John. John had met Pershore once before, in a dark Greek restaurant in St Martin's Lane. It was the twilight period just before the Election, when the Civil Service hold surreptitious meetings with emissaries of the Opposition, in an attempt to find out how seriously they might have to take the rhetoric of the hustings. (Contrary to the popular impression, they usually find that they have to be taken very seriously indeed – this is one of the main complaints of the Civil Service against the way that Britain is governed.) Over the second glass of sour retsina wine John had handed over in a manilla folder the first draft of the Conservative Election manifesto. It was not of course to be shown to Wellcome, but only to senior Civil Servants. Pershore had throughout the meal, for which he had paid, shown himself shrewd but patronizing, the man in possession listening patiently to the aspirant. Now John felt that the roles should be reversed. After all Pershore could not be sure that Sir James would keep him in his present position for more than the two or three weeks needed to get the new machine running smoothly. But John was not too sanguine. He felt subtly inferior to Pershore in the same sort of way that he felt inferior to all Frenchmen. For the first time in this triumphant day he was conscious that, as Antony had noticed, his suit was shiny and his shoes unpolished.

'Let me show you your office.' Pershore led the way down the corridor and then left into a pleasant room overlooking the garden. The Gainsborough portrait of Burke above the desk was not quite a Gainsborough, but the Norfolk fishing boats on the opposite wall were homely in a sombre sort of way. There was a bottle on the side-table, with a finger of sticky Polish vodka at the bottom, and an unwashed tumbler beside it. Pershore grimaced.

'I told them to make sure everything was cleared up,' he said. 'As a matter of fact, I think your predecessor has done quite well to clear out so quickly.' He flipped open a couple of drawers in the desk. They were empty except for a few stray paper clips.

'That door leads straight into the Cabinet Room.' It was covered with purple baize anchored with brass studs. 'Your predecessor used it occasionally' – a faint tone of disapproval here – 'but on the whole he found it answered better to use the door in our office, the Civil Service office. Then we all knew where we were.'

'It's very pleasant.' The trees in the park beyond the garden wall were still bare. The lake had been drained for cleaning, and some primeval machine belonging to the Department of the Environment was lumbering along its muddy bottom. The daffodils in the Prime Minister's garden were less advanced than those in Trevor Square.

'The Wellcomes are packing their things, and their furniture will be moved out of the upstairs flat tomorrow. I don't suppose Sir James will want to . . .'

'No indeed.' John began to speak with authority. 'He'll go back to Trevor Square tonight to sleep. He asked me to say

13

that of course Mr and Mrs Wellcome are free to use Chequers for the time being if they wish.'

'I gather that won't be necessary,' said Pershore. 'Their house in Essex is available straight away, and to tell you the truth, neither of them was ever really fond of Chequers.' To judge from Pershore's tone the domestic tastes of the Wellcomes were already a rather distant and peripheral matter. 'That is the lavatory which the Cabinet use.' He pointed to the two doors as they passed back into the corridor out of John's office. 'Of course you are free to use it yourself as appropriate. But not for lady visitors if you don't mind. And that other door is the waiting-room. Not for Ministers, you understand, they wait here immediately outside the Cabinet Room. It is for others, party officials, clergymen who want to be bishops, that type of person. The Patronage Secretary usually makes them wait ten minutes to test their spiritual qualities.'

On the other side of the corridor they paused in front of a news agency tape machine. A girl in a tweed skirt and flowered blouse had her back to them as she lifted the chattering paper.

'Ah, Clarissa, well met. This is John Cruickshank, the Political Secretary under our new dispensation. – Clarissa Strong, my colleague in the Private office, who specializes in Parliamentary questions and Northern Ireland.'

The girl turned round, and she and John muttered at each other. She held out her hand, he hesitated for a second, and by the time they shook hands it was clear that it happened only because she had started it. They covered up this typically British embarrassment by some typically British conversation.

'Ah yes, of course,' said John, 'you knew Antony Percival at Oxford didn't you?'

She went slightly pink. 'For a few months – my first year, his last. He'll have forgotten what I look like now.'

John thought she was wrong. She was a strikingly pretty girl. Plenty of soft fair hair strictly brushed, a long straight nose, a brown pleasant complexion and grey eyes with just the beginning of a wrinkle underneath.

'Belfast doesn't look too good,' she said to Pershore, tearing three inches of paper off the tape. For a moment John

14

thought she must be talking about an Election result; no other kind of news had interested him for three weeks now. Pershore handed him the paper.

'URGENT. Ulster riot on detention rumour. Troops fired rubber bullets to disperse riot by a crowd estimated at three thousand in the Falls Road area of Belfast. As outgoing Secretary of State Jack Rogers, before leaving by air for London, following his party's General Election defeat, issued a statement calling for calm. Riot started when teenage youths overturned four buses and set fire to shops. The cause was reported to be a rumour that an incoming Tory Government in London would reintroduce detention without trial.'

'Mild compared with the old days,' said Pershore.

'Yes, but worrying, don't you think? It's been quiet for so long.'

'Could you ring up the Ministry of Defence and the Irish Office straight away?' said Pershore, asserting himself. 'We ought to give the PM an up-to-date report as soon as he arrives.'

Pershore and John continued their tour up the angled staircase lined with likenesses of all past Prime Ministers – prints till you got to about 1880 and the first landing, after that signed photographs. There appeared to be no room for any more.

'Some minor adjustment will be necessary,' said Pershore, pointing to the wall. 'We shall have to elevate Mr Topping to make room. But we shall have trouble. I'm afraid Mr Wellcome has an aversion to personal photography. His campaign portrait looked as if it had been taken at least ten years ago. I gather that Transport House found it at the back of an old drawer when they were close to despair.' His smile was supposed to convey to John that his loyalty transplant was complete.

'I'm not sure Sir James has ever really got to grips with Northern Ireland – he's had no occasion to,' said John. 'As I told you on the phone he wanted to see the CDS on the security side tonight.'

'I have arranged that for 9.30,' said Pershore. 'I thought the PM would wish to spend the first few hours working on the first list of appointments – including of course the new Irish Secretary.'

They were in the second of the drawing-rooms now –

three exceptionally pleasant rooms, one blue, one white, one gold, with the doors connecting them thrown open so that each room caught the evening light from the western window overlooking the park. The other windows commanded the Horse Guards.

'Difficult to keep clean,' said Pershore. 'By tradition the children of foreign diplomats are allowed to watch the Trooping the Colour from here.' He picked up a slightly stained window-seat cushion. 'The daughter of the Cyprus High Commissioner was sick on this cushion last year. She was apparently suffering from a surfeit of Coca-Cola. I have been asked to authorize that it be sent to the cleaners for the third time. It is not an easy decision. The same small girl will be with us again in a matter of weeks.'

'But what about Ireland?' asked John.

He had not yet got used to the Civil Service habit of discussing small and big things with the same apparent seriousness.

'It could be difficult, it could be very difficult quite soon.' Pershore carefully put back the cushion in its exact place before turning to the next item on the agenda. 'In one sense direct rule has been a success for too long. The same moderate leaders, Catholic and Protestant, have been making the same speeches for five years now. They all say they want direct rule to end, but of course on their own terms. Since they know they can't get their own terms they privately prefer direct rule by Britain to someone else's terms. But I'm afraid the extremists have been gaining ground again lately, partly for economic reasons, but partly I fear through sheer boredom.'

'How did Jack Rogers really do?'

Pershore shrugged his shoulders. Direct comment on Ministers of the outgoing Government was not in his style.

'Let me put it this way. He didn't do much, but he was always ready to listen to anyone. That wasn't a bad combination.'

'But he's very colourless?'

'You could put it that way.' Pershore led the way into the next room. 'Whether that is a criticism or not, depends on your point of view.' The two men were still near the start of a long process of sizing each other up. It was too early for Pershore to give hostages in the form of snap judgements.

'This is the small dining-room,' Pershore went on. 'The larger one is just beyond, for more than eight. Incidentally, I had to take a decision about supper arrangements tonight. Sandwiches, you said, and I am sure that is sensible. A set meal wastes so much time on an evening like this. Normally of course the housekeeper here would do it, but in the circumstances I did not think I could ask Mrs Wellcome . . .'

'No, of course not.'

'Nor is it strictly a function for which Government Hospitality could be asked to take responsibility. It was not an easy problem. I consulted the Cabinet office mess, and they offered lager and pork pies. Very good, I am sure, but I did not feel that for an incoming *Conservative* administration . . . So in the end I cut a corner. I have ordered a cold chicken and a large quantity of smoked salmon sandwiches from my club. They also have a passable hock. I have asked for four bottles.'

'That is very good of you.'

'Not at all, not at all. We can discuss later exactly how the bill should be divided.'

They were out on the landing of the first floor. Two large glass cabinets contained Mrs Wellcome's array of shepherdesses.

'I shall miss this collection. The messengers christened them the Land Army,' said Pershore. 'I do not know how Sir James will fill these cabinets. In my experience most Prime Ministers collect something, if it's only gift ashtrays or silver trowels. That is the door into the study, and this staircase leads up to the private flat on the second floor – Perhaps we should have a word about your own access to classified papers. Of course once you have gone through all the security procedures . . .'

Pershore was interrupted by one of the messengers, panting slightly from the steepness of the stairs.

'Excuse me, Mr Pershore, I'm sorry to bother you, but there's a gentleman downstairs who says he's Mr Antony Percival. The policeman at the door let him in, but he wasn't too sure, and I thought I'd better . . .'

Pershore cut him short rather testily. 'It must be the Prime Minister's son – surely you could have spotted that. You know him of course, John – may I call you John? My name is William. Well in that case let's go down and greet him together.'

17

Antony was standing, feet apart, in the centre of the main entrance hall. He carried a tightly rolled umbrella and wore a bowler hat, slightly askew. He waited till they reached him, then spoke with quiet precision.

'They wish to relieve me of my hat and my umbrella. They mean kindly, I am sure. But without my hat and my umbrella, how am I to remember that I am to be a merchant banker?'

John saw that he must take charge.

'Come along to my office, and we'll talk about it.'

'It's a bit awkward,' whispered Pershore. 'The PM will be here at any time now. The custom is to get the whole staff lined up along the corridor to welcome him. It would be a pity if there were any incident . . .'

'There won't be.' He steered Antony down the corridor, but they ran aground opposite the bust of Pitt, which stood in a recess half-way down.

'Good afternoon, Billy, I will trust *you* with my hat,' said Antony, placing his bowler on the white marble forehead. 'Were you a good butcher?'

'What do you mean?'

'Isn't that what it's called when a Prime Minister sacks his colleagues? Billy, you knew about the bottle. You know that I have just drunk half a bottle of bad brandy. But girls, Billy, girls, I think not. You would not understand how I feel. So I will retrieve my hat. I have sacked my mistress and got myself a job. What do you say to that for an afternoon's work?'

John managed to steer him forwards.

'I heard Helena had a surprise for you.'

'Ah yes, but I have a surprise for Helena, bless her black heart. I've butchered Trisha, I'll take the job, do everything she asks. But I'm damned if I'm going to sleep on the streets. I'm going to live here.'

'For God's sake, Antony. And anyway I'm not sure there's room. It's a small flat, and . . .'

'Not room? For the Prime Minister's only son? No room for a cot and my toys and Teddy, and perhaps a bit later my pin-ups of football stars? You must be joking. The newspapers wouldn't like that story one little bit. Twenty rooms for typists, none for the prodigal son. No, no, Helena will have to . . .' He swayed into the wall.

18

'Here's your father now.'

John had heard the sound of clapping and cheering from outside in the street as the front door opened to admit the new Prime Minister.

'Excellent. I'll go and greet him, and then we can get down seriously to the fatted calf.'

Given his condition, Antony moved fast. Sir James was still near the door. He turned from waving to the crowd and as the door closed began to shake hands one by one with the line of secretaries and messengers who had been quickly assembled.

His brand-new detective towered uneasily behind him. Pershore was doing the honours expertly.

'This is Miss Jones, of Honours Section. Miss Jones has been with us for eighteen years now, isn't that right, Miss Jones?'

Antony slipped into a gap in the line, and fell to his pin-stripe knees.

'I am no more worthy to be called thy son,' he said to an astonished grey-haired lady on his right. 'Isn't that how it goes?'

John, following fast, had an idea, and pressed a button. By good luck the lift was there, and the doors opened. He pulled Antony quickly up and back, and the doors closed behind them.

Antony was in no way put out.

'That was quick work,' he said. 'You've come on a lot since you were at Merton. Now, if you press button 2 we can go and choose my bedroom.'

## CHAPTER FOUR

'The only possible explanation is that the Department of the Environment are mean with fertilizer. I don't wish to be unreasonable, but the Prime Minister of England is entitled to a decent lawn.'

It was true that there were bare patches, particularly under the trees where they sat in a little circle of cane chairs. It was hot, and though he was in the shade Sir James was in his shirtsleeves. The Civil Servants sat in the sun with their coats on, though Pershore acknowledged summer with a large yellow rose in his buttonhole. They had only twenty minutes to brief the Prime Minister before he left for the House of Commons. There were some tricky questions for him on the order paper today, but as usual he was in no hurry to start discussing them. All of them in the circle – Pershore, John, Clarissa, and the rest of the private office, had learnt from experience that it was no use rushing him.

'I understand the soil is impacted below the turf,' said John. 'So the roots don't get enough air. The builders' sheds stood here for years while Harold Macmillan was doing the place up.'

Although they worked reasonably well together, Pershore rarely missed a chance to show that John as Political Secretary could not grasp the infinite complexities of truth in the same way as a Civil Servant.

'There may be some truth in that,' he said judiciously, 'but I doubt if it is the whole explanation. Lloyd George and his Garden Suburb may well have started the trouble.'

'In my experience every Government has trouble with the grass roots,' said the Prime Minister. They made appropriate laughing noises. Since becoming Prime Minister he had fallen into the habit of making little jokes. They were not particularly funny, but they came as a welcome sign that he was having one of his good days.

'Now, we must make a start,' said the Prime Minister, as if it was the others who had been holding things up. 'Question No. 1, Mr Cornwall.'

'He's striking dangerous form,' said Richard Newings, MP for Andover and the new Parliamentary Private Secretary. His job was to look after the Prime Minister's relationship with all Members of Parliament. He was a precise little man with pince-nez, a lawyer who used his slightly absurd appearance and stilted voice to conceal lively ability.

'What do you mean?'

'I mean double whiskies all round in the Smoking Room, and a lot of shouting "I'll see you right, boy, when my day comes" – that sort of thing. When I came in he said "Here comes the spy" and ordered another round of whiskies for everyone except me.'

'He's going mad. No one can take him seriously,' said John.

'I don't agree,' said Clarissa unexpectedly, but didn't expand. She was wearing a fawn trouser suit cut close to show off her slim figure.

'As it happens Mr Cornwall has not tabled a question about his own mental health, but about whether I intend to visit Belfast,' said the Prime Minister. He poured himself another cup of coffee. 'What will his supplementary be?'

'I think it may be about force levels. There was a story in the *Belfast Telegraph* yesterday that we were going to reduce the Army in Ulster from twelve to nine thousand. He'll want to stir up trouble over that.'

'You would have to deny that absolutely,' said Newings. 'The Party's pretty sensitive already on any thought you're going soft on Ulster.'

'Yes, I see.' The Prime Minister seemed to agree, but John saw him catch Pershore's eye. Damn. Something was going on that he hadn't been told about. It didn't happen often, but was always annoying. He looked at Clarissa, but her head was bent over the briefing notes.

'There was a rather good bit in my last Party Conference speech about what the Army was doing – John, can you lay your hands on it quickly? It might come in quite effectively.'

'I put it aside – I'm pretty sure I've got it in my cupboard. I'll go and see.'

'I'll go too,' said Clarissa. 'I ought to check with the Ministry of Defence if any troop rotations are planned in the next week or two. It might affect how you handle the supplementary.'

In John's office the curtains were half-drawn against the afternoon sun, and it was pleasantly cool.

'Why do even clever politicians always want to quote from their own speeches?' asked Clarissa after she had made her telephone call. 'There's nothing more boring.'

'For the same reason that men like to wear an old suit. It's familiar, and they know it fits.' For some reason John was having difficulty in finding the Blackpool Conference speech. Had his filing system slipped up? Or was it because half his mind was flustered because Clarissa had followed him out of the garden so unnecessarily?

There it was, in the right folder after all. He locked the security press and turned round.

'Shall we go back?'

'It's not worth it. It's just on three. They'll have to come in in a minute if they're to get across to the House in time.'

Clarissa was sitting with both legs swung over one arm of the big black leather armchair in which John's visitors made themselves comfortable. Because it was an uncharacteristic pose he saw her as a girl not a colleague. This shift of focus had happened a good deal lately. He liked it, but did not in the least know how to progress beyond it.

'What was that coming and going between the PM and Pershore about force levels?'

'Oh, so you did notice. I only know because the CDS rang up the PM late last night. William Pershore had gone home, and I listened in.' It was routine in the Private Office that unless the PM specifically instructed otherwise all his important telephone calls inward and outward should be monitored by the senior private secretary present. There was no tape recorder, but the Private Secretary made a record if they thought it necessary.

'What did he say?'

'He warned the PM we were coming under strong pressure in the NATO Military Committee to bring the Army of the Rhine up to strength. The Allies don't see how we're justified in keeping so many units in Ulster when things are so quiet there.'

'But they're only quiet because the Army *is* there.'

'Maybe. But the CDS wants to move at least two battalions out to Hanover before the next NATO review of force levels. He thinks otherwise the Americans will cut their own forces again.'

'He's mad.'

'Well, he's bitten the other generals. The Army has always hated Ulster.'

'It's not safe. There's plenty of violence just below the surface.'

John sat quickly down at his desk and scribbled on a stray sheet of paper.

'What are you doing?'

'Just a possible answer to a supplementary. It'd make a small headline.'

Clarissa came and read over his shoulder, standing rather close.

'The fact of the matter is that never in peacetime has the British Army had such a worthwhile role in terms of the welfare of the British people. A patrol in Belfast is worth a dozen exercises in Hanover or on Salisbury Plain.'

'D'you really believe that?' she asked.

'I do.'

'Yes, I think you do.'

Rather clumsily she touched his cheek, and for a moment held the gesture. He sat very still. Clarissa's hand was dry and warm from the sun in the garden.

'Oh, I'm sorry to interrupt.' It was Helena. She had opened the door very quietly. 'I've just come to look at your pictures, John. I thought you'd be over at the House. I've got a greedy eye on that watercolour of Cromer, it might go better upstairs by the piano.' She produced a tape and began to measure the frame. By this time Clarissa was busy bundling her papers together.

'Come on, John, they're in from the garden, we'll miss the car to the House unless we hurry.'

Outside in Downing Street a small knot of tourists waited curiously. The Prime Minister's car was waiting with the engine running and the Inspector holding the door open. Sir James always ran it fine, but had never yet been late. Pershore was already sitting in one of the back seats, separated from where the Prime Minister would sit by four stacked red boxes full of papers to be read and decisions to be taken.

Clarissa and John bundled into a second black official Rover, which a minute later swung out into Whitehall, almost colliding with a white Mini turning into Downing Street. Antony was at the wheel with a cigar unlit between his lips. When he recognized them he hooted derisively.

23

# CHAPTER FIVE

After parking the car Antony went straight through the house into the garden. At first he had used the door out into the garden from the Cabinet Room, but Pershore had protested on security grounds. Ponderous minutes were exchanged, and in the end Antony was barred from using the Cabinet Room as a passage to the garden. Instead he was allowed to use what was called the Garden Room door, which was reached by a staircase down from the corridor where the ticker tape stood. To her intense annoyance the same restriction had been applied to Helena.

Once outside Antony took off his coat, shirt and shoes and piled them neatly by the side of a deck chair already pitched in the sun. He lit his cigar, but after four puffs was overcome by drowsiness. He laid the cigar gently to rest on top of a dandelion, closed his eyes to the sunlight, and felt happy. The Vouvray he had been given at lunch worked pleasantly through his body. There were still some advantages in being a Prime Minister's son.

He was woken almost at once by pain, violent enough to force him from the chair. 'For Christ's sake. Helena!' She had jabbed the lighted end of the cigar against his bare stomach.

'That is my chair. I set it out this morning where it would annoy Pershore most. Put on your shirt at once. You're putting on weight. You look obscene and ridiculous. You're in full view of the girls in the Garden Room.'

He recovered himself. 'In that case I'll take off my trousers as well next time.'

'Then next time it won't be your belly that gets the cigar. Why aren't you at the Bank?'

He had his shirt on by now, and was sitting on the ground putting on his shoes. If this was to be a serious bout with Helena, he would do better with his clothes on.

24

'The Hesperian have sent me to Brussels for a couple of days. They're involved in a property deal that's coming to the boil. They think I'm there already, but I decided to catch the night plane, and have a bit of a rest first. It's quite an interesting negotiation really – do you know that big block of flats overlooking the park just down the street from the Embassy? Well, they . . .'

'Spare me,' said Helena. He saw that her mood had changed. She wore a yellow and black check shirt and narrow black trousers. The figure thus on show was too young for her hard set face and harsh red hair with wires of grey running through it.

'Get up, I want to talk to you.' She picked up a shallow gardening basket which she had been carrying and strode off towards a lilac bush against the wall.

'I'm not going to move out of Number Ten.' It was some weeks since Helena had last tried to get rid of him.

'No, no, it's not that. Though why the hell you want to stay around here I can't imagine. The place is far too small, you're a thorough nuisance, you can't bring your friends here when you want, you can't bring girls here . . .'

'I thought you were against girls.'

'I was against Trisha because she was just a sex machine so far as I could see. But, for Christ's sake you're twenty-seven . . .' She pulled herself up short, and turned to face him. She had a pair of secateurs in her hand now, and jabbed the point towards his shirt.

'Look, we don't get on, never have, never will. It was a clever joke of yours to move in here. It turned the tables on me. Of course your father was glad and stood up for you. But you've made your point, don't spoil it. You ought to go out now, and spend the afternoon finding a nice flat. You can afford the rent now, you can afford to get married if you want to.'

'Who would have me?' He opened his arms mockingly. He suspected that his good looks irritated Helena.

But this time she refused to be provoked.

'You could marry almost anyone you pleased. That Clarissa girl, for example, in the Private Office. Brains, a good face, a bit of money. You knew her at Oxford, didn't you? I've

25

put you next to her at official meals more than once, and you've barely passed the salt.'

'Clarissa's only interested in her job. No sex, no small-talk. Like John.'

Helena pounced on this. 'Yes, like John. And that's the point. John's got freckles, dingy suits, no money, no small-talk, not much sex – but he's got that girl, just because he's taken a bit of interest in her.'

'Got that girl? What the hell do you mean?'

'Ah, so you were interested after all.' Helena turned to attack the dead lilac blooms with the secateurs. She saw she would have to embroider her evidence if it was to convince. 'I saw them just now in John's office, as I came out. Five minutes to go to Prime Minister's Questions. But what were they doing? Different sort of question entirely. Good luck to John – at least he's got a bit of guts. I've always liked him. They'll have clever children.'

'You're making it up.' But Antony believed her and was cross. Not because he was particularly attracted to Clarissa – she was pleasant enough, but there were prettier girls in the building. Yet it was galling to be surprised by anything Helena told him.

'Wait and see. But that's not the point. Are you going to stay here or not? You've had your joke. You could go.'

'No, I mean to stay.'

He had come as a joke, she was right. But he liked the place, and he would stay. Helena snipped on in silence at dark brown shrivelled heads.

'I've got a particular reason for wanting you to go.'

'What is it?'

'I'm not sure I shall tell you.'

'Please yourself – but I can guess.'

'Guess then.'

Antony drew a deep breath. He was pretty sure he was right. He was feeling bloodyminded. The wine, the sun, the few puffs at the cigar had turned sour inside him. His stomach hurt where this repulsive woman had burned him.

'You want me out because you find me too attractive.' Without hesitating for a moment Helena threw the secateurs at him. Because she had to swing round to do it, her aim was not quite accurate, and they missed his left ear by three inches. She banged at his head with the basket, and this time she connected. He staggered back.

'You bloody arrogant bastard.' She set off back across the grass towards the door. Antony stood half-dazed, rubbing his head. She changed her mind and ran back to him.

'If you've ever had a thought for anyone else in your life, just get this on board. Your father is ill, ill, ill. Ellerman was here yesterday morning. They don't know what it is yet. His leg is swollen and painful and won't get better. He thought it was just a bruise but of course it isn't. So he's got to have quiet – as much as he can get in this madhouse. You and I will row and racket for ever so long as we live under the same roof. I'm staying – so you can bloody well get out.'

'Are you telling me my father's got something seriously wrong with him?'

But she had marched away, and slammed the Garden Room door behind her. Antony picked up the secateurs which she had thrown. He walked over to the border which ran along the wall. Within three minutes he had beheaded the whole neat regiment of roses and carefully trampled the flowers and buds into the soil.

## CHAPTER SIX

John was always depressed by the Prime Minister's room in the House of Commons. He disliked the dark panelling, the dull engravings and the view through massed pigeon droppings on to the absurd underground car park which Parliament had inflicted on itself in the early seventies. Above all he disliked the atmosphere of rush and bother with which he associated the room. The Prime Minister never used it except for occasional interviews with Members of Parliament; but he came here for five minutes each Tuesday and Thursday before going into the chamber at 3.15 to answer questions. They were usually the most confused minutes of the week. Last-minute facts and statistics were phoned through by government departments, often contradicting those provided with complete assurance in the briefs they had been discussing at No. 10 half an hour before. The Chief Whip or some beleaguered Minister would appear with morsels of news which seemed to them of consuming importance. The main trouble with the House of Commons, thought John, was that no one was any good at relating their activities to those of other people. Six hundred one-man bands seemed to him to make more noise than sense. He had long ago decided that his own place was behind the green baize door, influencing decisions rather than taking or defending them. Sometimes he felt the PM had come to the same conclusion. Certainly Sir James showed less and less appetite for the small beer of politics. He often escaped from the hubbub of triviality into the lavatory which led out of his room, emerging only just in time to walk rapidly into the Chamber before the Speaker called the first question on the Prime Minister's list.

But today the panic was a real one. Bernays had been in the room when they arrived. Of all the colleagues he knew the PM best and worked most easily with him. As Irish Secretary he had the hardest job in the Government, but he did it well.

'Bad news,' he said. 'An ambush in the Falls Road. Three trucks of the Greenjackets. Front one blown up by a mine, the two behind it gunned from an empty house. Twenty killed. A shambles.'

John felt sick. It had all happened so often before long ago. Then there had been a lull, blessed at the time, but perhaps cruel in the end. For everyone seemed to have forgotten what they had learnt. Once again young men would blow themselves up with bombs, women curse and spit at their protectors, troops travel in vulnerable convoy, just as they had done when the last troubles started after 1969. The names in the headlines and on the gravestones would change, but not much else.

The Prime Minister moved heavily to his chair. John had noticed for some time that sitting down had become important to him. He no longer seemed ready to talk, listen, or even think except in a chair.

'No advance intelligence?' he asked.

'None, so far as I can find. I'm waiting for the final casualty list now.'

'Any terrorists hit?'

'No. They got away. A shambles, as I said.'

The Prime Minister sat quiet. The two folders of briefs were on the table in front of him. Luckily he had been through them fairly thoroughly. The Leader of the Opposition had been in poor form lately. He should not have much trouble. Then John remembered Cornwall's question. He spoke from the Gothic embrasure where he stood.

'Is it on the tapes yet?'

'No,' said Bernays. 'They're ringing next of kin now. The Press are usually willing to hold it an hour or so. I shall have to make a statement in the House tomorrow.'

He looked at the Prime Minister enquiringly. Sir James nodded, then gestured towards his political Secretary.

'John's thinking of Cornwall. He's got the first question to me, and it's on Ireland. But he won't have heard?'

'It happened just after 2. He could have heard from a bystander – a relative who's been reached already – or the IRA themselves. But it would be bad luck.'

'There'll be some awkward questions tomorrow.'

'I'll have to say there'll be a thorough enquiry into the whole affair and promise to report again.'

'An outside enquiry?' asked the Prime Minister.

'From outside Ireland, yes, I think so. Probably from outside the Army too. I'll try to think of a sensible QC and let you know. I'll have to talk to Joe Mercer.'

Joe Mercer was the Secretary of State for Defence. Under the new arrangements Bernays was responsible for all security in Northern Ireland, including the Army there, but Mercer's consent would be needed for an enquiry of this kind.

'D'you want me to speak to Joe?'

'If you would . . . then the Northern Ireland committee can take a decision tomorrow.'

'Arrange that, will you?' the PM said to Pershore.

'Of course, Prime Minister.'

The necessary kaleidoscope of telephone calls, talks and meetings was Pershore's business, and he was very good at it.

'It's just on quarter past.' It was Newings's job as Parliamentary Private Secretary to get the PM into the chamber on time, and he too had become an expert.

'Questions to the Prime Minister,' said the Speaker from beneath his wig at precisely 3.15.

The Under Secretary for the Environment who had been answering previous questions sat back against the bumpy leather of the front bench. He hoped the sweat on his forehead was not too obvious to the TV cameras or to the Prime Minister. He was safe. He had spun out his answer to question 24 in the hope that the clock would save him. Question 25, about the route of a much-hated motorway in the Lake District, was a stinker.

Jeremy Cornwall bobbed up towards the Speaker. He always sat at the end of the third bench below the gangway on the Government side.

'Number One, Sir.'

The Prime Minister rose to the despatch box and opened his folder. Cornwall did not have to read out his question, because every Member in the House had it in front of him on the order paper. '1. Mr Jeremy Cornwall (Mid-Staffordshire). To ask the Prime Minister whether he will pay a visit to Belfast.'

'I have at present no plans to do so, sir.'

The Prime Minister's voice was deeper and more effective in public than in private.

Several Members on both sides of the House stood up. But it was the rule that the author of the original question had the right to the first supplementary. Indeed this was usually the main point of putting down the question.

'Mr Jeremy Cornwall,' said the Speaker.

There was an audible shifting and nudging in the galleries. Because of television Jeremy Cornwall was known throughout the nation. Lately he had come to wear his sweeping black hair rather longer over his collar, to draw attention away from a thinning scalp. His shoulders in the bright blue suit were hunched, and the attractive strong voice was clearly aimed at the television audience rather than his fellow-MPs.

'Is the Prime Minister aware of the terrible, the unprecedented disaster in which thirty-two of our young soldiers

30

were barely an hour ago mown down like helpless rabbits in the streets of Belfast?' The order paper shook in his hands as he worked himself up. 'Will he at once fly to Belfast and sack those senior officers who by their complacency brought about this disaster? What has he, the chief spokesman of the Government, to say this afternoon to the relatives of those who died in this hopeless slaughter?'

The House was surprised and appalled at the news. In the public gallery there was a round of applause for Cornwall, quickly stifled by the tailcoated attendants. A young woman was hustled out.

John, sitting in the cramped Civil Servants' box alongside the Speaker's chair, could see the Prime Minister hesitate and grope in his mind for the right line of reply. Across the gulf of ten yards which separated them he willed him to get it right.

'Yes, sir, I was informed of this terrible tragedy just before I entered the House this afternoon. The full details of what happened are still coming in, and my right honourable friend the Secretary of State for Northern Ireland will be making a statement at the end of questions tomorrow. I am sure the whole House will wish to join me in expressing our deep sympathy with the relatives of those who died and our sense of shock that this brutal act of mass murder should have been committed.'

The House expected him to say more. There was nothing final about the way he pronounced the last few words. But after a second or two of indecision he sat down.

John knew in his bones that it was not enough. Nothing about an enquiry, no anger against the terrorists, no re-assertion of policy, no feeling of any kind. Even Mr Well-come, the Leader of the Opposition, still shell-shocked from his Election defeat, felt that something more was required.

He lumbered to the despatch box opposite the Prime Minister.

'The whole House will associate itself with the Prime Minister's words of sympathy . . . We will of course await the Secretary of State's further statement . . . but can the Prime Minister give an assurance at once that no effort will be spared to track down these cowardly assassins' (a murmur of approval from all sides of the House) 'and that an enquiry will be held to establish by what error our forces found themselves in such a vulnerable and unprotected position?'

The Prime Minister, recognizing his mistake, made it worse. It usually took him several seconds to lose his temper, and John knew the symptoms well. He ran his hand quickly back through his white hair, he twitched the lapel of his coat, his pale face turned sallow and set.

'There is no evidence yet of error, and the right honourable gentleman knows that quite well.' His soft hands tightened on the despatch box. The voice was still good, but the edge in it was out of harmony with the feeling of the house. 'Of course there will have to be an enquiry, but it does no good to leap to conclusions in advance. It is typical of the right honourable gentleman that he should seek political profit from a national tragedy with ill-informed criticism of this kind.'

There was a dutiful 'hear hear' or two from his colleagues on the Front Bench, but most of the Conservative Party sat quiet and embarrassed behind him. From the box John heard one young MP at the end of the bench nearest him mutter a sentence to his neighbour which ended with the words: 'Losing his grip.' There was a muttered response which John could not catch.

The Speaker called the next question, and the questioner bobbed to the Chair.

'No. 2, sir.'

No. 2 was about the rate support grant and John sat back relieved. The ten remaining minutes of question time should be plain sailing. But before the Prime Minister began his answer to No. 2, Jeremy Cornwall was on his feet again.

'On a point of order, Mr Speaker.'

'Mr Cornwall.'

John had noticed before now how Cornwall's voice acquired something of a brogue when he spoke on Irish matters. The lilt was very evident today.

'Mr Speaker, in view of the wholly unsatisfactory nature of that reply, may I make it plain that I and many others are reduced to despair? Up to now I have urged the Government to send more troops to Northern Ireland, and to take their security responsibilities seriously. This terrible tragedy shows once more that they refuse. Well, I take that refusal as final.'

'Order, order,' shouted some Conservatives. Cornwall was clearly not raising a genuine point of order but the Speaker made no move. Beneath his huge wig he was mortal, and Cornwall in a temper was not a safe man to stop. He now raised his voice to a bellow.

'And so I have changed my purpose. From this moment on I shall spend all my energy, all my waking hours, to campaign for the immediate and total withdrawal of British troops from Ulster. On behalf of the youth of Britain I say we cannot allow one more drop of English blood to be shed in this dishonest and shameful charade. As a young man, I cannot sit idly by while they risk their lives. I shall not rest till all my young countrymen are safely home.'

There was a scatter of hear, hears from some left-wing Labour members opposite who had always argued for withdrawal. Cornwall swept his black hair back across his forehead, and strode down the gangway. His chin jutted with determination, and he threw his order paper on to the floor of the House as if it represented a way of life which he rejected. He was the picture of honest youthful indignation, John could see the two authorized television cameras swivelling to follow him. He marched out of the House without turning to bow to the Speaker. It was an effective piece of instant history.

'Mr Atkins.'

'No. 2, sir.'

'I am not yet in a position to add to the reply which I gave to the honourable gentleman on May 13.'

'But is the Prime Minister not aware . . .' John and Pershore, sitting side by side in their narrow box, by common consent stopped listening. Their man was safe for a minute or two.

'Cornwall did not carry the House with him,' whispered Pershore. 'Only a few Labour members.'

'It's not the House he's after,' said John. 'Wait for the Press tomorrow.'

# CHAPTER SEVEN

And the Press the next morning was indeed lousy. Antony could see this even standing in the doorway of his father's dining room. The Prime Minister sat as usual surrounded by newspapers. It was just past eight o'clock. He was a tidy man in everything except newspapers. Once he skimmed through a paper he let it fall spreadeagled to the floor. There were ten of them. He spent three minutes each on *The Times,* the *Telegraph* and the *Guardian,* and ninety seconds on the rest. So in twenty minutes he'd gathered everything he needed to know, and he never looked at a newspaper again until he glanced at the two London evenings with tea and toast at five o'clock. Antony could remember when his father after reading the papers had exclaimed, cursed and rung up editors or even proprietors. But years had brought the philosophic mind.

'Not too good?' Antony said, standing in the doorway. He had listened to the Press summary on the eight o'clock radio.

'Good morning,' said the Prime Minister, putting aside the last newspaper politely. 'It is bad enough to deal with Ireland. To deal with a bogus political crisis at home is absurd.'

Sir James was fully dressed. Although the day would be hot again he wore a waistcoat with his pale grey suit. Soon he would go downstairs through the Cabinet Room into the garden and choose a rose for his button-hole. Antony thought guiltily of the bushes he had butchered the day before.

'Jeremy Cornwall, you mean?'

'Yes, that's right, do you know him?' The Prime Minister always spoke as if Antony knew nothing whatever about the political scene. Antony could see a banner headline staring up from the carpet of newspapers on the floor.

BRING THE BOYS HOME
CORNWALL'S SHOCK CHALLENGE

'Yes, he's a shit, a prize shit.'

He never remembered in time that his father did not like bad language, even watered down. The Prime Minister picked up the telephone on the floor as if to finish the conversation.

'Chief Whip, please, if you can find him.'

There was a pause, but a short one, for the Downing Street switchboard is famous as the best in London.

'Good morning. How are you, David? Had any reaction to yesterday? . . . Well yes, that's hardly surprising. I'm worried myself. He's had far too much space in the Press, and that always makes the back-benchers nervous . . . No, no, of course they don't like him, his strength has never been in the House. Wait till they come back from the constituencies on Monday. That's when the Whips will start hearing from them . . .'

'. . . Do you want me to talk to the 1922 Executive?'

'. . . Yes, I think you're probably right. I'll have a word with Paul Bernays. We can talk about it again tomorrow. We don't want to give an impression of panic. Goodbye then David, see you later, my regards to Sylvia.'

While this conversation went on Antony screwed up his courage. He could hear stately splashing as Helena took her bath behind the door to his right. He did not have very much time. He tightened the cord of his silk dressing gown, and talked rather fast.

'Look, Father, Helena tells me you're ill. It's nothing to do with me, but shouldn't you pull out now? You won the Election for them, you've started them off in the new Parliament. Now it's going to be rough with Ireland and Cornwall and the rest of it. You're not strong enough any longer to do it well. You'll simply destroy yourself. Whereas if you resign now you can have proper treatment, and you and Helena can find a nice house in Hampshire or somewhere where you can fish to your heart's content.'

It all came out in a rush, and because he had thought about it too long, the words were stilted. He knew he had muffed it before he stopped speaking. He stood in the doorway, unshaved, wearing only his dressing gown, thrown back into a teenage awkwardness which he had hoped never to feel again.

'Fish?' said the Prime Minister. 'I haven't fished for years. It bores Helena to tears. It's only my leg. I've strained a muscle, it's taking time to heal. You mustn't believe everything Helena says.' He paused. 'Would you mind bringing over that red box from the dressing-table? There are some briefs I must read before the Northern Ireland Committee meets. When's your plane to Brussels?'

So it was no good trying to get through to his father. Maybe Helena had been lying, trying to catch him on the raw and his father wasn't really ill after all. Certainly he looked brisker and less tired this morning, and a man of 65 was entitled to have his boxes brought to him.

But even if he was ill, Antony could no longer get through to him. Antony remembered how it had felt before this was true. He remembered in particular how there had been a wedding reception on the terrace of the House of Commons. He could not recall which girl it had been, though it was only twelve years back. It had poured with rain and they had all been penned uncomfortably into the long narrow tent lined with tables of sandwiches. The rain had lifted just as the bride and groom went off to change. He and his father had slipped through the join between two lengths of canvas and stood and sipped their champagne away from the stifling hubbub, leaning over the stone parapet which bordered the Thames. For five minutes his father had talked freely to him about his hopes in the House, about his dead wife who had been Antony's mother, about whether he should marry Helena. The sun had broken through the clouds, brighter for being unexpected, transforming the river and even the thick lump of St Thomas's Hospital opposite. It must have been the champagne. Not since then had they talked as friends. Now they had both lost the art.

Antony could hear the water swishing out of Helena's bath. He fetched the red box, and his father fished a bunch of keys out of his waistcoat pocket.

'My plane's not till ten,' said Antony. 'I'll be back tomorrow. It's a routine loan for property development in Brussels.'

'Ah, yes.' His father was already browsing in the box. The papers were carefully separated into five folders marked Urgent Action this Day, Urgent Information, Action, Information and Foreign Office Telegrams. The Prime Minister usually picked out the least urgent folders first. He believed that a certain measure of exasperation was good for Civil Servants.

'I'll be off, then.'

'All right, see you tomorrow.' The Prime Minister seemed far away. Next door Helena brushed her teeth noisily. But as Antony turned to go his father looked up from the box.

'You wouldn't understand, Antony. It's a drug, worse than alcohol. Once you are Prime Minister it's impossible to give up. Either you're kicked out or you're carried out. Have a good day in Brussels.'


# CHAPTER EIGHT


'Did I tell you he'd asked my parents over to tea?' asked Clarissa.

'I saw it on the diary card,' said John. 'How did that happen?'

They sat side by side in the back of the black official Rover, their knees touching. The front seat was piled high with boxes, including John's own black box for political papers. Though the traffic on the M40 was light in the middle morning Jack the driver never took the car above 50 miles an hour. There had been a circular from the Department of the Environment recommending this as the most economical speed even on motorways. At this rate they would hardly get to Chequers in time for lunch.

'My mother is a shameless snob. She wrote directly to the PM saying they'd heard so much about him from me and they did live only twenty miles from Chequers. Instead of showing the letter to me silly Pershore put it straight in the box and it came out last week with a scribble on it "Invite tea". My father is as embarrassed as I am. You'll like my father.'

'It'll be splendid to meet him,' said John.

He took her hand and held it squeezed down between them on the seat so that Jack the driver could not see in the driving mirror. One or two people on the No. 10 staff had smiled knowingly at him lately. Helena must have talked, and talk spread rapidly downwards. The lady who brought his coffee every morning had taken to putting at least a dozen sugar lumps by the saucer. 'Need to keep your strength up,' she had said knowingly, as if he spent each afternoon wrestling with Clarissa in one of the beds provided on the third floor for staff who worked late.

Glancing sideways at her face and the way her throat fitted into the old-fashioned silk blouse, he wished that he did. But in the two weeks since Helena had found them together he had not got further than a squeezed hand and a good night kiss. Suppers, yes, Chinese and Italian, in Fulham Road restaurants or in Clarissa's flat off Notting Hill Gate. Talk, certainly, gallons of it, about everything except the future of each of them. If this was courtship, it was extraordinarily middle-class and old-fashioned, thought John, like something out of a Julian Slade musical from the 'fifties. He was hopelessly old-fashioned himself, he recognized that. He had slept with a girl at Oxford for a few months, and later with another on a holiday in the Aegean. Each time the girl had made the running, and he wondered if Clarissa would ever do the same. He squeezed a little more, and thought again of those hard beds at the top of No. 10. Were there locks on those doors, he wondered? Not that it mattered, for if they ever did get up there, they would probably sit side by side on the bed discussing Proust. He felt that they behaved as if they had been married for four years already, and in the circumstances this was ridiculous. He envied Antony, who had many problems, but not this one.

'Is it a typical Saturday lunch?' asked Clarissa.

'Yes, the usual mixture, two tycoons, an MP, a don and the Chairman of the Bucks County Council. Plus wives.'

'The wives are always the hardest.'

'Lady Cloyne's quite fun, I met her the other night.'

They were on the last stretch now, the long winding road which leads from Great Missenden into the green depths of the Buckinghamshire countryside. Jack had slowed to 40 miles an hour. Famous people in big cars often got lost on this stretch, puzzling over the Gothick sketch-map sent them with their invitation, searching vainly for Chequers in a maze of byways and beechwoods. But not Lady Coyne, who had been before. There was her dark green Rolls parked on the verge ahead of them. She sat on a wicker chair by the side of the car, partly hidden by the surrounding cow parsley, wearing a white dress and a tiny red hat. Lord Cloyne and the chauffeur were fiddling with glasses and a bottle of champagne.

'She'll be late,' said Clarissa as they passed.

'She likes to be half an hour late.'

'He's the man Antony works for, isn't he?'

'Yes, he's an old flame of Helena's. Extinguished by now, I reckon.'

'D'you think I should have brought a hat?'

'Of course not, you're staff.'

He leaned across, and kissed her on her high cheekbone. Jack stepped on the accelerator, and they took the last corner at a giddy fifty-five.

'Why does Lady Cloyne get asked so often? Is she as amusing as all that?'

'No, but she has a loud voice and a kind heart. She's his secret weapon against Helena.'

'Helena's not coming, of course?'

'You know she never comes to Chequers unless she's forced to at gunpoint. Nothing less than a Head of State will get her here.'

'Poor PM.'

'Not at all. He's devoted to her. He just likes to get away from time to time, that's all. It works out pretty well.'

They were passing the main entrance road, set between two lodges. The drive rose, dipped, rose again to their left, and beyond it they could see the dusky Elizabethan mass of Chequers, set deep in its landscape. No one used the main drive now; it belonged to older and safer days. For security reasons they had to take a side road half a mile farther on, where the police would stop them and check their names and car numbers against the details telephoned through from London. Then they joined the main drive again and drove into the courtyard of the house past the big tulip tree.

It was an idiosyncrasy of the Prime Minister to open his own front door. He was not allowed to do it at No. 10, but for his small parties at Chequers he insisted.

'You're late,' he said. 'The Chairman of the County Council is here already.' He was smiling, but he meant it. Every member of the staff was expected to arrive fifteen minutes ahead of his guests.

John noticed a small chair pushed out of its ordinary position into the middle of the entrance hall. The Prime Minister had been sitting there waiting for the front door bell to ring. A few weeks ago he would have stood.

John and Clarissa carried the boxes from the car into the office immediately to the left of the entrance. A Garden Room girl was on duty there, guarding the telephone and the chattering telex machine. There were so many Garden Room girls that John had not yet mastered all their names. He thought this one was called Mary, but was not sure enough to try it out. She looked at John and Clarissa knowingly.

'Had a nice drive down?' she asked.

John understood and was cross. No. 10 was a family, and a family gossiped.

'No, Jack drove like a snail with a hang-over. Anything happened we should know about?'

'William Pershore has telexed down a draft itinerary for the Foreign Office for the Far East tour. The PM wants to settle it after lunch. William Pershore and Richard Newings are coming to talk about it at 3.'

She gave Clarissa and John flimsy copies of the draft, and of the Prime Minister's programme for the rest of the day. John jammed his in his pocket. He had clear ideas about the Far East tour already. He did not know if anyone would share them.

'That's a bad idea,' he said. 'We shan't start lunch till 2, and anyone who thinks we'll be shot of Lady Cloyne by 3 is out of his mind.'

'Stop being such a bear,' said Clarissa. 'And your hair's standing on end. You can't get through to the loo without bumping into the County Council. You'd better comb it here.'

She produced a little blue comb from her handbag. John ignored it, and smoothed his stiff hair fiercely with his hand. She had no right to mother him in this way in front of other people.

'There's another thing,' said Mary. 'John Stebbings, the Liberal MP who was coming to lunch, cried off a couple of hours ago. Very apologetic, but he woke up this morning with mumps. Typical Liberal childishness, the PM said.'

'So?'

'The PM told me to see if Mr Jeremy Cornwall could come in his place.'

'Good grief.'

'He was charming on the phone.' It had obviously been an experience for Mary. 'Asked me my name and all that Said he had been going to his constituency, but an invitation to Chequers was a command, and so on.'

'And then?'

'He'll be a bit late, but promised to be here by 2.'


## CHAPTER NINE


It was in fact just after 2 that the main course entered the dining-room by one door, and Jeremy Cornwall by another. He stood for a moment framed in the dark panelling. At a range of ten yards he looked a picture of energetic youth, charming but strong. He had picked a deep red rose from the bed outside the front door. Pinned to his lapel it set off admirably the sweep of black hair and the light grey suit. He easily won the competition with the saddle of lamb for the attention of those present. He did not blur his entry with any apology for being late.

'Ah, Jeremy,' said the Prime Minister, shifting round in his chair. 'I'm so glad you were able to come at such short notice. Forgive me if I don't get up. D'you know everyone? We've put you over there, next to Lady Cloyne.' Then turning back to his other guests. 'This is Mr Jeremy Cornwall, of whom you have all heard.'

'Thank you, thank you,' said Jeremy Cornwall, as if acknowledging applause. 'It's a real pleasure to come to a quiet old fashioned lunch in the country after the week I've had. Pardon me if my voice is hoarse.'

It was the height of impertinence, given that he had spent the week at packed meetings in three cities denouncing the Irish policies of his host.

John could see the PM bestir himself. He had been silent over the soup, but now he chatted eagerly to dim ladies on his left and right. Jeremy Cornwall was at a diagonal to him, just within the radius of his charm. John, sitting at the end of the table, winced at the sheer weight of flattery which the Prime Minister heaped on his enemy. Surely he did not believe that Cornwall could be bought so easily.

'How is the book going then, Jeremy?' Cornwall had just published a selection of speeches and essays under the title *Young for England*. It appeared simultaneously in hardback and paperback.

Cornwall was helping himself to red currant jelly, and the Prime Minister hurried on. 'You've read them, of course, Mrs Earle?' to his right. 'Really, what a shame. You should lose no time. Put together in this way, they have the most remarkable impact. What about you, Lady Cloyne? Yes, of course you read everything. The most forceful oratory of any young man since Canning, I should say, and the remarkable thing is the speeches are just as exciting to read as they are to listen to.'

'May we quote that on the jacket of the next edition?' asked Cornwall. His dark eyes were bright, and John supposed that he would always be thirsty for praise from any source. His voice, so effective in public, in private conversation sounded harsh and coarse by comparison with his elegant appearance.

'Of course, of course, anything to keep you off our backs in the House of Commons.'

Lady Cloyne had been munching Brussels sprouts through this exchange. She evidently did not like what she heard.

'How old are you, Mr Cornwall?' she asked between mouthfuls.

'I was thirty last month. You may have read of the party we gave at the Savoy.'

'I am told I too appear in the gossip colunms, but I never read them. You look older than that. Your hair is getting thin. Why is your wife not here?'

The Prime Minister chipped in, speaking deliberately so that Lady Cloyne could catch the point.

'Mrs Cornwall is up in Staffordshire. Of course she could not be expected to come down at such short notice. I was very lucky that Jeremy happened to be free. Tell me, Jeremy, what is going to happen in the French elections? I gather you were there during the recess.'

'The Left will miss it by a hairsbreadth.'

'How can you be so certain?' Lady Cloyne was not in a mood to be put down, even by the Prime Minister. She laid down her knife and fork in a very definite manner, as if indicating that she would not be needing them for several minutes. 'If it is true that you are only thirty, you have not had time to become so definite about such an indefinite subject. I have studied the French all my life, and still know nothing about them.'

'That is because you are not a politician yourself,' said Cornwall. He was not quite sure who she was, and did not bother to be polite to her, but raised his voice to bring more people within range. 'In politics the only thing that counts is absolute certainty. You must make up your mind on the best evidence, then throw away all qualifications, and never hedge your bets. I'm sure you agree, James.'

For a second the Prime Minister allowed himself to show surprise at being addressed in this way by a man half his age. There was a clatter of plates being cleared, and John caught Clarissa's eye at the other end of the table. The sleek young man on her left was leaning towards her, pressing some question which John could not catch. By process of elimination John deduced that this must be the managing director of a big furniture firm over the hill in High Wycombe. He might have felt jealous, except that Clarissa was obviously straining to catch the conversation around Cornwall. She returned his wink.

'The French are the only people who still frighten me,' said the Prime Minister. 'The Italians used to till I spent a year in Rome. The Chinese, I suppose . . . but they are so likeable that I forget to be alarmed. You lived in Paris for a time, I think, Jeremy?'

'Yes. I did, for six months, long enough to speak the language perfectly. I saw no point in staying any longer. It was expensive, and at that time I had no money.' He implied that he was now enormously rich.

'Tell me, how long did it take you to learn Chinese?' asked Lady Cloyne, apropos of nothing. A diamond glinted on her white chest as she turned to bring him into her sight.

'I have never thought that worthwhile,' said Cornwall.

'But surely by the time you are Prime Minister we shall all have to speak Chinese. Isn't that right, Prime Minister? A thousand million people, the best communists in the world, *and* the best capitalists. I thought better of you, Mr Cornwall. You should look ahead, you really should.'

'You underestimate him, Jane,' said the Prime Minister. 'Jeremy is waiting till they romanize their script. Then he will master it in a couple of nights, just in time to save Hong Kong for Britain.'

John could see Jeremy Cornwall stiffen at this hint of irony, then relax again as Lady Cloyne turned away from him.

'Hong Kong is not worth the life of a single British soldier,' he said to the table in general.

Lady Cloyne leant across to John, obliterating a don eating strawberries between them.

'Why is this pompous young man here to spoil my luncheon?' she asked in a stage whisper.

'I can only suppose it's a peace initiative,' said John.

'Suppose, suppose – you ought to know, you're the Political Secretary. You're falling down on your job. The PM should have learnt by now you can't feed a tiger on olive branches. This one will never change his spots.'

The don between them giggled nervously into his cream. John wondered if lunch would ever end.

It ended five minutes later, with an agreement to take coffee on the terrace. As the guests moved, John fished out of his pocket the revised programme for the afternoon which Mary had given him when he arrived.

1 for 1.15. Luncheon party.
3.      Meeting to discuss Far East Tour.
        PM
        Mr Pershore
        Mr Newings
        Miss Clarissa Strong
        Mr John Cruickshank.
3.30.   Rajnayan Ambassador.
4.30.   Brigadier and Mrs Strong to tea.
5.30.   Open extension to Princes Risborough Secondary

School. Mr Pershore will accompany. (Department of Education and County Council briefs in box.)

7.      Return to London.

8.15.   Arrive No. 10. Family dinner.

It was ten to three : as usual they would be trailing behind the programme all afternoon. The Prime Minister, moving slowly out of the dining-room behind his guests, motioned to John to join him.

'I've agreed to see Cornwall in the study for a few minutes,' he said. 'You and Clarissa will have to keep the rest of them happy outside till we come out. Show them the swimming pool, it's open, I think.'

'You don't want me to sit in with you?' John was no good at disguising his disappointment at being shut out from this kind of occasion. It simply wasn't safe for political adversaries to meet without a witness. The Prime Minister noticed his tone and slightly shrugged his shoulders.

'Better not, I think,' he said. He looked exhausted by his efforts at the lunch-table, and he was definitely dragging one leg.

As he opened the study door he seemed to lean upon the handle. 'Go and get him, will you?' he said.

Jeremy Cornwall was standing on the terrace in the sun, talking to Clarissa, a glass of brandy already in his hand. He had picked another of the Prime Minister's roses and started to pin it on Clarissa's blouse; but he broke away, giving her the flower, as soon as he saw John approaching. Politics must always come first.

'Pretty girl, that,' he said, in her hearing. 'Is the boss ready, then? He'll be wanting his afternoon snooze after all that wine and food. Looks a bit run down. I won't keep him long. Nothing particular to say, in fact.'

As they passed into the short map-lined corridor which led from the garden door to the study, he held John by the sleeve for a moment.

'Look, your name's Cruickshank, isn't it? The boss asked if you could sit in on our talk. But I said better not, much better not. He and I are the principals, we'll do better with no staff. Nothing personal of course, no offence meant.'

45

John felt like dropping a curtsy and saying, 'And none taken, kind sir.' He seethed, muttered, and held the study door open. He could see the Prime Minister sitting in the big leather armchair by the empty grate.


# CHAPTER TEN


Lady Cloyne was dead-heading the roses with a pair of ancient secateurs which Lord Cloyne had had to fetch from the Rolls. Lord Cloyne watched her from a deck chair, nursing a glass of port, wondering whether he could smoke a second cigar without being rebuked, wondering how long this blessed interlude of peace would last. Apart from Jeremy Cornwall, the rest of the guests had left, the Prime Minister having reappeared briefly from the study to say goodbye and receive their thanks. Then he had gone back in, but John, passing and repassing the door on minor pretexts, could hear very little in the way of conversation. The three o'clock meeting was already assembled in the Hawtry Room, across the great hall from the study. Since it consisted only of No. 10 staff it did not matter when it started – except that the Rajnayan Ambassador would be crunching up the drive in about twenty minutes.

'What's His Excellency coming to Chequers for on a Saturday afternoon?' asked Richard Newings. 'He wasn't in the programme for the week.' He looked over his pince-nez accusingly.

'He's been kept hanging about for weeks for an answer to their invitation to the PM to go to Rajnaya,' said Clarissa. 'He rang up day after day, and eventually the PM said he could come this afternoon to get his answer.'

'Chequers was left to future Prime Ministers by the late Lord Lee of Fareham as a place of tranquillity and rest,' said Newings. 'Lord Lee, though a foolish man in many ways, was quite right in this respect. If he had known his house was being turned into a cross between a slave labour camp and a doss house for black men he would have annulled the bequest. And quite right too.'

'Doss house is a bit hard,' said Clarissa. 'The poor Ambassador will only get a cup of tea. If he lingers, we can shunt him on to my parents when they arrive. My father served in Rajnaya for a time.'

'But the real trouble is that the PM hasn't made up his mind about going to Rajnaya. At least not so far as I know,' said John.

'That is one of the purposes of this meeting,' said William Pershore primly. He wore a discreet fawn-coloured suit and highly polished brown brogues. He did not let pass any suggestion that the process of taking decisions at No. 10 was disorderly.

'What meeting?' asked John, looking at his watch. It was nearly quarter past 3.

Then they could hear Jeremy Cornwall's voice in the entrance hall.

'Goodbye then, James. I should think it over if I were you. Think it over, that's the thing. Thanks for the meal. The cooking's better than under poor Topping.'

They heard the main door close, and John went out into the entrance hall. He found the Prime Minister staring at the newly-closed door in front of him, as if examining for the first time its different generations of heavy bolts and hinges. He was leaning back against a big oak chest behind him. Little blue veins were clearly marked on his sallow cheeks.

When he saw John he jerked himself together. 'I'll just go and write a short note about all that,' he said. 'You can take it back to the Chief Whip this evening. I'd like him to see it tonight.'

'Any excitements?' asked John.

The old man hesitated. 'What do you want excitements for? It's not excitements we're short of.'

'You won't forget our meeting on the Far East tour? We're all here in the Hawtry Room. And of course the Rajnayan Ambassador is due at 3.30.'

'Yes, yes, I know all that.' Unusually, he was irritated. 'There are plenty of rooms he can wait in. They can give him tea, Ambassadors like cakes. It's no good rushing any of these things. They must take their course, you'll learn that one day.'

He disappeared into the small writing-room called the White Parlour, and it was five minutes before he joined the impatient group in the Hawtry Room. He gave an envelope to John, who saw that it was unsealed and addressed to David Bross, who had taken Bernays's place as Chief Whip.

'You can read it,' the PM said, 'so that you know where we are. But no one else need know.'

John could not prevent himself flushing with pleasure; trust like this made his job worthwhile. He did not mind now that Jeremy Cornwall had kept him out of the talk in the study.

'Now, what have we got to decide?' The Prime Minister was on the sofa, his bad leg stretched in front of him. The afternoon flow of energy into his system had begun. Already he looked different from the old man sprawling against the oak chest whom John had seen outside in the hall a few minutes ago. But it was worrying that these tides of energy should ebb and flow so strongly through him.

Pershore took charge.

'I should perhaps explain first, Prime Minister, that Clarissa Strong is here because as you agreed for the next six months she will be in charge of the foreign affairs desk at No. 10 pending a new appointment by the FO.'

'Not at all,' said the PM. 'Clarissa is here because I asked her to lunch and because her parents are coming to tea. But let it pass.'

'Quite so, Prime Minister.' One of Pershore's strengths was that he took no notice of teasing. 'We need really to settle finally the itinerary for next month's Far Eastern tour. It's been hanging fire for some time. You approved the outline immediately after the Election, and here' – handing him a blue double spaced minute, 'are the detailed proposals. The main variation is that you spend three nights in Hong Kong instead of two. The Governor is anxious that you should have a working dinner with the Urban Council, instead of including them in his lunch for the Executive Council.'

'It sounds like hard work.'

'The Governor was particularly keen.'

'Very well.'

'The other point is more difficult, Prime Minister, and also more urgent. The Government of Rajnaya want you to spend two days there on the way home. You remember the message from President Revani, it was in your box last week-end. Revani is obviously putting great pressure on his Ambassador for a favourable answer and you agreed that the Ambassador should come here this afternoon to receive your decision.'

'What do the FO say?'

Clarissa took her cue.

'They say it's really up to you. Our relations with Revani have improved lately, but of course Rajnaya has no special importance for us any more. Revani is having mild communal trouble, Indians shutting shops and banks, that sort of thing, and a visit from you would show the Indians that he had finally turned his back on his revolutionary past and become respectable in the outside world.'

'And has he?'

'He thinks he can run Rajnaya, and nobody else can. I doubt if his beliefs go much further than that.'

'He's probably right. He was at Cambridge, wasn't he?'

'Yes, that's right.'

'Which college?'

It was one of the Prime Minister's habits to drift off into inessentials while making up his mind.

John judged that this was his moment. He looked at Newings, willing him to give support, then spoke to the gathering as a whole.

'Surely the PM should look at the whole idea of this tour again. After all it was agreed in principle just after the Election when things were very different. I'm not sure that he should go at all.'

Clarissa and Pershore looked at the floor, with severe expressions, and John knew why. Their cast of mind was different from his. He knew even Clarissa was thinking that in a perfect world political secretaries did not butt in at the last moment trying to overthrow the careful work of Civil Servants over several weeks.

'Why do you say that, John?' The Prime Minister's tone was neutral.

'Well, to start with, end July is a terrible time to visit the Far East. It will be very hot indeed, and the programme is bound to be extremely exhausting.'

'We did go into all this before,' said Pershore, his irritation showing. 'The FO has taken particular trouble to insist on proper air conditioning in the various guest houses and meeting places, and to set aside at least one hour a day for rest. If the tour is to take place at all it has to be after the House rises in the third week of July.'

'After all, it was you, John, who insisted I shouldn't go in September because you want me to do those political tours in Scotland and Lancashire.' The PM smiled, but John could see he was losing. He looked again at Newings, who did not yet know the PM well, and came in with the wrong argument.

'John is surely right, it will be very exhausting whatever precautions are taken. I wonder if you should consult Dr Ellerman whether he thinks it would be entirely prudent. I gather Helena will not be able to come and support you, and in the circumstances . . .'

The PM cut him off.

'Thank you, I know my own strength and weakness. I shall be able to manage very well. The doctor can come with us. I don't doubt it will do me good to have a complete break from this terrible prison routine.'

John decided to weigh in.

'Let's face it, the political situation is quite different now. I don't know whether you managed to head off Jeremy Cornwall just now, but it doesn't sound like it. He's a thoroughly destructive man, with a flair for oratory, and on the Irish business he's stumbled on a sizzling popular cry. If he carries through the speaking campaign he's announced for July, we could be in real trouble by the end of the month. He had three thousand in the Colston Hall at Bristol two nights back, and they cheered him for ten minutes. Bundles of petitions for pulling out the troops are pouring in at No. 10 already, and those are just the oddments, quite apart from the main petition he's organising himself. Yet you mean to be away just when his campaign is at its peak. I think it's too dangerous.'

'Surely this can be left to the Secretary of State for Northern Ireland,' said Pershore, crossing his thin legs as he sometimes did when he felt he was on to a strong point. 'It is not for me to comment on a political problem, but Paul Bernays is, as they say, no slouch himself when it comes to oratory. I should have supposed that he could keep young Mr Cornwall at bay quite satisfactorily until you return. The violence has died down again for the time being. Mr Matheson's report on the Greenjackets massacre won't be ready for weeks yet. I agree that the underlying position is still tense, but there's no reason to expect any sudden deterioration.'

John could see the PM look at him quizzically. He knew they both had the same thought. Paul Bernays certainly had the authority to keep Cornwall at bay, but would he use it? Lately he had fallen very silent, using reasons of pressing business to excuse himself from television appearances and even from debates in the House. John did not know quite why. He did know that the old easy personal friendship between Bernays and the PM was for the moment clouded.

'Would the Parliamentary Party be upset if I went East as soon as the House was up?' The Prime Minister asked Newings the question which lay within his particular sphere as Parliamentary Private Secretary. But Newings had been bitten once, and would not fight again that day.

'No, they'll scatter at once, and most of them won't look at a newspaper or a television set for at least a fortnight. If they do, they'll be glad to see you getting some head-lines abroad. Publicity is hard to get at home at that time of year.'

There was a pause, broken by the noise of tyres taking a corner too fast on loose gravel. A Rolls with a green, white and chocolate flag stopped outside the door. From where he sat near the window John could see the licence plate below the back bumper: RAJ 1.

'Then that's settled,' said the Prime Minister. 'The itinerary for the trip as a whole is approved. I shall tell the Ambassador that I shall be delighted to go to Rajnaya – two days only. The FO must make sure that the programme there doesn't involve me in Rajnayan politics. Anything else we need to settle now?'

'There's the composition of your party,' said Pershore, consulting a list. 'We've told the FO you want to keep it as small as possible. May I take it that Lady Percival will not be coming?'

'Helena will stay at home, but I shall take my son Antony to help me over personal matters.'

Pershore opened his mouth and shut it again. They were

51

all taken by surprise, and none of them was pleased. If Antony was to look after the PM, who was to look after Antony? Helena, though stormy in private, looked splendid and behaved well on all public occasions.

'It's time he learned how the real world works. And strangely enough he seems keen,' said the Prime Minister. Now I must go and see the Ambassador. Clarissa, you'd better come and take a note. Ask Mrs Jennings for a pot of Indian tea in the White Parlour. And cake of course, a great deal of cake.'

Pershore and Newings disappeared towards London in a black official Ford slightly bigger and newer than the one allocated to Clarissa and John. John looked at his watch – still three-quarters of an hour before Clarissa's parents were due. He wanted to think. He wanted to bring his relationship with Clarissa to a head. He wanted to go to bed with her, but it was hardly an overriding passion. He wanted to marry. He wanted to marry her – but then again, it wasn't overpowering. He didn't want to make a mistake. Why the hell couldn't a wave come along and sweep him off his feet, as it did other people? How could he find time to sort out all these dim feelings into some reasonable pattern? And anyway, was it possible to sort them out just by thinking about them? Each time he dredged one of his emotions to the surface of his mind it trickled away like sand, and he couldn't be sure it really existed.

The Cloynes were still in the garden, he could hear her shouting at her husband across the rosebeds. John decided to have a swim. The PM kept the water too warm for his liking, but even so it helped thought. Once on an Easter morning in the cold Aegean five minutes' swimming had brought him to a clear decision about another girl. Would the two detectives be in the pool? He was in luck, they had gone, leaving large wet footmarks in the changing cubicle.

John emptied his pockets before he undressed. On a day like this he acquired many stray bits of paper, telephone messages, notes scribbled at a meeting, maybe a newspaper cutting – the flotsam and jetsam of official life. But there of course in his jacket pocket was the unsealed letter to the

Right Honourable David Bross, MC, MP, Government Chief Whip, 12 Downing Street. By hand.

The PM had said he could read it, and he did, standing in the cubicle with his shirt still on over his bathing trunks.

'Dear David,

As I told you on the telephone this morning I decided on the spur of the moment to speak to J.C. today. He came to lunch, and showed off. Then we had half an hour in the study.

You know that my powers of flattery are considerable. I asked him for advice on sterling, on the common agricultural policy, on whether we should buy the Boeing fighter. I praised his wife, his book, his courage. Then I offered him the Ministry of Defence (I decided after we spoke that Joe Mercer would after all be the right man to promote. Between us we could have persuaded him to go to the Treasury with enthusiasm).

Nothing worked. He is deaf to anything except the cheers he gets on Ireland. He is drunk on Ireland. Ireland is turning him mad. Once we had decided to bring the troops home, yes, he would take the Ministry of Defence, keeping of course, full freedom to break the Government and the Party at any time he wished. But nothing would deflect him from his present campaign.

So from now on there is to be no compromise of any kind with Cornwall. I know the difficulties in the Party, for you point them out every time we meet. But I rely on you to overcome them. When you need my help it will be there. The man is wholly destructive, and he must be destroyed.

Yours ever,
James Percival.'

John pulled his shirt over his head, and hung it untidily on a hook in the wall. That was all very well. John was fond of political memoirs and knew that Prime Ministers often wrote in this vein. Short sentences and a brusque brushing aside of difficulties seemed to go with the office. But did the PM really understand the weapons Cornwall was using, the deep core of defeatism in the British nation which he was tapping? And did he have the counter-weapons which were needed? He himself was visibly flagging. The decision to go to the Far East, to escape from it all, was a bad sign. Who else was there? Bernays, now worried and silent: David Bross, sleek, worried, loyal, but limited: and a lot of people like Newings, able enough but shut in on themselves, having no gift with any audience more than thirty strong.

John stood on the edge of the pool in his badly fitting red trunks. There was an old half-crown on the bottom of the pool. This had been passed on from one Prime Minister's detective to another for many years now as a talisman. They were not supposed to use it for diving practice, because it interfered with the filtering, but they did. John dived, felt for the bottom, fumbled with the half-crown, missed it and spluttered to the surface. So many questions, too few answers. Back to Clarissa, then. He tried to think of himself living with her. She would want to go on working, so no children for a time. He thought the bed part of it would work out well. It was the talk that would worry him. Now they talked as colleagues, jokey, easy talk born out of shared work. But man and wife, lover and mistress, either state would need a new way of talking. John tried to remember when his own parents had last talked in any real way to each other, but it was so long ago he could not grasp it. Perhaps Clarissa's parents had done better.

And there on cue they were, standing by the group of cane chairs at one end of the pool. At least it must be them, for Clarissa had often described them. Her father tall, erect, very thin with sparse grey moustache and Clarissa's deep grey eyes, her mother equally thin, with a strong heavily powdered nose.

'Don't get out,' said Brigadier Strong. 'We are early, and the girl said we could find you here. You must be John Cruickshank.'

Of course he had to pull himself out, but he did it clumsily, flopping back into the water once because his arm muscles were not strong enough. He wiped the water off his right hand and shook hands with them both. He knew exactly how he must look to them – a white rather feeble body going flabby about the waist, untidy thinning hair, a dull pleasant face, old-

54

fashioned bathing trunks, a poor breast stroke. Not what they would hope for in a son-in-law.

'I'm so sorry not to have been there to meet you. I expect Clarissa and the PM are still with the Rajnayan Ambassador.'

'That's right,' said the Brigadier.

'That's a big car for a black man,' said Mrs Strong.

'He's an Arab,' said John, feeling tired. 'They have bigger cars than anyone.'

'Oh,' said Mrs Strong. There was a pause.

'I'll go and change,' said John.

He took his time, and a button came off his shirt. The swim had settled nothing, done him no good. He was not sure he could add to his other problems the burden of twenty years' conversation with Brigadier and Mrs Strong.


## CHAPTER ELEVEN


The main sitting-room of the Rajnayan Government guest house shone with the evening light flooding in through embrasures from the sea. But it was not because of the brightness that Antony was wearing dark glasses. He found them a psychological protection against noise, and the room was full of noise. The air conditioner let into the wall thudded and shook. But mainly it was the sound of tired humans trying to do business in a hurry, competing for the precious half-hour available before they had to leave for President Revani's farewell banquet.

John, unusually, was the noisiest, for he was shouting into a telephone which stood on the corner table by an enormous basket of fruit and toffees garnished with red and yellow paper flowers.

'Tell them it's urgent, URGENT. Is . . . is that No. 10? Thank God, at last. I can hardly hear you, speak up. This is John Cruickshank here. Look, we're in a hurry and the PM must speak to the Secretary of State for Northern Ireland straight away. Can you get him while I wait? No, I daren't lose the connection, I couldn't start all that again . . . Yes, of course I know it's lunch-time in England but his office should know where . . . Right, I'll hang on.'

In the centre of the room was a heavily marked rosewood table loaded with little white coffee cups and flanked by two immense sofas. On these Clarissa, Ian Hanning the Press Secretary, and the British Ambassador in Rajnaya were working on the Prime Minister's speech for the banquet.

'We really can't have this bit on page 3,' said Hanning. 'My boys will see it as Revani hooking the PM right into his domestic squabbles. And they're gunning for Revani after that mix-up over their hotel bookings.'

The Ambassador looked pained. There were no British journalists normally resident in Rajnaya. He disliked the ragtag of scruffy media people who were tailing the Prime Minister on his tour. For the Ambassador, who had not served in Britain for eight years, public opinion was still adequately represented by the correspondence columns of *The Times*.

'I am not sure you understand the position,' he said stiffly. 'The Rajnayans attach great importance to a reference to the President's multi-racial policies. I fear they will deeply resent any attempt to delete this paragraph.'

He looked for support to the Prime Minister sitting in the next armchair. But the Prime Minister had abstracted himself from the discussion. Antony watched his father as he sat absolutely motionless, just smiling, one of his shoelaces undone.

Antony saw that the old man was deliberately trying to cut out all unnecessary expenditure of mental thought and physical energy, trying for a few minutes to recharge the batteries run down during the last ten punishing days. Not for the first time Antony cursed Doctor Ellerman for falling off that dry dock in Hong Kong and breaking his leg. Painful no doubt, and everyone except Antony felt sorry for him. Antony simply knew that his father needed a doctor.

'How would it be,' said Clarissa, 'if instead of "congratulating the Government of Rajnaya" we put "notes with sympathy the efforts made by the Government of Rajnaya"?'

'OK, OK, have it your way, but it'll still be taken as a sellout. The main thing is, we must get the bloody thing cleared. We've been fooling around with it for days. It'll take half an hour to roll off even if the Embassy machine hasn't broken down again.'

The Ambassador stiffened. 'There are some consequential amendments on later pages, I suspect. And of course the Prime Minister has not yet given final approval.'

'No, no, we can clear it without him,' said Clarissa as if the Prime Minister was not sitting three yards from her. She was reading through the text rapidly, jotting in punctuation marks here and there. Getting bossy, thought Antony. But the back curve of her neck as she bent over the paper was an attraction he hadn't noticed before. He wondered if at the banquet she would be wearing the rather low-cut scarlet dress with the tight waist that had been a triumph in Hong Kong.

'Here's the copy for the Ministry of Foreign Affairs. The Rajnayan interpreters want it as soon as possible.' She gave the paper to the Ambassador as if he were an errand boy, then realized a little too late that he wasn't. She smiled and Antony watched her switch on her sex. 'I'm so sorry, but it's all a bit of a fluster, and there doesn't seem to be anyone else around. D'you think you could possibly arrange for it to be delivered to the Ministry?'

'I'll see if the Head of Chancery is still here,' said the Ambassador huffily. 'It's his responsibility. I've got to go home and change. The traffic across the town is terrible at this time of the evening.' He glared round the room at the spread-out newspapers, the full ashtrays and empty coffee cups, the red husks of the lichees which Hanning had munched, Antony slouched with one leg over the arm of his chair, the sheer mess and indecorum of it all.

'Someone ought to be on time for the banquet,' he said, 'even if it's only the poor Ambassador.'

On his way across the room he almost collided with John. John's hair was messy, and the rich food had produced a boil on the left side of his neck.

'They can't find Bernays anywhere,' he said to the PM. 'They've tried the Northern Ireland office, his home, the House – no one seems to know where he's lunching. I've told them to keep going, and ring us as soon as they've traced him.'

'Have they tried the Carlton?' murmured the Prime

Minister. No one took any notice. Clarissa flared out at John.

'You can forget the telephone call. The PM's not changed, he hasn't read his speech for tonight, Revani's car will be here to collect him in ten minutes, he certainly won't have time to talk to Bernays. For Christ's sake, let's put first things first.'

John in turn was angry.

'All right then, which comes first? A bloody useless banquet in this God-forsaken dump of a country, or what's happening at home? If the radio is even half right, there's an uproar at home. Ireland, the cities, Jeremy Cornwall, the lot. And all you can think of is getting to the canapés on time, and putting the commas in your great big boring speech, which no one will either listen to or read.'

Clarissa shut her mouth very tight, and looked hard at John.

Antony's head was knocking with their noise, the clamour of the air conditioner, and the three glasses of whisky which he had drunk while the rest of the party had been at the afternoon round of official talks. He was the only person in the room who had had time to change. He looked again across the room at his father and saw that the old man was asleep. Not absolutely asleep, for he was fighting to keep his eyes open to say some sort of goodbye to the Ambassador who was still hovering over him. But his chin was right down and his eyes when he did open them were without expression. Blast Helena, why had she not come? A prodigal son was one thing, but a wife was another. Damn Dr Ellerman, couldn't he see where the railing ended on that dry dock? Damn and blast himself, for being so full of whisky. He should have accepted the offer of a visit to that collective farm instead of sitting alone through the steamy afternoon with the bottle and his thoughts. Antony rose to his feet. For a long few seconds he could not bring out the words in his head.

'I shall go to the banquet because I like banquets,' he said slowly and loudly. 'The Ambassador will go to the banquet because it is his duty. Messrs Hanning and Cruickshank and Miss Strong will go to the banquet because they've got nowhere else to go. But the Prime Minister will not go to the banquet. Nor will he speak to Mr Bernays, nor to Mr Bross nor to

Mr Cornwall nor to the hall porter at the Carlton Club. The Prime Minister is going to bed at once, immediately, and now.'

They all looked at him. Antony stood in his white sharkskin dinner jacket, swaying very slightly. They saw someone they had never known before. Then they looked at the Prime Minister, but he sat motionless in his chair with his eyes shut. For the moment he was not a person but a body to be contended for.

There was a moment's confused babble, led by the Ambassador. Then the Prime Minister opened his eyes as if a thought had just occurred to him.

'I think I shall go to bed.'

And so it was that Antony Percival entered politics.


# CHAPTER TWELVE


'And so I give you a toast – to the health of President Revani, to the lasting prosperity of Rajnaya, and to the growing friendship between our two Governments and peoples.'

There was a scatter of applause, and the pretty girl interpreter began to translate the speech into Arabic, while the Ambassador backed away from the microphone to his place at the top table. He had a good resonant voice, and had read the Prime Minister's speech as if it was his own – which of course it was.

John drank more of the grain spirit which was one of Rajnaya's contributions to civilization. In the old Sultan's day the spirit had been brewed in filthy stills high in the mountains and brought down to the city sloshing in barrels tied to the flanks of weary donkeys. Now it was mass-produced on the industrial estate alongside the oil refinery and shipped to all parts of the world in bottles with charming labels showing a smiling Arab girl stooping to pick up a sheaf in a sunny field. John had drunk a good deal more than usual. The top table was round. President Revani had of course backed out of the dinner himself as soon as he heard that the Prime Minister was not coming. There were thus only ten places set at the table instead of the expected twelve, so that the space between each guest was wide. This suited John. Normally he was chatty on these occasions, and would have been eager to glean facts and figures from the Director of the Harbour and Stevedoring State Corporation on his left, and the Vice-Chancellor of the University of Rajnaya (ex-Milton Keynes) on his right. But it was the last evening of the tour, and once again he wanted to think about Clarissa. Ten days ago in the Alcock and Brown suite at Heathrow as they waited to board the special RAF VC10 for the flight to Hong Kong he had promised to himself that he would clear up the whole Clarissa business before they returned. Freed from the usual chores of No. 10, the daily round of minutes and meetings and casual intimate chat, he and Clarissa would be able to sort themselves out. But it hadn't happened, it hadn't happened at all. If anything the pace had been more strenuous, the work more insistent than at home. Now it was almost too late – almost, but not quite. He had one night in hand. John looked at Clarissa across the table, and she raised her glass of fizzy orange towards him. That was a relief. The row between them in that terrible sitting-room before dinner was over. John's flashes of temper were rare and never lasted long, but he knew that Clarissa sometimes smouldered. She was wearing the long low-cut scarlet dress for which Antony had hoped. Its harsh colour and fierce angles did not suit her figure, but they helped John to make up his mind. It was not talk that he needed from Clarissa. Talk would be useless, because he had still not made up his own mind what he wanted of her. There was only one thing which would make up his mind, and perhaps hers as well.

John looked round the crowded hotel room. The Rajnayans had attacked fast and silently the heaped plates of rice, boiled meat, fish and fruit in front of them. They were almost all Arabs, for very few Rajnayan Indians were asked to Government banquets. For many of those present this occasion provided the only decent meal of the month. Interspersed with the Rajnayans, distinguished by pink faces and dinner jackets, were members of the British community – oil men, three or four bankers, a couple of British Council school teachers, and the diplomatic staff of the Embassy. The last speech had been interpreted, and on the dais in the far corner of the room a Rajnayan Army band in green tunics and white trousers bounced into a selection from *Mary Poppins*.

John tried to fix every detail of the scene in his memory – the music, the plates still heaped with fruit and sweetmeats, the three glasses by each place, the movement of Antony's hands as he talked to the Vice-Minister of Foreign Trade. He lingered on Antony, envying once again his smooth black hair, his ease of manner and the way his white dinner jacket hung on his body without creasing. The drink inside him brought back the moment at Oxford, now eleven years ago, when he had first met Antony and found him physically attractive. He pushed the memory away from him. Antony had amazed them all tonight with that sudden burst of authority, but John felt no jealousy. What mattered in life was sustained work and steady judgement, and he knew that Antony was capable of neither. Now Antony was talking to a Rajnayan sitting to his left, between him and Clarissa, a tall anxious man wearing the dark grey tunic of the Rajnayan revolution. The two men rose and changed places, smiling meaninglessly at each other. Antony began to talk urgently to Clarissa, and through the array of glasses John could see his hand touch her wrist. He could not hear what Antony was saying.

John found himself on his feet without really meaning it. He went round to where the Ambassador was sitting, and bent confidentially over him. 'I don't know who should make the first move, but I think we ought really to go back and check that the PM is all right. I'm sure the Garden Room girl would have rung us if there had been any thing he needed, but even so . . .'

Ten minutes later they were all back in the guesthouse. The Prime Minister had been sleeping soundly ever since they left him. John and Antony went together into his bedroom without turning on the light. The room was cool, dark and quiet except for the chuntering of the air conditioner. The old man had unhooked the folds of the mosquito net round his bed. They peered down at the sallow old face with the dark moustache through the white net. He was sweating slightly in his thick English pyjamas, but breathing easily.

A pile of routine telegrams had come round from the

Embassy, and been delivered to John's room in an envelope with a red seal. It took John some time to read through them and make sure that none of them needed action that night. Then he undressed and lay on his bed in his underpants, drinking a final whisky out of the bathroom tumbler. It tasted of chlorine from the tap, but it did the work required of it. After five minutes John put on his dressing gown and slippers, having first consulted the list of room numbers with which they had all been provided.

The corridor outside his room was dark, but a dim light showed from an alcove where the passage turned, following the outside ramparts of the old palace of the Sultans of Rajnaya. A sentry stood motionless in the alcove, facing inwards, his rifle held stiffly by his side. Behind the soldier's cap John could see an oil tanker at her moorings, and the sea glittering under a full moon. The man did not stir as he passed. There was just enough light to see the room numbers painted in white on each door. 21, 22, 23 – he was getting close.

Then he heard a door open at the end of the corridor he was approaching, and dimly saw a figure emerge and move towards him, still twenty yards away. John stopped where he was and froze against the cold stone wall. There was a light under one of the doors ahead of him, and the light broadened as the door was opened from inside at the sound of the approaching footsteps. John's eyes were by now acclimatized to the semi-darkness, and he had no difficulty in seeing Clarissa welcome Antony to her room.


# CHAPTER THIRTEEN


'Well, then, how is he? He looks terrible.'

Helena, her fiery hair piled on top of her head, was wearing a green and orange dress more suitable for a cocktail party than for the reception suite for VIPs at Heathrow Airport. She had broken away from the Rajnayan Ambassador to waylay Antony, who had been shaving in the gents. There had been no time for this during the stop-over at Zurich, and after that the queue outside the wash-place in the VC10 on the last leg of the flight had been formidable.

'Very tired. You should have come.'

For once she did not hit back.

'What went wrong?'

'Nothing went wrong. He's old. The trip was a killer. It was too much. In Rajnaya he just flaked out.'

A customs man approached, holding a cardboard list.

'Excuse me, you are Mr Percival, Mr Antony Percival? Did you make any purchases while you were in the East?'

'Yes, that young girl over there,' he pointed to Clarissa, 'and two years' supply of contraceptives.'

The official smiled, ticked the name off his list and passed on to harass the secretaries.

'You haven't changed anyway,' said Helena.

'Nor has all this. What a bloody country.'

The room was polite pandemonium. The Rajnayan Ambassador had come, according to diplomatic custom, to welcome the Prime Minister back from his country. Robbed of Helena and unable to approach the PM, he was gobbling chocolate biscuits in a corner to disguise his chagrin. At the far table, littered with coffee cups, Ian Hanning the Press Secretary was sitting with the Prime Minister, John Cruickshank, Clarissa and Pershore. Various other persons wandered about counting red boxes and suitcases.

'There are about thirty of them in the usual interview room,' said Hanning, breathing uneasily through his moustache. 'There's a good deal of interest. Both BBC and ITN want separate television interviews afterwards.' He tried to make all this sound like good news.

'It's really quite intolerable,' said Pershore. He had enjoyed lording it at No. 10 when the PM was away. 'The Prime Minister has had a long journey and needs several hours rest. It is not reasonable to ask him to give a Press conference. I cannot think who authorized these people to be present.'

'No one authorized them, they don't need authority, they just come.' Hanning had been round this course many times before. 'And they won't be pleased if they're sent away without a story. It could be dangerous.'

'What do you mean by that?' asked Clarissa. Everyone present tended to despise Hanning because he was frightened of his job as Press Secretary. But John tried to remember that Hanning was frightened of his job because he knew it well.

'Well, there have been those stories about the PM's health. There's plenty in the mornings today about the banquet he missed in Rajnaya. If he skips a Press conference today there'll be resignation rumours and requests for a medical bulletin by tonight.'

They spoke as if the PM was not there. He was two feet away, flicking through two days' worth of newspapers and throwing the wrecks on the floor, as they had seen him do so often at No. 10. John could see that he was only going through the form of it. The old man was too tired to absorb anything except the most superficial notion of what he was reading. But it protected him from having to converse with the Rajnayan Ambassador, the representative of the British Airways Authority, the Customs man, the waitress with the weak coffee, his staff, his son and his wife. Despite all the noisy evidence to the contrary, for a precious few minutes behind the shield of newsprint he could feel that he was alone.

Pershore continued his argument with Hanning. 'At least you could rule that they only ask questions about the Far Eastern trip, nothing about Ireland or Jeremy Cornwall or any of that.'

'I suppose I could.' Hanning's eyes began to water, as always happened when he was on the run. He was good with journalists, bad with his colleagues, and terrible with his superiors. He was twenty years older than John, ten years older than Pershore; this too was a great handicap.

'Of course you couldn't.' John was used to defending positions which Hanning had prematurely abandoned. 'The Far Eastern trip is inside page stuff now – even in the heavies – they're not really interested. No one in Britain is interested in anything outside this country except football and sex.'

'It's really a choice between an unrestricted Press conference and nothing at all,' murmured Hanning, edging back into the discussion now that he had an ally.

'Of course it must be nothing at all.' Antony had detached himself from Helena and stood behind Clarissa's chair.

Alone of the party he had no tie and two buttons of his dark blue shirt were undone. A wave of Fagergé after-shave enveloped everyone within range.

Pershore looked startled, for he had not yet heard how the Prime Minister had been persuaded to miss the banquet at Rajnaya. The others had got used already to the idea of Antony as a person having authority. John watched Antony's long hands touch Clarissa's hair as she leant over the back of the chair.

'My father must go straight back to No. 10, and rest until tomorrow morning. He is far too tired to do anything else.'

'Antony is quite right,' said Clarissa.

'That would present very substantial difficulties,' said Pershore, glaring at Clarissa and piling on the syllables to buttress his authority. 'The Secretary of State for Northern Ireland is insisting on a meeting of the Northern Ireland Committee this evening to consider Mr Matheson's report of the enquiry on the Greenjackets shootings. He is particularly anxious . . .'

'Then either Bernays must take the chair or it must wait till tomorrow.'

For a moment Antony thought he had won. He knew exactly why. He did not fit into the structure of Pershore's world. John, Hanning, Bernays, even Helena had labels round their necks. They were the Political Secretary, the Press Secretary, the Secretary of State for Northern Ireland, the wife. Because of their labels Pershore knew how to handle them, just as he could handle dozens of other tidily ticketed personages. The Prime Minister's son – that was a label Pershore had not recognized up to now. To mix the metaphor, Antony was a comet streaking through an ordered constellation and for the time being Pershore was baffled. It was in Pershore's character to draw back until he had satisfactorily classified the new phenomenon.

'Everything's in order now, Prime Minister.' The Airports Authority approached deferentially. 'Whenever you are ready . . .'

'For God's sake, let's get going then.' Helena too had joined the group. She reserved her tough talk for her own immediate circle, and had spent the last few minutes rescuing

65

the Rajnayan Ambassador from his chocolate biscuits. She had charmed him with questions about his family and the state of the weather in his country. So long as she was able to grumble about her job she did it well.

Antony saw Hanning's face and, because he was learning fast, understood why he was dismayed.

'If you like I'll come and explain to your journalists why there's no Press conference,' he said. 'That'll give them a story.'

'But there will be a Press conference.' The Prime Minister had emerged from the stockade of newspapers. He spoke without enthusiasm but firmly. 'I'll just go and wash,' he said. Antony went with him to the door of the washroom. The rest of them did not hear his father's next words. 'You are quite right,' the old man said. 'But so are they. Either I do the whole job or I leave it alone. It's not a part-time occupation . . . Do you think you could lay your hands on a toothbrush?'


Hanning had insisted that questions on the tour should be taken first, but they were few and trivial. The diplomatic correspondents were not there. They were a tribe apart, and would get a long off-the-record briefing later in London. Hanning in the presence of journalists was a man transformed. He took the chair briskly but without causing offence. He even from time to time supplemented an answer from the Prime Minister with a quiet comment of his own. Antony and Clarissa stood together at the back alongside one of the camera crews. Their lights were not on because they were getting a separate interview immediately afterwards, but the press of bodies was already making the room oppressive. Antony watched his father carefully. He looked better than he had in the VIP lounge. His sparse white hair was carefully combed, and he had more colour in his cheeks. But he was husbanding his words.

'Al Hostage, *Toledo Blade*. Would the Prime Minister comment on reports that he went to Hong Kong to prepare the locals for talks on the surrender of the colony to Red China?'

'No such talks are in prospect.' The Prime Minister smiled

briefly to soften the briefness of his reply. Hanning stepped in. 'The lease on the New Territories still has several years to run, and of course the island itself is a Crown Colony with full British sovereignty . . . So far the Chinese have shown no desire to change the status quo.'

The status quo. The phrase jerked Antony into one of those trains of thought which a year or so ago would for him have been unthinkable. Perhaps it was all those hours flying over sea and mountains. Perhaps it was the sight of his father starting the doomed fight for normal health. Perhaps it was the recollection of Clarissa leaning sleepily over him a few hours earlier, the shape of her shoulders outlined against the warm grey dawn of Rajnaya. All these things were much more important than the restless nonsense which interested the people in this room. If only politics could stand still, and let everyone else get on with what mattered. But it could not be, and what was worse he knew that he himself was now hooked. He felt for Clarissa's hand and squeezed it. She had said nothing to him through the flight from Rajnaya or since they reached Heathrow.

'All right?' he whispered.

She still said nothing, but squeezed back. Her hand was dry and warm. The television cameraman spotted them and grinned.

'Now we'll move on to domestic matters. But I'm afraid the Prime Minister will have to leave for London in twenty minutes flat, and he has two television interviews when this is finished,' said Hanning. There was a stir in the room. Several people woke up, others clicked their ballpoint pens into the action position.

The questions came fast.

'John Fleetwood, *Daily Telegraph*. Have you yet received the Matheson report on the Greenjackets massacre?'

'It's in one of those boxes over there.' The Prime Minister pointed through the metal-framed window to the waiting car outside. Two drivers supervised by a girl secretary with fat legs and white stockings were loading boxes out of a trolley into the boot. 'The third red one from the top, I think, to judge by the markings. You observe, gentlemen, there's nothing wrong with my eyesight.'

But he failed to deflect them. Fleetwood jumped up with

a supplementary. He was spectacled, cadaverous and fiercely right-wing.

'How come you haven't seen the report before?'

'Because there was no need. A summary was telegraphed to me in Hong Kong. I shall now read the full report and discuss it with my colleagues. Then as we promised the House before the recess the report will be published with our observations on it.'

'Isn't that rather a leisurely procedure when the lives of British soldiers are at stake?' This came from a young man in the second row, carroty and fat in his purple shirtsleeves.

Hanning intervened to give the Prime Minister time. 'I must ask you all again to give your name and paper before putting your questions.'

'Adam Silver, *Western Mail.* I think the PM knows me pretty well.'

'Yes, indeed, and it's a fair question. There will be no delay at all over this. My colleagues and I will meet to discuss the report this evening or tomorrow, and if we accept that there are changes to be made in Government policy, we can set the necessary work in hand straight away.' He hesitated, then took a risk which ten years before he would have avoided. He had flipped through the summary late at night a week earlier, sleepy with Government House whisky, and had not read it again. 'I have no reason to believe that any major changes of policy are indicated.'

'Then why do we hear stories that Mr Bernays is considering resignation if his views on the report are not accepted? Geoffrey Roper, *Belfast Telegraph.*' A grey, dour, hard-working man, staunchly Orange but not given to fancy.

The Prime Minister snapped at him.

'Where did you get that nonsense from?'

'You can't expect me to answer that, Prime Minister.'

'And you can't expect me to comment on unsubstantiated rubbish. I don't suppose there has been a government in modern times which has stood so well together, and this is particuarly true of the very difficult decisions we have had to take on Ireland. So let's hear no more talk of resignations, if you please. It is mischievous, damaging and untrue.'

There was an embarrassed silence. A Prime Minister in a public show of temper was something the British Constitution did not readily accommodate. Antony looked hard at Pershore, who was standing next to the Inspector by one of the doors, near enough to the Prime Minister to come forward with any information which might be required, far enough away to preserve his anonymity. Pershore had stayed at home, he would have caught any uneasy whisper running through Whitehall. Either at lunch in his club, or chatting in an anteroom before some interdepartmental meeting, or discreetly over the teacups with his colleagues at No. 10 — somehow he would have heard anything there was to hear. But Pershore stood motionless, attentive, silent.

'Jacob Ridsden, *Newcastle Journal*. What about Jeremy Cornwall, then? You've read his big speech at Newcastle while you were away, calling off his campaign for the time being?'

'He didn't favour me with a copy, but I read a Press report, yes.'

'Did you agree this with him when you gave him a lunch at Chequers?'

'I don't think I should reveal what passed on a private social occasion.'

'But you're aware of course that he threatens to renew his campaign and organize mass demonstrations in September? In effect he's given you a month to change your policies and start bringing the troops home. What's your comment on that?'

'The only certain thing I've read is that Mr Cornwall doesn't propose to make any speeches in August. If I may say so, that seems admirably sensible and in tune with the best British traditions.'

'You don't see any link between Jeremy Cornwall's change of tactic and these stories about Paul Bernays?'

'None whatever. I've dealt with both these topics at length. Can we have one more question please?'

'Robin Smillie, *Daily Mail*. Is it true, Prime Minister, that you collapsed yesterday evening just before you were due to attend President Revani's farewell banquet in Rajnaya?'

Hanning was ready for Smillie always gave trouble.

'I must rule that out of order, I'm afraid. I said all there was to be said about that incident before we left Rajnaya. It does no one any good . . .'

The Prime Minister interrupted him. 'No, I will answer it.' He ran his hand back through his white hair. The room became very quiet. 'It is not true that I collapsed. It is true that I was tired that evening. Perhaps that is not surprising after the tour we have had. Nevertheless I was preparing to go to the banquet. Then my son Antony intervened. In case any of you do not know him, he is standing at the back there, by the cameras. He said very firmly that it was more important that I came back fit and vigorous to face our problems here than that I go to the banquet. I thought about it for a minute or two, and discovered he was right. So, you see, ladies and gentlemen, it was really very simple. After a certain stage of life a man must learn to take his son's advice. And now if you don't mind . . .'

The Prime Minister got up and left quickly, to do his television interviews in a smaller adjoining room, followed by Hanning. Antony with Clarissa made to follow the Prime Minister through the crowd, but the journalists enveloped him. They flashed bulbs at him, shouted questions at him, pressed and scurried round him. By the time he reached the big black Rover the television interviews were over, and the car engine was already running. The Prime Minister and Helena were in the back seat, Pershore in one of the jump seats, and the second set in position for Antony. As they drew away behind a police cyclist the Prime Minister said :

'They seemed to take quite an interest in you, Antony.'

Antony pulled his coat straight on his shoulders. A woman journalist trying to detain him had pulled it askew. He was learning fast, and saw what his father had done.

'That was a good story,' he said.

'A true story,' said the Prime Minister, leaning back on the cushions.

'Good enough to distract them from the rest?' The Prime Minister laughed, actually laughed for the first time in months.

'We shall see, we shall see. It's always worth remembering, there's only one big headline in a paper. And now,' his tone changed as he turned to Pershore, 'and now, what's all this about Bernays?'

# CHAPTER FOURTEEN

The next morning John reached the policeman outside No. 10 at five to ten, exactly half an hour later than usual. He liked to be precise in such matters. Half an hour was a reasonable credit of leisure to claim in return for all the extra work during the Far Eastern tour. He did not enjoy travel for its own sake. Indeed he did not really enjoy any break from the set pattern of his life, which was overwhelmingly composed of very hard work. Holidays were a worry, not a relief. But half an hour at the beginning of a morning was welcome, and particularly on that morning. He had not spent it asleep, although he was still tired. He had used it walking from his flat in Notting Hill Gate across Hyde Park, then Green Park, then St James's Park, and up the steps to Downing Street. He carried the locked black Downing Street box with 'Political Secretary' stamped on it in gold. He liked the London parks in August; the dusty plane trees, the grass worn thin, and the waste paper bins overflowing with the bottles from which tourists had sucked fizzy drinks. Young bearded persons employed by the Department of the Environment were very slowly putting out stacks of folded deck chairs, wearing the air of kindly scorn which Englishmen reserve for tasks below their intellectual status.

John wanted to think about himself, something he found much more difficult than thinking about affairs of state. First, Clarissa. He had lost her, or so it seemed. She had hardly spoken to him the day before. She had stayed close to Antony on the plane, at Zurich, again at Heathrow. Of course she could not know that he had seen Antony go into her room at Rajnaya. It seemed much more than thirty-six hours ago. Perhaps she would be willing to slip back into their old routine together – cheap meals, concerts, the midnight glass of scotch in his flat or hers, the educated jokes, the friendly kiss. Once, he remembered, she had actually

71

sewed on a button for him. That, to date, was their climax.

He laughed at himself, startling two Japanese in the act of photographing Apsley House. He would miss her, the hole in his life would be hard to fill. But that particular way of running the relationship was certainly exploded. Either he must marry her, or sleep with her, or let her go.

Marriage, yes, in principle he was in favour of that. Children, yes, he certainly wanted them. He would really like to skip fifteen years and move at once to being a comfortable husband and father, grey-haired and well settled, taking a small boy and girl to the local middle class comprehensive school in the mornings, living close to a friendly wife who looked nice and talked well, but who made few demands because she had friends and interests of her own. But those fifteen years could not be skipped. To get that far he would have to change himself, enter into her personality, give up his self-sufficiency, love and be loved. He doubted if he could do it, with Clarissa or with anyone.

He found a way through the traffic in the Mall, angry with himself, and scuffed his shoes through the gravel on the opposite side. He began to make excuses. He was tired still from all those hours of flying, he must give himself another day or two, then it would all come clear. As he came into St James's Park he turned with relief to think of the political situation. Politics was about people, but at one remove from himself, and that made it easier.

Now for some tidy analysis. He leaned against the balustrade of the bridge across the lake looking towards the towers of the Foreign Office, the white elegance of the Horse Guards and beyond them the imperial pinnacles of Whitehall Court. It was a view which always impressed and soothed him.

First, the things that were going wrong. The PM's health. Something *was* certainly wrong, though it was hard to pin down. During the tour the old man had performed well, buoyed up by that extra strength which comes to anyone who holds the centre of the stage. But his performance before he left had been very ragged, and on that last evening in Rajnaya he had almost collapsed. He was consciously saving his energy, economizing on words, movements, emotions. Serious illness was a private affair, and John shrank from prying. He could not ask the PM, he was afraid of asking Helena,

72

Dr Ellerman would not tell, Antony almost certainly did not know. But he must find out somehow. Obviously the PM meant to soldier on, but if John was to give the right advice he needed to know.

Second, Ireland. Outwardly, the pressure had relaxed since the disaster to the Greenjackets. In Ireland itself political killings were down to two or three a week. There was still no sign of the two communities agreeing on institutions, and the White Paper setting out its own ideas which the Government had promised for the autumn would be a limp affair. But direct rule under Bernays as Secretary of State had gone on as smoothly as could be expected. Given the essential bloodiness of Ireland and the Irish the situation on the ground could be much worse. It was the shift of attitude in England which was worrying. The ambush of the Greenjackets in the Falls Road had done it. It had rammed under people's noses the brutal prospect that the whole weary effort in Ireland would have to start all over again – the shots from the empty houses, the mine under the culvert, the bomb in the parked car, the parades of murderous bigots, the flood of empty eloquent deceit. Above all, the harvest of plain military coffins returning one by one to England, the body in the coffin, the bullet in the body, the waste of someone's son and someone's husband. And Cornwall, dark handsome Jeremy, without a scruple or a decent motive in his heart, had seized these decent emotions of worry and indignation so that he could carve out of them the block of his political career. John knew that this was what politics ought not to be, a playground for the morally destitute.

John scowled at the regatta of ducks manoeuvring under the bridge. He had worked himself into one of his moralistic moods, from which no good would come. Back to the grindstone, the nitty gritty, the files. He picked up the black box, balanced it gingerly on the rail of the bridge, and opened it with an old-fashioned key from a ring in his pocket. He was not supposed to take any confidential papers home, even in the locked box, and usually he was scrupulous. But he had found such a pile of reading matter waiting in his in-tray at No. 10 on his return that he had filled the box without looking too closely at the security classifications. Here it was, near the bottom, a printed White Paper with the words 'Draft –

confidential' stamped across it. Trouble, but trouble not yet brought to birth. He read the full title : 'Report of an Enquiry into the shootings in the Falls Road, Belfast, on June 19, 19—, conducted by Mr Robert Matheson, QC'. He relocked the box, jammed the report into his pocket, walked across the bridge, and sat on an empty green bench on the edge of the path. He looked at his watch. It was still only a quarter to ten, he had ten minutes of his self-appointed leisure in hand.

Matheson, a safe lawyer past his prime, had written a pedestrian document, telling a tale of neglected precautions, rules grown rusty and ignored, information received but not acted on. The dull prose made the tale more damaging. Years before, at the height of the previous troubles, the Army would never have sent three truckloads of men unprotected like that down a notorious street. They would have checked the phone call which had warned of a likely ambush, and there had been codes with which bona fide IRA informers validated themselves. The men themselves would have reacted quicker, the survivors would at once have stormed the empty houses, and some of the gunmen would have been caught or killed. The report made these points in the calm measured tones in which a judge might criticize a lawyer's handling of a case.

There would be a row, yes, quite a big row, though by the time the House came back in October the report would be stale. That was an argument for publishing it early. In any case, if they didn't, it would begin to leak. But the row would be a Ministry of Defence matter. It was about security tactics, not about Irish policy. The Government should be able to keep the argument within those bounds and so prevent Jeremy Cornwall running away with it. Indeed it looked as if Cornwall had drawn back for the moment. Why then was Bernays said to be so upset? The PM had slapped down the story at his Press conference. Certainly it had seemed absurd. No doubt they would find out today if there was any truth in it.

John's eye fell on para. 37 of the report headed *General Considerations.*

'37. It is possibly for consideration whether the general concept of a policy role for the Army in the likely circumstances in Northern Ireland needs overall review. Such a review would be beyond the terms of reference of this enquiry. In the previous troubles the need for this police role for the Army obtained general acceptance, and if there is to be a resumption of similar troubles the same considerations might again prevail. But the evidence which I examined and my own judgement point in the opposite direction. In the interests of service morale and of avoiding confrontation a much more restrictive definition of the Army's role would be required.'

What did that mean? It had not been in the summary which had been telegraphed out to them in Hong Kong. It should have been, but he could understand how its importance had been missed. John could see it at once. Of course it was gobbledegook, and devious at that. But what the dull safe man was saying was that the Army should be kept off the streets and out of the tangle of individual murder and violence which might once again make up a normal day in Northern Ireland. It was a familiar point, argued over many years and there was something in it. But now there it was, peeping out of the verbiage of an official report, a gift to Jeremy Cornwall and to the whole tribe of those who look for intelligent arguments to justify an act of cowardice. Perhaps this was what was worrying Bernays. John stared again at the imperial skyline in front of him, as formidable in its way as the Kremlin or the Forbidden City. But a brave skyline was not enough if the offices and conference rooms which it sheltered were full of timid men.


## CHAPTER FIFTEEN


Good morning to the policeman, who had already pressed the bell so that the doorkeeper inside swung the door open exactly at the moment when John reached it. Though the No. 10 staff carried passes they never showed them because they were so few that the policemen, also few, recognized them without difficulty. No document was as difficult to forge as a man's face. It was one of the pleasures of a small establishment. You felt part of the time as if you were working in a private home.

But not all the time. The telephone rang as soon as John reached his office. He dumped the black box on the pleasant mahogany desk with the green leather top and grabbed the receiver.

'Oh, Mr Cruickshank, we've been ringing you for some time now.' That was as near as anyone in No. 10 would come to telling John that he was late. 'The Prime Minister asks if you could go up to the flat straight away.'

Not by the lift, that was too slow. He walked fast across the open space in front of the Cabinet Room, glanced at the tape, and poked his nose round the door where the three junior Private Secretaries and the Duty Clerk sat. Over by the window Clarissa's desk was empty.

'She's up in the flat,' said the Duty Clerk, a freckled snub-nosed young man who made a speciality of answering questions before he was asked them.

'When's the first engagement?'

'Secretary of State for Northern Ireland, ten o'clock. But he's just rung to say he'll be a bit late. Pershore's up there too.'

'Still going to Putney this afternoon?'

'So far as I know.' Putney was the Prime Minister's constituency. A visit to Putney counted as political and so came within John's responsibility as Political Secretary.

The tiny drawing-room upstairs in the flat was crowded. Pershore and Clarissa sat at opposite ends of the sofa and the middle cushion between them was piled with the papers which they had brought upstairs with them – or more likely which they had rescued from one of the urgent red boxes in the bedroom next door because the Prime Minister had failed to read them overnight. Antony sprawled across the armchair on Clarissa's right. He had neither shaved nor dressed, and was wearing a purple silk dressing gown and red slippers. One leg bare to the thigh swung over the arm of the chair as he flipped through the *Sun*. He paused for a few seconds before a particularly ample display of buttock, on an inside page.

'Riper yet and riper
Shall her bounds extend.'

he said to Helena as she passed his chair, a vase of roses in her hands.

'Why the hell aren't you at the Bank? Why do I keep on having to ask you the same question? You're in everyone's way. You can't spend all day here drooling over Rupert Murdoch's nudes.' She spoke without rancour, and stopped above him to look down at the paper.

'The Bank are civilized, not like you lunatics. They give a man an extra day off after ten hours flying time.'

'Or, rather, you told them your father still needed you today,' said Clarissa, breaking away from a subdued official palaver with Pershore. She stretched out her arm to turn Antony's paper to that she could see what he was looking at, and for a second her hand touched his knee.

'And so he does. He popped his head round my bedroom door with the morning tea and asked if I'd go with him to Putney this afternoon. You'd better watch out, John, or I'll be taking your place.'

'It looks as if you've taken it already,' said Helena, who had noticed the hand on the knee. She laid the roses side by side on a tray on the side-table and bashed the bottom of their stems with a small hammer from her apron pocket. Helena had learnt not to intrude on regular scheduled meetings, even if they were held upstairs in the flat. She had fought several battles with Pershore on this in the early days, but had found the Prime Minister on Pershore's side. But she had reserved the right to come and go as she wished through her own flat in the morning before the official timetable of the day began. This was the time when Private Secretaries or John or Hanning or a Minister who knew the Prime Minister well would look in for a quick informal word, using their closeness to him to steer a discussion towards their own opinion, or pre-empt a decision which they thought was going wrong. It was thus an important time, and Helena made the most of it.

'But he can't go to Putney this afternoon. He must rest, rest, rest. That clumsy fool Ellerman's still on his back in Hong Kong, but I talked to his partner on the phone. Half Ellerman's age and twice his sense. He quite agreed with me. After a trip like that, with the PM in his present condition, you're going to have to thin out the afternoons and leave the evenings absolutely free. It is meant to be August, you know.' She spoke to the roses, though the message was clearly for Pershore.

'Where actually is the Prime Minister just at the moment?' asked Pershore, meaning that he was not prepared to discuss these matters with Helena.

'In the bath,' said Antony. 'Why do you think I am sitting here with an inch of bristle spoiling my beauty?'

'There's a perfectly good basin in your bedroom,' said Helena.

'But I was brought up to have a bath in the mornings. And stone cold too, unless there's an R in the month.'

'The place is full of steam whenever you leave it.'

The advisers were used now to this kind of pointless bickering between Helena and Antony. It had no venom in it. Clarissa began to talk to Pershore again about the Irish papers they had brought up with them. John slipped out of the room, hoping to catch the Prime Minister before he reached the others. The manoeuvre worked.

'Good morning, sir, how are you?'

'Tired, John, tired. I'm always tired these days. Who have we got in there?' The PM was in his shirt and trousers, carrying the coat of his suit on his arm, with a tie draped over it.

'Just the usual lot. Bernays is going to be late.'

'Yes, I know. You'd better stay on when he comes. Often useful to both sides to have a witness on occasions like this.'

John was flattered. It made up for the fact that the PM had asked Antony to go to Putney with him.

The Prime Minister was in the sitting-room putting on his tie. 'Don't get up,' he said, as he always did. But only Antony continued to sprawl.

'Good morning Prime Minister. Perhaps we could clear up one point of mechanics at the outset,' said Pershore, speaking quickly to get in first. He wore his smart grey suit and his cream shirt was long enough to show bright green jade cuff links. 'You have had in your diary for many weeks a constituency surgery at Putney this afternoon starting at 3. I understand from John that the usual two hours of appointments are fully booked. On the other hand,' he pressed his fingers together, 'there is a great deal of business waiting for you here, and Lady Percival quite rightly points out that after all your exertions you are still in need of rest. On balance I think . . .'

'Cut out Putney, cut out the business waiting for you here, an omelette and salad for lunch and then bed for the rest of the day. That is, if you want to stay alive.' Helena was gripping her hammer, but she spoke more quietly than usual, and John had the impression that this was just a skirmish in a battle she knew she was losing.

'How long is it since I had a constituency surgery?'

'Two months,' said John, 'and that was in Roehampton, not Putney proper.'

'Too long,' said the Prime Minister.

Pershore tried again. He alone knew the pressing burden of paper, the Ministerial meetings which had already been delayed, the decisions which were hanging fire. Usually the main decisions had been taken by the time Parliament rose at the end of July, Whitehall shifted into neutral gear, and senior Ministers and Civil Servants went on the holiday they badly needed. The Prime Minister's Far Eastern trip had upset the rhythm of the seasons, and here they were in the second week of August cross, tired and behindhand.

'You look after your constituents remarkably well, Prime Minister,' said Pershore. 'You sign every letter to them yourself, you entertain them here, you and Lady Percival take a keen interest in all their activities. I'm sure you could postpone your surgery just this once. Perhaps Richard Newings could go down and take it for you, promising to report to you personally on each case. I'm sure they'd understand.'

'They wouldn't understand at all. They'd simply say that I was too busy to bother with them, and it showed what a mistake it was to have a Prime Minister as your MP.'

'Nonsense, they love having you where you are,' said Helena. 'They tell me that every time I see them. We're a long way off a General Election and you can perfectly well afford to forget Putney for a year or two.'

The Prime Minister thought for a moment.

'They want to have it both ways. And they're quite right. A Member of Parliament who forgets his constituents is no good. A few do, but they're wrong. It's the first rule. I shall go to Putney. John and Antony can both come with me. And

I'll go to the Cosy Club tea-party in Disraeli Road afterwards as arranged. And now, what's next?'

They were all looking at him, judging how he felt that morning. John noticed the short sentences – they were new since a few weeks ago, as if words had suddenly become valuable. As usual he was trimly shaved, the silver hair and dark moustache were well brushed, and his suit hung well. Perhaps a little more loosely than a few weeks back? Perhaps the sallow skin on his cheeks was beginning to collect in more visible folds. It was hard to be certain. When he was tired, as yesterday, you would say that the Prime Minister was so ill that he could hardly continue. His leg dragged and he was reluctant to move. When he had rested, as today, you could not say more than that he was ageing. In either condition he had kept that strong will which was his main asset.

John did not in his heart believe that Sir James Percival was a splendid man. He had no real humour, little imagination, and no interests outside politics. Professional politics was his whole life. But he had steel in his character, and that made him worth serving.

Pershore moved unruffled to his next subject. 'The Secretary of State for Northern Ireland will be here at any minute. As I mentioned in the car yesterday I have grounds for supposing that he is seriously perturbed at one aspect of the Matheson Report and its possible bearing on Irish policy. In Clarissa's absence abroad with you I had the task of mastering the draft report, and I have discussed it with her this morning in view of her greater knowledge of the background. We both came to the conclusion that it is almost certainly paragraph 37 which perturbs the Secretary of State. Although obscurely drafted . . .'

The telephone rang and John, sitting nearest to the receiver, took the call.

'It's the Duty Clerk. He says the Secretary of State is here. He's taking him up to the study as you asked.'

'Quite right. Well, William, if you'll just give me the report and your brief on it . . . I think this will be mainly political talk, so I've asked John to sit in.'

It was a bad morning for Pershore. John, having been excluded from many meetings in his time, knew how he must feel. And it was worse for Pershore, whose colleagues across

Whitehall would expect him as Principal Private Secretary to have the Prime Minister well under control.

'There are a number of detailed points which might come up, Prime Minister . . .'

'Yes, indeed, and if they do I'll ask you to join us. Come along, John, we mustn't keep a colleague waiting just because he's twenty minutes late. Helena, I wonder if I could have something light for lunch, an omelette perhaps – Antony, have a word with Miss Glossop about the surgery appointments, will you? There's probably background to some of them that I should know. And do for heaven's sake get dressed. This is supposed to be my levee, not yours.'

## CHAPTER SIXTEEN

Paul Bernays had grown sleek with success in a dangerous job. His face was redder and fuller than it had been, and the stiff white collar now bit into his neck. He wore a dark blue striped suit and a red carnation. About his ability there was no doubt, but John was not sure about his personal loyalty. He was now a potentate in his own right, no longer dependent on the Prime Minister.

Bernays was not pleased to see John.

'Good morning, James. I'm sorry to be late. I had a series of calls to Belfast, and the line was shocking. I had hoped we could have a private talk.'

'About the Matheson Report, is it?'

'Well, yes . . .'

'Then if you don't mind, I'd rather John stayed. He knows the ins and outs of it better than I do.'

This might just be true, thought John, but if so they were in for a rough ride. So far as he knew the Prime Minister had gone straight to bed the night before, and read only the newspapers that morning. Certainly Pershore and Clarissa had failed in their attempt to brief him about paragraph 37 at the levee.

Bernays still looked unhappy.

'If you want a private word or two with me at the end . . .' said the Prime Minister. And so John stayed.

The Prime Minister had rearranged the study on taking office. The cavernous sofa and deep leather armchairs had been moved, and replaced by a number of small gilt chairs borrowed from Lancaster House. Only the Prime Minister's modern swivel-chair behind the big desk offered any comfort. The staff at No. 10 assumed that his intention had been to keep meetings with his colleagues short and to prevent Helena and Antony from intruding. The study, poised on the first floor between the domestic life in the flat above and the hurly burly of the Cabinet Room and the private office below, belonged particularly to the Prime Minister himself, and had taken on his character – stiff, impersonal, hard to read.

'I think Matheson has done a reasonable job. It could be much worse,' he said.

Bernays took no notice of this remark. He had worked out his offensive, and was not going to be deterred. John could imagine him striding up and down his bachelor flat in Millbank, rehearsing the phrases he would use.

'We have to look at the background. First, we have made no progress at all in finding a political solution. You know how I have listened to them all time and time again. So did Rogers before me, to do him justice. But there is no common ground, nothing whatever to build on. It's still a hopeless hand to play.'

'You've been very clever in getting them to sit down quietly under direct rule. And you're working on your new initiative.'

Bernays eased his finger along inside his collar.

'I take no credit for that. They know perfectly well that direct rule is acceptable to almost everyone in Northern Ireland so long as there is no violence. But now we've got to face the fact that violence is going to start again. The lull is almost over. The Greenjackets massacre was just the beginning. You see the intelligence estimates. Every report shows that the IRA has bought its arms, built up its network and is ready for a new campaign.'

'We can beat them again.'

'I doubt it. I doubt it very much, and I'll tell you why.

This time they hold the trumps. The Army has been through all this before too recently. So have the British people. And the big difference from last time is Jeremy Cornwall. He has shown what he can do when things are relatively quiet. When it comes to the crunch he can stop us. Demonstrations, riots, even mutinies, not in Northern Ireland, but here. I'm not prepared to fall into that trap.'

'You're running rather wide, Paul.' The Prime Minister lit a cigarette. It was the first time John had ever seen him smoke. 'All this hasn't much to do with the Matheson Report.'

'Indeed it has, it has everything to do with it. The moment Cornwall reads paragraph 37 he will ask us to undertake that this time the Army won't have a police role. He'll want us to promise they'll be kept in barracks. If he doesn't get that promise he'll start his campaign up all over again. And then we'll be sunk, because he's on to a winner.'

The Prime Minister flipped through the report until he reached para. 37. He read it carefully. John sat back in the window seat so that both men could forget he was there. He guessed that the Prime Minister was reading para. 37 for the first time. He wondered if Bernays guessed the same thing.

'I still think you're leaping ahead too fast,' said the Prime Minister. 'Cornwall's called a truce. His campaign was beginning to run out of steam. This paragraph is pretty obscure. You can't be sure he'll seize on it.'

'Yes, I can. I showed it to him three days ago. He said he would.'

There was a pause. The Prime Minister watched the smoke twisting away from his cigarette. Then he said quietly:

'Was that wise? He is a dangerous man.'

'That is why I showed it to him. And I suppose that is why you asked him to Chequers before you went to the Far East.'

Another pause, and this time Bernays broke it.

'His weakness is his vanity. If you flatter him he shows his cards before he plays them. We mustn't break with him completely.'

'If you hadn't shown it to him, we might have persuaded Matheson to drop para. 37. It's strictly outside his terms of reference.'

'I tried that too. Before I saw Cornwall. Matheson wouldn't budge. All I got was an undertaking that he wouldn't say anything more once the report is out.'

'That's something.' Another long pause. John was used to these silences. He knew that the Prime Minister wanted Bernays to show more of his mind.

Bernays got up and went over to the window next to the one where John was sitting. He looked out at the trees and a phalanx of tourists clustered round the pelicans on the lake.

'I suggest that we should fix a date for the withdrawal of the Army,' he said abruptly, 'and use this to force the politicians there to reach an agreement. I see no other chance for our initiative.'

'That's an old gamble. It's always been rejected in the past. It's very dangerous.'

'In the past other paths have seemed open. They're all blocked now. We'd knock the cards out of Jeremy Cornwall's hand.' He turned to face the desk, and spoke more formally. His short but bulky frame was suddenly formidable. 'I must ask you to face the real facts of the situation, Prime Minister. It's something I'm very sure of in my own mind.'

The Prime Minister looked quickly at his watch.

'Good God, it's nearly eleven, the Soviet Ambassador must have been waiting ten minutes.' He picked up the telephone on the desk beside him. 'Is the Ambassador there? . . . You should have told me, please give him my apologies, and ask Clarissa to bring him up straight away.' He got up slowly. 'I'm so sorry, Paul, but I know he has an urgent message to deliver. What you say is very important, and we must have a long talk about it very soon. You're not taking your holiday yet, are you? Then we must have a quiet meal together. I'll get Pershore to arrange it. We've got a week or so while the Report is being printed.'

Bernays hesitated. John could see him debating with himself whether to persevere. John left the window seat and held the door open.

'Take the Secretary of State down, would you John?' said the Prime Minister.

Bernays said nothing at all on his way out to his car, where his tall thin detective was waiting. On his way back John watched him clamber into the back and disappear. As he turned back into the house the doorkeeper was taking a message from the telephone, and motioned John to stop.

'The PM says would you step up to the study again, sharpish.'

The Russian and Clarissa were on the landing outside the study. The Ambassador was examining the prints of old Whitehall on the panelled wall, and looked cross.

'You're to go straight in,' said Clarissa. 'For God's sake don't be long.'

The Prime Minister was back at his desk. He looked pleased with himself. 'D'you think he was going to threaten to resign if I hadn't broken it up?'

'Not quite. Not yet.'

'Probably not. But he's thought a lot about it. Did you notice that he talked of it all in terms of a card game? It's a bad sign when people do that. It means they've been in politics long enough.'

And it's a bad sign, thought John, when they chatter too much to their Political Secretaries. It was very unlike the Prime Minister to unbutton like this.

'The Ambassador is outside. He looks a bit fretful. Is there anything else you want?'

'Yes, about para. 37. It wasn't in the telegraphed summary we got in Hong Kong, was it?'

'No.'

The Prime Minister had been badly let down. The responsibility had been Pershore's. The Prime Minister would have been justified in exploding. But an explosion would not necessarily produce the best result. It might have been a mistake, or conceivably not. John could see the old man weighing all this up. Finally he said:

'Find out what happened and let me know.'

'I will.' And as John reached the door, the Prime Minister added:

'No record of that talk of course. Tell William Pershore about it. Not the others.'

# CHAPTER SEVENTEEN

John found Pershore in the Cabinet Room, sitting at the big table with papers spread in front of him. When he wanted to be alone he sometimes moved in there from his own office, which he shared with the private secretary who dealt with economic affairs. John noticed that he was in his shirt sleeves and that his hair was ruffled, both unusual. But he greeted John with his normal rather empty courtesy.

'Come in, I wanted a word with you, it is good of you to spare the time. I am afraid something very unfortunate and disturbing has occurred.'

'You mean paragraph 37.'

'Paragraph 37?' He had genuinely forgotten there was such a thing. But he quickly brought the right file to the top of his mind. 'No, not that at all. But what happened about that?'

'The PM covered up beautifully. But he is upset.'

'He remembers that it wasn't in the telegraphed summary?'

'Of course.'

For the first time in John's experience Pershore felt constrained to explain himself.

'The summary came across from the Northern Ireland Office late one evening. It was a busy evening and I sent it off to you at once in Hong Kong before I had read the Report itself. Because of leave arrangements I was alone in the office that day. I took the Report and the summary home that night meaning to read them both together. If the summary was in any way inadequate I intended to send you a supplementary telegram. I am afraid I fell asleep with the papers strewn on top of my bed. I read the Report next day, but I never re-read the summary, and the important omission of any reference to paragraph 37 escaped my attention.'

When Pershore was tired he looked younger than his years, like a haggard schoolboy. John felt a wave of sympathy for him. His was a job where you could make a dozen important mistakes each day without being a fool.

'Is the Prime Minister furious?' asked Pershore.

John shrugged. 'You know him. The milk is spilt. So long as we do not spill it again . . . But I think he would like to feel sure that the bad drafting in the NIO was a genuine mistake.'

Pershore digested this. 'I am sure in my own mind that it was. Conspiracies in Whitehall are less common than people suppose in novels and newspapers. I cannot see why anyone should wish to keep the PM in the dark.' He thought further. 'What you say seems to imply a lack of confidence in the Secretary of State . . .'

John told him briefly what had happened in the study. Pershore ran his fingers again through his sleek grey hair. Then he took off his glasses and rubbed his eyes as he stored this information in his tidy brain.

'I will speak to the Prime Minister about the summary,' he said, rather sadly. 'But frankly that isn't the matter which gives me most concern this morning. Since we met in the flat I have received a most disturbing message from Rajnaya.' He took up an orange paper, but did not give it at once to John. 'Frankly, I am very reluctant to show you this. Not because of its high classification, I know that you are in every way qualified to see highly secret papers. My hesitation is of a different nature.' He got up, holding the paper, and walked round the Cabinet table. John could see that he was slightly flushed. 'I have supposed for some weeks that you and Clarissa have been seeing a good deal of each other, perhaps becoming fond of each other. I have heard . . . but that is neither here nor there.' He came to a halt by John's side. 'Suffice it to say that I would not have shown you this if there was any other sensible person to whom I could turn for advice.'

'What the hell are you talking about?' John was jolted out of his natural politeness. But Pershore took no notice. He pushed the flimsy paper across the table.

It made no sense at all. A jumble of figures and what appeared to be times, and at the end the words 'Pass to K'.

'It's a code?'

'Let me explain.' Pershore collected himself. In spite of his anxiety he still enjoyed making things clear to others. 'This document comes from Rajnaya. Rajnaya is in one respect unique among the countries which you visited. It is the only one which has a reputable intelligence service. It was the first piece of technical assistance which President Revani obtained from the Russians when he took over. One of their main duties is to monitor very thoroughly the activities of their foreign visitors.'

'We were given a general warning before we left.'

'I wish it had been more precise. We have of course ourselves penetrated the Rajnayan Intelligence Service. That is normal. The Russians can provide a country like that with modern techniques and equipment. They cannot supply it with committed incorruptible personnel. Unfortunately we have since last night a full account of the material which they gathered on the Prime Minister's visit.'

'Unfortunately?'

'The material shows that on your last night there Antony Percival entered Clarissa's bedroom in the small hours and spent the rest of the time making love to her.'

'There was a sentry in the corridor.' John remembered the grey uniformed figure in the alcove, stiff against the moonlit bay.

'He was of course on duty in more senses than one. His serial number is the first entry in this report. Then follow the exact times at which Antony entered and left the room.'

'You run ahead a bit far. He might have gone there to talk. He was very worried that night about the PM's health.'

'There are microphones in each room, behind the portraits of Revani in each case. They were full on. The quality was not good, and I gather there are gaps in the transcript. But even so, it is possible to distinguish between a casual late night conversation and the violent seduction of a young woman.'

John bit his lip and felt blood. But he felt he must do his best for those who had been his friends.

'Bloody hell,' he said. 'I had no idea of this. I am very fond of Clarissa. But I don't see why it should upset *you* so much. It's really nothing to do with the Government or the Civil Service whether those two sleep together.'

'These reports go to the Soviet Union. That is a condition which the Rajnayans had to accept in return for the shiny hardware.'

'Even so . . .'

'Even so, even so – I thought you had some political sense.'

'I still don't see.'

'We're not still living in the 'seventies, you know. The kind of messy conduct that was taken for granted ten years ago is not permissible today. You know that as well as I do . . . I understand that up to the Election Antony had an affair with some girl in Fulham, and that he was made to break it off. At least that was not an affair under the Prime Minister's roof with one of the Prime Minister's most trusted staff.'

'What are you going to do?'

'I think we need to be precise about the danger. It is not primarily a security risk. If the Russians use this information it will not be to blackmail secrets out of Clarissa. It will be to inflict through tendentious publicity maximum damage on the PM and the Government. The risk is political, and therefore essentially one for you rather than me to assess.'

'So you're washing your hands of the problem?' John spoke bitterly.

Pershore looked at him. The grey suit was crumpled. 'We have not always understood each other very well,' he said, 'but I think you know me better than that. So long as I work at No. 10 the Prime Minister's problems are my problems. But they cannot all be solved by Civil Service methods.'

'I never thought I'd hear you say that,' said John.

'That just proves my thesis.'

'Your thesis?'

'That we do not understand each other very well – But I am getting away from the main point. I do not want to bother the Prime Minister with any of this. There must be a limit to what he is asked to carry . . . you understand that. I do not believe Helena could handle it. I know that I myself could not. So the question is, can you make sure that the liaison is brought to an end?'

John tried to think hard. He did not come to a conclusion. Pershore knew better than to press his luck. He simply said: 'Think about it.' Then as John moved to the door Pershore had the last word:

'They were rather lavish with their microphones. Do you realize that, at least in tropical climates, you have a strong tendency to snore?'

## CHAPTER EIGHTEEN

'Good afternoon, I'm Antony Percival, the Prime Minister's son. What is your name please?' asked Antony.

'Randall, Susan Randal, Mrs., 23 Lower Richmond Road, Putney.'

Antony filled in the form.

'Can I ask you how you knew the Prime Minister was holding a surgery here this afternoon?'

'Read the ad. in the paper.'

'Which paper was that?'

'Same as usual, we only take the *Putney Herald*. And the *Mirror*, of course.'

'Thank you very much, Mrs Randall. I'm sorry we've kept you waiting, but some people ahead of you have been taking rather a long time. Ten minutes is what we allow for, and we've had some nearly double that.'

'Long-winded lot round here. Can't abide them.'

'I'm sure you won't run over *your* time, Mrs Randall.'

'Got better things to do than spend all afternoon nattering.'

'Quite right. Just one more question, Mrs Randall. My father usually asks Miss Glossop, his agent, to stay in the room with him when he interviews a constituent. It makes it easier for her to help him with the follow-up action. Would you have any objection to this?'

'Makes no odds. Long time since there was anything private in *my* life.'

'That's all right then. If you'd like to follow me upstairs, it's just one flight, I'll show you in to my father.'

When Antony came downstairs into the waiting-room he said to John :

'Widow's pension?'

'More likely husband missing, police won't help.'

'Husband behind with maintenance payments, court won't help, I'll lay you three to one.'

'Anti-bloodsports.'

'Pro-hanging. She had that glint in her eye as she shook hands upstairs. Measuring my father for the big drop.'

'You were good with her.'

'I was good with them all. Why did no one tell me? I'm a born receptionist. Does Miss Glossop keep any scotch locked away?'

'Certainly not in the waiting-room. And it's only five o'clock. Cosy Club tea to come yet.

'That's exactly what I mean.' Antony sat on the edge of the table and swung his legs in the direction of the photograph of Churchill inspecting blitz damage in the East End. 'D'you know, John, I enjoy all this caper, I enjoy it much more than I thought I would.'

'You're much better at it than I expected. I think you like this side of it more than I do.'

'You're interested in ideas, I'm interested in people.' He turned to look seriously at John, who sat uncomfortably on the round cane-bottomed little chair beside which Mrs Randall had left a dark green umbrella.

'Tell me, does it do any good?'

'Does what?'

'Fill in your name, upstairs for ten minutes, shake hands, I want a council house, a bigger pension, a fairy godmother, someone to stop my bloke giving me a black eye every Friday night.'

'Sometimes.'

'How come?'

'People need someone new to listen when they talk. Not their husband or wife, not a priest any more, doctors are in too much of a hurry. So they come to their MP. If he's their Prime Minister too, that's a bonus. And one in ten times it's something bad he can stop, something good he can shove along.'

'That's not much of a ratio.'

'And of course the MP learns. He can sit up all night all week listening to housing debates in the House and learn less than he could from a couple of cases at his surgery. Because this is where it actually happens.'

'You're really keen, aren't you?'

John looked out through the diamond panes on to the laurels and scattered ice cream cones in the front garden. Miss Glossop did not regard it as one of her duties to tidy the approach to the Association's headquarters.

'Yes, I'm keen. It's a bug. Considering everything, it's surprising how many people catch it.'

There was a pause. Mrs Randall was still at it, but if she was as laconic upstairs as downstairs she wouldn't be long. He didn't have much time.

'What about you?' he asked.

Antony sprawled back on the table and gazed at the light fitting in the middle of the ceiling, blue and red glass in the Venetian style.

'No bug here,' he said. 'Or rather so many they cancel each other out.'

'There's one you've got to get rid of. For her own sake.'

Antony sat up smartly. 'You mean Clarissa?'

'Of course.'

'Did she tell you?'

'No, I saw you that night in the corridor. You weren't exactly discreet.'

Antony let it pass. For a moment he was really serious. 'You don't mind, though. She said you wouldn't.'

John dodged. 'It's not what I mind. Pershore knows, and he minds like hell. No, not through me. There was a sentry behind the door and a mike above the mantelpiece.'

'Christ. We might just as well have stripped off between courses at the banquet.'

'It would probably have been a shade less public.'

'So there's a tape, then?' Antony laughed. 'Has Pershore actually heard it? He'll have learnt a thing or two. Life in Hampstead should be hotting up before long.'

'Not actually heard it. In fact it's on its way to the Soviet Union.'

'You're joking. These things only happen in naval commanders' memoirs.'

'And in real life. That's why you've got to give up Clarissa. Either that, or leave No. 10. Or else you'll bust her career. Either Pershore or the Russians or both will see to that.'

'Career girls have had affairs before, you know. More affairs than marriages, in fact.'

'But if they have affairs with a Prime Minister's son under the Prime Minister's roof, the Press won't let go once they hear of it. That's the point. We're close to it now. But if you give her up, no story.'

Antony stood up. 'The dirty tricks department,' he said quietly. 'Is this all because you want her back?'

'I've never had her.'

'No, indeed. So I learnt. She doesn't even know if you sleep naked. I asked her.'

'Look, Antony, if I thought Clarissa didn't mind about her career, I'd never have mentioned all this. I'd have let Pershore set about it in his own way. But you know she does.'

'Of course she does.' There was a silence.

Antony picked up a heavy glass ashtray. John could see that he was stirring himself up, as he had done before the banquet at Rajnaya when he had told the Prime Minister to go to bed. But when he spoke it was quietly, and the ashtray moved gently from one hand to another.

'You are all mice,' he said. 'Some of you are rats, but mostly mice. You scurry about the corners of rooms, looking for holes, thinking always what the other mice will think or what the cat will do. Usually there isn't a cat at all, but the mice can't believe that, because if they believed that they'd have no excuses, they'd have to come into the middle of the room and think and feel for themselves.'

'It can't be wrong to try sometimes to think about others.' John thought his best chance was to keep the conversation as banal as possible.

'Yes, it bloody well can. If it stops you being a real person, it can. Think of Pershore, just think of him. A first class public servant, they say. And what does that mean? Not a real thought, nor a real emotion from dawn to dusk. A mouse, a sawdust, squeaking, well-dressed clockwork mouse. He thinks so much about other people's feelings, he destroyed his own long ago. And you've just proved you're exactly the same. If you were a real person, you'd be down here hating my guts and fighting as hard as you could to get back your girl. Instead of that you've got an unselfish smile on your face and you're talking like a Whitehall minute.'

'Pershore is genuinely worried about Clarissa.' John was determined not to be drawn on the subject of himself.

'Genuinely worried . . . that's just the sort of inhuman crap you all talk. He's worried – well, I'm not.' Antony leant forward and tapped John on the knee. 'Get it straight, and put it to him straight. Clarissa can look after herself. I don't love her, and I don't think she loves me. She finds me several times more exciting than she does you, in bed or out. Pershore sent you here, I send you to Clarissa. You're one of nature's go-betweens. I don't want to put any pressure on her in any way.' He raised his voice. 'But you can tell her that if she wants to stay with me, she can. It's up to her. She's free, educated, and only slightly dull. I'm not going to shove her out of my bed just because they've got our love talk on tape in the Kremlin. I'll move out of No. 10 and get a flat. Then she can come to me or do the other thing.' He paused.

'Will you put that to her for me?'

'Why the hell should I do that?'

'Sorry to intrude,' Mrs Randall had clearly heard the last sentence. She showed no sign of curiosity, but walked straight to the cane-bottomed chair, where she recovered her green umbrella.

'Anything to pay?' she asked abruptly.

'No, no, nothing at all, Mrs Randall,' said John.

'Thought there might be a charge. I had a cup of tea.'

'No charge, not even for tea. Did it go all right?'

'Suppose so. He told that Miss Glossop to get on to the Housing Department first thing in the morning.'

'What's the trouble?'

'Mice. Everywhere. Nothing but mice.'

# CHAPTER NINETEEN

The date was August 14 and the Cabinet had its longest agenda of the year. The two facts were closely connected. It was a tidying-up session. Ministers were being asked to take a lot of decisions before they left for their holidays. God willing, the Cabinet would not meet again for at least a month.

Some of the decisions were small. But small decisions were not necessarily easier. Sometimes, indeed, the reverse. Faced with the great issues of finance or foreign policy smaller Ministers kept quiet. But everyone, it seemed, knew exactly when pubs should open and shut in Scotland.

'6.  Licensing hours (Scotland.) Proposals for legislation by the Macintyre Committee (Paper circulated by the Secretary of State for Scotland C(84) 136 dated 3 August.)'

As the clock on the Horse Guards struck twelve thirty the Prime Minister gazed round the coffin-shaped table. The deeper more distant note of Big Ben followed two seconds later. The Lord Chancellor was explaining how, twenty-five or possibly thirty-five years earlier, a relative of his, now deceased, had been debarred from ordering either a brandy or a scotch without a meal at a hotel, whose name now slipped his mind, at Ballachulish, or was it Fort William? The Prime Minister leaned back in his chair. This chair, identical with the others except that it had arms, tactfully underlined his position as first among equals. He reminded himself of the two remaining items.

'7.  Security in Northern Ireland : publication of the Matheson Report (Oral statement by the Secretary of State for Northern Ireland.)'

'8.  Public Lending Right for Authors (Paper circulated by the Secretary of State for Education and Science C(84) 138 of 9 August.)'

Old Basil Proudfoot, Secretary to the Cabinet, was a master at deciding the order of the agenda. Item 7 was the only important decision of the day. He had put it late, so as to discourage long discussion – but not at the very end, where anyone with strong views might try to exploit the desire of his colleagues for lunch. Item 8 had been on the agenda of every Cabinet which the Prime Minister could remember – a project eminently worthy, and eminently expendable at any given moment.

He decided to chance his arm over Item 6. He waited for the Lord Chancellor to pause, then cut in.

'This has been a useful and interesting discussion. There is no doubt that the pressure for more liberal licensing laws in Scotland is now very strong, particularly in the new middle-class areas in the north and east. Most of my colleagues believe this pressure to be justified. On the other hand it is also clear that new legislation on the lines now proposed will not achieve the two-thirds majority in the Scottish Assembly which under the new arrangements would enable the Assembly to pass it without reference to Westminster. The question is therefore whether we should offer to bring forward a Bill ourselves in the Queen's Speech for the next session. Opinion in the Cabinet is divided on this point, but the prevailing view appears to be that the Secretary of State should be asked to hold further consultations with the different interests concerned and with the Party leaders in the Assembly at Edinburgh, and report back to the Cabinet before the end of the year. I hope that we shall then be able to take a definite decision.'

He glanced at the Secretary of State for Scotland sitting at the far end of the table, but only just gave him time to nod. The young man from the Cabinet Secretariat who was taking the minutes at the other end of the table scribbled hard, with a satisfied look on his face. The Prime Minister's summing-up was the crucial part of any Cabinet discussion, and it was a joy to work for a Prime Minister who expressed himself so readily in the natural language of Whitehall.

'Now, Item 7. Before I call on the Secretary of State for Northern Ireland, it would perhaps be for the convenience of colleagues if I said a word of a procedural kind. Mr Matheson's Report obviously has implications for the whole range of Irish policy. We are all anxious about the prospect of renewed violence. The Secretary of State for Northern Ireland, the Secretary of State for Defence and I are in close touch as the situation develops. We are not yet ready to put any firm conclusions to you about changes in general policy. There are day to day operational plans, which will come before the Northern Ireland committee in the usual way. I suggest therefore that this morning we should confine ourselves to discussing the actual item before us, namely the arrangements for publishing the Matheson Report and the comments which the Government will have to make at the time of publication.'

He looked round the table. There was a shuffle at one end as Clarissa took her place alongside the Cabinet Secretariat. As the member of the No. 10 staff who dealt with Irish matters she was entitled to be present, but not of course to speak, when this item was taken. The Prime Minister noticed that she looked pale and puffy in the face. Something was going on, but he didn't know what. Why had he not seen Antony for two days now? Irritated, he forced his mind back to the agenda. One of the maddening things about being Prime Minister was that your staff tried to protect you by not telling you things which you wanted to know.

Paul Bernays was shifting in his chair, looking at some manuscript jottings in front of him. Perhaps it had been a mistake to try and head him off. The Prime Minister knew Bernays well enough to read his mind. His pink, fleshy face, over-neat clothes and portentous manner made him unattractive in the House and on television. He acted older than his age. He would never become Leader of the Party unless there was some crisis which made his gifts more important than these trivial defects. Bernays was a hard and genuine worker. He was fascinated by problems and wrestled with them until he had found a solution which satisfied him. Usually you found long before that stage some semi-solution which for the time being would satisfy most people. Bernays rejected semi-solutions.

'I accept what you say, Prime Minister, of course,' said Bernays slowly, fiddling with a cuff-link, 'and it is getting late. On the other hand the Cabinet will not be meeting again for several weeks. By that time, I don't know . . .' He glanced round the table, as if expecting support, but no one had any idea what he was driving at. Of the others present only the Prime Minister and Mercer at Defence saw the intelligence reports.

He pulled himself together and fell into his most sententious manner.

'The immediate problem need not detain us for more than a minute. Arrangements are in hand to publish the Matheson Report next week in pursuance of the undertaking which I gave to the House of Commons in May. We can accompany this with a very brief statement, accepting the specific criticisms of Army tactics and procedures and saying that these have already been corrected. I gather that would be acceptable to the Secretary of State for Defence.'

'Of course,' said Mercer. 'I've posted the officers concerned. New orders are in force for patrols in Belfast and other towns. That's all there is to it.'

'With respect, I wonder if that is wholly correct,' said Bernays. It was perhaps natural, thought the Prime Minister, that longwinded men should dislike men who used monosyllables. Bernays and Mercer were often at odds. 'The difficulty is that the Matheson Report opens up the general problem of the role of the Army in Northern Ireland. In paragraph 37 Matheson questions the assumptions which have governed that role for many years now. He does this at a time when violence is on the increase, and when all the evidence suggests that it will increase further to a point where the Army will become involved day by day on a scale which we have not seen for several years. It is equally significant that a powerful member of our own Party is succeeding in making considerable political capital out of this very issue at our expense.'

'This is not the place to go into that,' said the Prime Minister. It was a mistake to discuss Party considerations at formal Cabinet meetings with Civil Servants present. And anyway there were one or two colleagues who were still on chatty terms with Jeremy Cornwall.

'I don't see where all this is heading.' Mercer was a small freckled red-headed man. He had been a regular soldier and then a farmer before entering the house. He brought a pipe to

Cabinet and clenched it between his teeth even though the no-smoking rule introduced by Mr Heath was still applied. He had just been made Chairman of the Conservative Party, and now he spoke more often in Cabinet.

'August is always a bloody month in Ulster. Certainly violence may grow. In that case the Army must deal with it as it has before. Ulster is a part of Britain, there can't be any mucking around on that. We've been through all this endless times before. Matheson has written some cautious lawyer's gobbledegook. I couldn't make head or tail of it. And if I can't, nor can the great British public. As for Cornwall, he can pull in the crowds because he's got sex appeal, money, and arrogance. But none of those will last long at the present rate. So I say, publish the Report, add as little comment as we can get away with, and for God's sake let's go on holiday.'

But Bernays was not to be stopped. He sipped from a glass of water, then pulled a large blue silk handkerchief from his breast pocket and wiped his lips.

'I must warn my colleagues that there is a serious risk that within days or weeks, if we take no action the Army may be dragged once again into a security role in which it cannot succeed and which we shall not be able to justify to ourselves or to others. I believe that the Matheson Report gives us an opportunity to rethink our policy and take a fresh initiative before it is too late. I have been thinking about the form this might take.'

The Prime Minister was about to intervene, but Mercer cut in, nettled that Bernays had ignored what he had just said.

'What d'you propose, then?'

'I propose that I should announce next week when the Matheson Report is published that I was inviting all the political leaders in Northern Ireland to a Round Table Conference to discuss self-government for Northern Ireland within the United Kingdom. I would add that if they failed to come or if they failed to agree at the Conference, British troops would be totally withdrawn from the province by December 31. I believe in effect that the threat of troop withdrawal is the only means available for us to head off violence and achieve a political solution.'

There was a silence round the table. It was a hopeless situation. An important proposal by an important colleague was being thrust at them at twenty minutes to one at the last Cabinet of the summer. They could not conceivably settle it there and then. They could not meet again that afternoon. They were unprepared, reluctant, tired.

'I really don't think we can carry this much further.' The Prime Minister allowed irritation to creep into his voice. 'If the situation worsens as fast as the Secretary of State fears, then of course we shall have to meet again, and it will be open to him to put his ideas to us in greater detail. Such a change of policy would need a great deal of thought and consultation – with the Chiefs of Staff, with the Opposition, and so on. It can't be done at the drop of a hat just because of some speeches by Cornwall and a paragraph in the Matheson Report.'

'And anyway, it stinks. It is cowardly and irresponsible.' Mercer never measured his language, and to some extent they had learned to live with this. 'I couldn't sit in a Cabinet which ran away in that direction.'

Bernays kept his temper. 'This is an awkward moment to press my proposal. There will always be awkwardness, great awkwardness and difficulty, whenever it is proposed. I will not insist on it being further considered this morning. I will of course bear in mind what the Secretary of State has just said, and I respect his convictions. In return I hope that he will respect mine. They are not the result of a sudden panic, let alone of Cornwall's speeches. This is a matter which I have pondered long and deeply. I shall circulate a paper and should be grateful if the Secretary of State and my other colleagues could find the time among their other many preoccupations this month to consider it with the care which I hope it will merit.'

It was well done in a portentous sort of way. There was a barb in it. Mercer had won much personal publicity by qualifying for an amateur golf championship which would keep him out of action for most of the rest of August. Mercer responded by gathering his papers together noisily.

'Thank you very much,' said the Prime Minister. 'I needn't sum up. We've no time for item 8 today. It only remains for me to say that I hope you will all find some opportunity for rest and a holiday. It has been a gruelling few months, and we deserve a break. Before we disperse I would like on your behalf to thank Sir Basil Proudfoot and his able and energetic staff for all the help they have given us in the Cabinet Secretariat. Without them we should, I fear, be simply sounding brass, or, in some cases,' he bowed towards the Energy Secretary, the only lady present, 'a tinkling cymbal. And may I finally thank you all for your unfailing support. Like most Cabinets, we have different views and different personalities. This sometimes shows here, but not, I am happy to say, outside. I do not believe there is a Cabinet in modern times which has pulled so well together with so little dissent. In a way that is a negative virtue. I hope we can also feel that we have in difficult times done some good for our country.'

That too was well done, but some of them were a little puzzled as they filed through the door out into the ante-chamber.

'What was the old man on about at the end?' said Mercer. 'All that goodbye stuff. Sounded more like the end of a Parliament than the end of a session.'

David Bross, the Chief Whip, paused in the act of collecting his umbrella from the hook with his name written above it. He was a quiet smooth dark man who attended Cabinets but never spoke unless specifically questioned.

'I don't know if you've heard . . .'

But they were interrupted by Clarissa.

'The PM asks if you would both come back for a quick word. Something political, I think.'

'Damn,' said Mercer.'Get someone to ring up my office, would you, there's a good girl? I'm giving lunch to the Iranian Chief of Staff in some hotel or other, they'd better start without me.'

Back in the Cabinet Room, the Prime Minister was pouring sherry from a decanter into six cut glasses on a silver tray. The Civil Servants had disappeared, but he had used his buzzer to summon John from his desk in the adjoining room. John and Richard Newings handed round the sherry glasses, taking one themselves. Outside beyond the garden wall, the plane trees were ruffled by the strong breeze which comes before rain in London in summer.

'Sit down a minute,' said the Prime Minister. 'I won't keep you.'

The table was still dishevelled. Ministers had packed their papers into their red boxes before departing, but had left behind jotting pads, paper clips, a couple of ballpoint pens.

'I just wanted you to know that I am going into hospital for a few days.' He paused. They waited.

'I've had a bad leg, a swelling that won't go down. You've all of you noticed it. I'm run down, I tire easily. You've noticed that, too. There is no reason to suspect anything seriously wrong. Ellerman is back now, and he's quite sure there's nothing malignant in the leg. But he wants me to have a check-up. That means two or three days in the Charing Cross Hospital, starting Tuesday.'

'I'm sorry . . .' began Bross.

'No need to be sorry. Hanning will simply say it's some time since I had a check-up and now I'm back from the Far East, there's a natural opportunity to fit it in. Nothing about the leg, of course. There'll be some Press speculation, particularly as I missed that banquet in Rajnaya. But if it has nothing to feed on it'll die down.'

John could see them looking at the man in a new way, sizing up what might actually be happening, known or unknown, in that strange mixture of flesh, bone and spirit which added up to a Prime Minister.

# CHAPTER TWENTY

'Come and have something to eat upstairs,' said the Prime Minister to John. 'I want to ask you about something. Helena promised to cook a Quiche Lorraine. She usually makes too much.'

Half way up the photographs on the staircase he had another thought.

'What about Clarissa? She looked as if she needed cheering up.' This was a most unusual line of thought.

'I'll see what's she's doing.' John ran down the stairs again and past the ticker-tape into the private office. The old man continued up towards the landing, slowly but steadily, leaning on the staircase rail.

In the private office Clarissa was at her desk, sobbing on to her blotting paper. In the corner behind his desk the duty clerk sat counting security keys and trying not to notice.

John put his hand on her shoulder.

'What's wrong?'

'It's all a terrible mess.'

'What's a terrible mess?'

'Everything. Everything I do. Everything I don't do.'

'You're to come and have lunch. Upstairs in the flat. He particularly wants you.'

She looked up at him, and the flood stopped. He noticed she had no make-up on, not even lipstick. It made her nose look longer and her eyes less deep. Her cheeks were blotchy.

'Will Helena be there?'

'I expect so.'

'Well, I suppose I must face it some time.' She found a hankerchief in her bag, and dabbed hard. 'I can't go like this.'

He waited outside the lavatory till she came out. She had combed her hair and put on powder.

'What have you got to face?'

'Wait and see.'

'I think I know already.'

They were opposite Ramsay MacDonald. She turned and kissed him on the lips, harder than ever before.

'I think you do,' she said. 'You're an odd person.'

'We're all mad in this place.'

'Except at our work. It's the work that keeps us sane.'

The door at the top of the stairs up to the flat was open and Helena stood on the landing wearing an apron.

'He told me,' she said. 'I've dressed another lettuce. More salad, less quiche. There's only one bottle of Vouvray chilled. So you'd better both start with gin.'

'Thank you. I had sherry downstairs.'

She made a face. 'I thought Wellcome's South African had all gone. They used to hide the bottles when the Labour Party Executive came. Apartheid and all that. One of the messengers told me. They were quite happy with it as long as it came from a decanter.'

When they were all at the small lunch-table the Prime Minister said :

'Not a bad Cabinet.'

'A long agenda,' said John.

'We got through it all except one item.'

He paused.

'It is pleasant to see you and Clarissa here. What I really want to know from you is what has happened to my son. I hope that is not an unreasonable request. One of you must know. He hasn't slept here for two nights.'

Helena chipped in.

'You mustn't upset yourself. It's not important. He couldn't control himself. He thought he should go for a time. He was quite right.'

'Stop treating me as an invalid. He is my son, not yours. I insist on knowing what has happened.' John had never known the old man snap so hard.

Clarissa emptied her wine glass and sat up straight in her chair. John thought she looked like a student nerving herself for a viva.

'He's taken a flat in Ennismore Gardens. I'm living there with him.'

'You silly fool,' said Helena in a matter of fact tone. She got up and began to clear away the plates. John and the Prime Minister waited.

Clarissa raised her voice slightly, and John had more and more the impression of a public performance.

'It's really quite simple. We fell in love a few weeks ago. The first time he spent the night with me was at Rajnaya, after that banquet. William Pershore found out, and let us know that for security reasons it wouldn't do for Antony to live here if I was to go on working for you. I want to go on working here, but I want to live with Antony. So he decided to go. I know that he meant to tell you himself, but I think he found it difficult to find an opportunity.'

The old man sat still, and John could not read his reaction. A Brie appeared, long and oozing, with Bath Olivers banged on the table by Helena in their tin.

'You all seem determined to make life complicated,' said

the Prime Minister. 'There is an estate called matrimony . . .'
For a moment he sounded almost wistful.

'I don't think that's in either of our minds,' said Clarissa.
She was far removed from the damp distraught creature
whom John had found half an hour before.

'You knew about this?' he turned to John.

'Yes.'

'And you?'

'Of course,' said Helena. 'He told me. I was honoured.
But it was because I had to send on his laundry.'

'I give up,' said the Prime Minister. 'The Irish are simple
and sane by comparison.' He thought for a moment, and
almost said more, but a veil came down. 'Let's have coffee
in the other room. The chairs are more comfortable.' Over
coffee they talked about summer plans and then about the
Queen's Speech. Nothing was said about the hospital, and
nothing more about Antony.

'Did he mind?' asked Clarissa on the way downstairs.

John could not resist trying to upset her.

'Of course he minded. He minded like hell.'

'It didn't show.'

'For a few months he got Antony back. Now you've driven
him away.'

They were on the landing outside the study. Clarissa turned
to face him. Her cheeks were full of colour now.

'I don't think he gives a damn about Antony. He's purged
himself of all that. Helena is a cook and a companion.
Antony is a problem he can do without. Politics is all that
matters to him, and he's quite right. He can't have it
both ways, and he's made his choice. It's the only choice
you can make if you want to do a good job. And don't you
forget it.'

Then she changed her tone.

'You're coming down to Redburn on Friday aren't you?'
The weekend had been pencilled in his diary for two months.

'I assumed you wouldn't want me to come.'

'Well, I do. My parents will be upset if you cry off. They've
asked people to dinner.'

'Will Antony be there?'

'Good God, no, they don't know anything about Antony.
And you mustn't tell them.'

'That means I'll be there under false pretences. They'll always be leaving rooms so that I can put the question.'

She laughed.

'They've given me up, I'm afraid. The estate of matrimony's not for me.'

'Why not?'

'It's a long story.'

'I don't think it is at all. Come into my office and tell it to me.' John felt exhilarated, and therefore pushing. He was relieved that events had settled the question whether he was in love with Clarissa. He wasn't. On top of that he was relieved that she wanted him as a friend.

'I can't. I've got the Overseas Policy Committee at 3. The PM agreed to take the chair.'

'He's going into hospital, you know.'

'I know. William told us just before the Cabinet.' There was either a whole lot or else nothing more to be said about that.

'I'll drive you down on Friday.'

'Fine. If we leave it till about 7 we'll miss the traffic.'

They had never been more at ease together.


# CHAPTER TWENTY-ONE


As a long-established bachelor and town-lover John was a connoisseur of middle-class weekends in the English countryside. They fell into two categories, active and passive, and each had its hazards. Active was tennis and swimming and people in for drinks before every meal. Passive was looking through the drawing-room windows at the rain, reading books, talking quietly and borrowing gumboots to go for walks among the puddles and dripping woods. John was no athlete and preferred the passive. But it was very hard work unless there were people under the same roof whom you knew well.

He did not know Clarissa's father well, but there the two of them were on Saturday afternoon, striding along a damp track which had once been a railway line, a terrier snuffling through the blackberry bushes on one side. The fields to left and right were white with ripe and battered barley. Another downpour threatened, and the boots which he had borrowed from the Brigadier were decidedly tight. Clarissa had contracted out at the last minute, saying she must help her mother cook for the dinner party that evening. John felt more and more that he was at Redburn under false pretences. At any minute his host would ask him about his intentions.

'Sorry to hear the PM is going into hospital,' said the Brigadier, slashing at a thistle with his stick.

'Did Clarissa tell you?'

'Clarissa, good God, no. She never tells us anything. It was on the eight o'clock news.'

The announcement was to have been on Monday for Tuesday's papers. Hanning must have had to bring it forward because of a leak.

'It's just a check-up.'

'So they said. He didn't look fit to me that day we were at Chequers. Very pleasant though, remarkably pleasant.'

'He's very fond of Clarissa.'

'Ah.' The Brigadier had his cue, but did not seem able to use it. A small rabbit lolloped along the track in front of them, undetected by the terrier, which appeared to be as old as the Brigadier and considerably less spry.

'That fellow, Cornwall, what do you make of him?'

This was something on which John was not prepared to trim, though he guessed what was coming.

'I think he's a thoroughly destructive person, no beliefs, no real character.'

'Do you now, do you, that's odd.' His host was nonplussed.

'Never met him myself, but it strikes me he's got guts. He talks in a way that ordinary people understand. Not afraid to speak his mind. Pity that he and old Percival can't make it up. Shouldn't let personal differences stand in the way. They were saying so in the pub the other evening.'

It was a familiar tramline. John knew he could not win.

'But it isn't personal. He and the PM disagree fundamentally on what ought to be done. In Ireland, for example.'

'Oh, Ireland. No good'll ever come of that.'

The rain had begun again, driving in their faces. Ahead of

them was the platform of Redburn Halt, unused for thirty years, overgrown with weeds through which pink rambler roses still thrust their way. The ancient waiting-room still stood at one end of it, yellow brick with a fretted iron roof.

'Coming on hard, and you've got no coat. Better stop a minute in there.'

There was a strong smell in the waiting-room. The door leading to the gents had fallen from its hinges, and through the opening John saw what he took to be the corpse of a hare. That was another thing about visits to the country. On the road, in the garden, round every corner and in each recess you came upon the sights and smells of death.

'I gather you're not going to marry her.' Brigadier Strong seemed to find this the most natural possible place to discuss his daughter's future.

'No, I'm not. In fact, I never asked her.'

'Oh.' The Brigadier spoke as if he had learnt not to be surprised by anything young people did. 'I thought you were going to. You seemed fond of her.'

'I am fond of her. But I thought she'd say no. Now I know she would have.'

The Brigadier pulled out a pipe, evidently ready for a long stay.

'A pity. My wife and I like you. Not that that has anything to do with it. The others have all been difficult, very difficult indeed. Is there anyone else now?'

'I think you must ask her that.'

'Oh. Yes, quite right. Sounds as if there is, though.' The Brigadier pulled at his empty pipe, producing a low wheeze. John shifted his position to avoid drips from a leak in the roof. The terrier shook its wet off on to his trousers.

'At Oxford the worst was the Irishman. Barry, I can't remember his other name. A real politician, he was. He came to stay here once, and that was a mistake. He talked about Ireland the whole time. I can usually keep a civil tongue in my head even when I disagree with people. With Barry what's his name, I remember, I just took my hat and walked out of the house. Middle of January and raining hard, much worse than today. I remember it clearly.'

'I think it's letting up,' said John. Certainly it was wetter inside the waiting-room than out.

'He was a cousin in a way,' said the Brigadier, poking a puddle with his stick. 'Did you know Clarissa had an Irish grandmother? On her mother's side, of course. I once met a man who told me that grandmothers were at the root of the trouble in Ireland.'

'Really?'

'They keep them at home, the Catholics, I mean. No question of old people's homes. So there they sit by the fire, night after night, telling all the old stories, spreading all the old lies. That's why the different kinds of Irish go on hating each other. If it was just their parents telling them, they'd soon find out different, learn to think for themselves. But because it's granny they take it as gospel. It's the same in Sicily, virgins and vendettas and the Mafia, you know what I mean.'

In the presence of his wife or daughter, Brigadier Strong was quiet, even tongue-tied, an upright man who carved, poured drinks, and mended small things in house and garden. Obviously there was another side to him which needed an occasional canter. John now understood one reason why Clarissa had invited him down.

'You probably know Clarissa deals with Ireland at No. 10.'

'Of course I do. The phone never stops ringing every time she's down here.'

'She's always very sensible in what she says.' In fact it would have been more accurate to say that he had hardly ever heard Clarissa make any comment on Ireland. Most senior Civil Servants were pretty free with their views among people they trusted, and so was Clarissa on most subjects – but not, he now realized for the first time, on Ireland.

'Good, good.' It wasn't his daughter's opinions which interested the Brigadier. 'D'you think she's happy?'

'Yes, I do, definitely I do.' This would have been entirely truthful except that he remembered the sobbing figure at her desk three days before.

'Rain's stopped. Time we were going,' said Brigadier Strong, as if John had been detaining him in idle chat. John wondered if all Clarissa's friends were taken this walk on Saturday mornings and cross-examined about her happiness. He could not imagine Antony getting farther than the garden gate. Certainly he would draw the line at the hare. As if guessing the question, the Brigadier cleared his throat.

'I don't usually go on like this,' he said. 'But I care for the girl. Only child, and so forth. When I was young people didn't have to go to strangers for the simplest questions about their children.'

'Happiness isn't simple,' said John.

The Brigadier vaulted from the platform back on to the weeds and cinders of the track, and started back towards Redburn.

'I think you're probably right,' he said after fifty yards.


'I've got to go.' Clarissa had run out on the lawn to meet them. John had never seen her run before. 'William Pershore rang. It's a special meeting of the Northern Ireland Committee. At Chequers, in an hour. I'll just make it.'

'Isn't there anyone else?' asked Brigadier Strong bleakly. 'It always seems to be you.' John could imagine the number of times this had happened, leaving him alone, growing old in a big house he couldn't afford with a tiresome woman who happened to be his wife.

'I'm afraid it must be me. But I'll be back long before dinner. Mummy's got everything organized.'

'I'm sure.' Her father was not consoled.

'I'll come with you,' said John.

'I did tell William you were here.' He could see her looking for words which would not hurt. 'He didn't think . . . it's a formal meeting of the Committee, you see, even though it's at Chequers. Just Ministers and the Chief of Defence Staff and the usual secretaries . . .'

'Of course.' John was not consoled either. He tried to think of a political weekend at Chequers which as Political Secretary he would control. He would ruthlessly exclude William Pershore.

'Come and talk while I change.'

'What's happened then?' he said when they reached her bedroom.

'Unzip me, then.' She stepped out of her dress. Her legs were the same soft brown colour as her face. 'The PM's going into hospital on Monday instead of Thursday. He wanted to get this meeting out of the way.'

'Why the change?'

'No idea. You can imagine William on the phone – "I understand the change of dates has no particular medical significance." Sit down. I won't be a minute.'

'What's on the agenda?'

It was absurd, but it was the first time he had seen her in underclothes only. They had swum together at Hurlingham, but that wasn't the same. She was much more attractive now than fully dressed. Because she dressed badly he had drawn some wrong conclusions about her. He felt desire – and remorse, for it was too late. He was only there in her room because it was too late.

'It's a security operation, it's been on the cards for some time now. It's called Operation Roughneck. I expect Bernays wants to bring it forward. He'll try to net some of the top Provisionals before their campaign really gets going.'

'Clarissa, I want to ask you two questions,' John said. He knew it sounded pompous.

'*Two* questions? A gentleman usually has one.'

'Don't laugh at me.'

She came over and stroked his head. He resisted a silly urge to pull her down to him.

'The first is, why were you crying the other day? I'd never seen you cry before. I didn't like it.'

'No more did I. Well, I'll tell you. It wasn't about Antony, and it wasn't about you. No guessing, you'll never get it.'

She was at her dressing table doing things to her hair and face. The mirror was askew and John could not see her expression.

'Second question: are you happy in the job, Clarissa?'

She swung round. She dropped the bantering tone and her deep eyes were fierce.

'Why do you ask that?'

'I want to know. So does your father. You never give any sign. Even at No. 10.'

'Then let me tell you. If Antony hadn't left No. 10, I'd have left Antony. Work that out, and it should make you feel better.'

He tried.

'You don't really love him?'

'He attracts me, he fascinates me, he's fun. But it's only in novels that love comes first.'

111

'And with you?'

'Any woman can have a beautiful lover. I've got a job at No. 10.'

'That can't really be the answer.'

'You're holding me up. I'll be late, I'll tell William you took longer seducing me than usual, and I couldn't get away.'

And so Clarissa left in her father's Vauxhall, leaving no one satisfied.

# CHAPTER TWENTY-TWO

*The Times August 23*

The Prime Minister left the Charing Cross Hospital yesterday morning after a four-day check-up and returned to No. 10. No medical bulletin was issued, and neither Sir James Percival's doctor, Dr Ellerman, nor any of the hospital consultants was available for comment. However the Press Office at No. 10 let it be known that the Prime Minister had been given a clean bill of health after a series of exhaustive tests. 'All he needs now is a good rest' said a spokesman. The Prime Minister himself seemed cheerful as with Lady Percival he posed for photographs on the hospital steps. 'The only medicine the doctors prescribed was a fortnight without newspapers' he told waiting journalists. It is understood that after a day or two clearing up papers at No. 10 the Prime Minister will go to Chequers for about two weeks. Cabinet colleagues and officials have been warned not to refer decisions to him during this period except in an emergency. A tour of marginal seats in Lancashire and Scotland which had been planned for the first week of September has been cancelled.

*Our Political Correspondent writes:* Friends and opponents alike will rejoice that alarming rumours about the Prime Minister's health have been dispelled. It is not surprising that so much emphasis should be laid on the need to rest. Sir James is after all nearly sixty-six and he has had a gruelling year. The victorious General Election in the spring, a hard Parliamentary session, and then a punishing tour of the Far East have inevitably taken their toll of his energy. August is a tricky month for Governments, and this year is proving no exception, with widespread anxiety about the growing violence in Northern Ireland. The publication last weekend of the Matheson report strengthens the arm of those who feel growing doubts about the British Army's commitment in the province, and this is likely to be a key issue when political life revives at the end of September in advance of the Party Conferences. Meanwhile it is good news that for the next fortnight Chequers is not to be the summer seat of Government, as so often in the past, but a real haven of tranquillity and rest for the Prime Minister.

'Glad to see you back, sir,' said the doorkeeper.

'Glad to be back.' He turned to wave to a small knot of tourists on the opposite pavement of the sunny street. Helena, Dr Ellerman and the Inspector followed him into No. 10. John, Antony and William Pershore stood inside to greet him.

'All well?' he asked.

'All well,' said Pershore for them all.

'Good. We'll have a proper talk about things this evening. Meanwhile I'm going straight upstairs to sleep. Those tests were fairly exhausting. Not to speak of the interrogations morning, noon and night. Now I know what the Lubyanka must be like.'

He talked easily, but they could see that he still pulled one leg behind him as he walked to the lift. They had a feeling of let-down.

Helena let him go up with Dr Ellerman.

'I should be very grateful if you could all come and have a word with me.' She spoke with an unusual formality. 'I think John Cruickshank's office would be the most convenient place.'

John, Antony, and Pershore followed her down the corridor past the bust of Pitt. They were joined on the way by Clarissa and Hanning and by a young Duty Clerk, who pushed past them to speak to Helena.

'I'm sorry to interrupt, but Lady Cloyne is on the line and wants to speak to you urgently.'

'I'll take it in here,' said Helena, continuing her march to John's office. 'No, no, come in all of you – nothing I say to Mary Cloyne can be in the least bit private. Hello, hello, I'm here, put her through . . . Yes, Mary, good morning – yes, just back from the hospital – fine, just fine, a little tired, but we'll soon see to that – oh, I see . . . Yes – I see, at Nice, how clever of you – how kind. No, Mary, I'm afraid it's out of the question. For one thing he mustn't fly. For another, he'll have a better rest at Chequers. All visitors will be kept out, officials, everybody. Yes, even friends, I'm afraid, Mary. Once we start allowing exceptions, you know how it is . . . I must go now. Thanks for ringing. Yes of course I'll tell him. Goodbye then.'

Helena moved over to the mantelpiece, and leant against it, knocking down a card inviting John to some official function. Her harsh face set in the wiry mass of orange hair had lost its usual sullen look. Authority for the moment had come her way, and she was enjoying it.

'I dislike Chequers, you all know that. But I shall go there for a fortnight to make sure that Lady Cloyne keeps out. She had the nerve to suggest that we spend the fortnight on her yacht. A real Mediterranean rest, she said. Eating rich food and listening to her rich friends jabber about their tiny problems. Nothing would be more exhausting. James would hate it.'

John thought the PM might in fact enjoy it. He was always amused by Lady Cloyne. Sun and rich food would certainly make a change. However none of them was in a position to argue.

'I mean what I said,' Helena directed herself mainly to Pershore. 'Of course a detective will have to be there. But no Garden Room girl, no meetings, no visitors and no telephone calls to him direct.'

'There will have to be suitable arrangements for the collection and delivery of boxes. And of course for the hotline telephones,' said Pershore.

'Those are details,' said Helena. 'But you get the point. The point is, keep out. And you understand why.'

'I don't,' said Antony. He had been the only one to sit down.

'The doctors found nothing,' said Helena. 'That's in the

114

papers. They said so. They didn't say there was nothing to find.'

'What does that mean?'

'It means they don't know. Something's wrong. We've all seen that. Perhaps just old age. Perhaps something not important. Something too small to show in their tests. Perhaps something rest will cure. Let's try it anyway. Then we can see.'

# CHAPTER TWENTY-THREE

'Serial No. 14, address 21 Inkerman Road. House deserted. Neighbours say no one there for at least a week. But signs of food consumed within last few hours.'

'What does that last sentence mean?' asked the Colonel, looking up from the slip of paper.

'Egg still sticky on the plate, sir. Great ones for eggs, the Provos. Cheap and quick. When the egg's fresh the mess left on the plate takes 24 hours to dry completely.'

'Doesn't look too good so far.'

'No, sir.'

'What's that blue civilian car outside?'

'Headmaster's car, sir. He asked permission to leave it here as usual. It was searched when we arrived last night.'

They were in the classroom of a Catholic school commandeered for the purpose of Operation Roughneck because it was close to most of the addresses of the men they wanted. There was a list of these pasted to the wall alongside the Virgin Mary. Sergeant Spencer marked X in red chalk, in the blank space opposite No. 14 and added '0840 hours'. Then he filed the slip of paper in a small green box on the table behind which the teacher usually sat. He took off his spectacles and rubbed the sweat from his face.

'Serial No. 7, address Sullivan's Garage, North Parade. No trace. Left work as usual 1730 last night. Was expected to clock in 0800. Detachment used authority in operation order to visit alternative address 16 Sandhills Road. Landlady reports 7 left for work 0730 as usual.'

'Coming in fast now, sir.' There was another sergeant at the special telephone, scribbling on a pad as the light beside the receiver flashed.

'Serial No. 1, no trace . . .'

'Damn. I hope the other units are doing better.'

'Serial No. 19, no trace.'

'Might I make a suggestion, sir?'

'Go ahead.'

'We should clear out of here at once.'

'Why?'

'Roughneck's been blown, sir, that's plain enough. If they've got the names we want, they've probably got our operational HQ as well. We'd be safer back at battalion.'

The Colonel thought for a moment.

'Right. Pack up at once and into the truck.'

'Very good, sir.'

They were almost in time. It took a few minutes to dismantle the telephone and pack the files. Sergeant Spencer, of 31 Reynolds Road, Northampton, turned back from the door as an afterthought and spent another minute putting the class-room chairs and tables roughly back in place. The bomb placed at dawn in the headmaster's car exploded just as he finally left the room. It killed him instantly.


'To sum up, then. Sixty-five names, and they only got two. One at the border under a load of potatoes in a truck, the other by chance in the street. He had quarrelled with his wife and left home without telling anyone. On our side a sergeant killed.'

'Bleak.'

'Worse than bleak.'

When news was particularly bad Sir Basil Proudfoot, Secretary to the Cabinet, usually came in person through the door which linked the old Treasury building to No. 10. He admired William Pershore and thought of him as a possible successor one day. It was useful to pick his brains informally at a moment of crisis like this.

'You'd better tell the PM.'

'Not till five o'clock. Those are the rules.'

'Surely for a thing like this . . .' said Sir Basil.

'Those are the rules. No messages between lunchtime and five o'clock.'

Both men had a vision of Helena, bored and fierce, prowling through the rooms of Chequers which she hated, daring the Downing Street staff to telephone in the prohibited hours so that she could turn and rend them.

'What about Bernays?'

'He'll know by now, of course.'

A light glowed on Pershore's desk, and he picked up the telephone.

'Yes, he's here, Secretary of State. We were discussing the unfortunate outcome of . . . Yes. Yes. Yes, you could put it that way . . . No, not yet, we have a rule that he isn't disturbed until 5 . . . Yes, I think he probably could . . . very well.'

'That was Bernays. He would like to see us both at once.'

'He didn't wait for you to find out if I could manage it.'

'I don't think he is in a particularly courteous mood.'

'Have you noticed how it is only second-rate Ministers who become angry at bad news? The third-rate ones do not feel it enough, and the first-rate ones rise above it.'

'There are not many first-rate Ministers these days.'

'Very true. Shall we go out by the street? It's a nice day.'

The sunshine was brilliant and Whitehall was almost deserted. A one-decker bus cruised slowly past the entrance to Downing Street while the guide gave its inmates a potted version of British constitutional history.

Sir Basil was pink and pear-shaped; he rolled slightly as he walked. Pershore slowed down to keep pace. They passed the bus stop, and turned into Dover House, which Bernays had managed to secure for the Northern Ireland Office in the latest reshuffle of Government buildings. A fluttering Private Secretary was at the door to meet them and escort them up the stately staircase to Bernays's office. It was one of the most splendid rooms in Whitehall. Bernays had hung a blue and gold French hunting tapestry of his own between two white Corinthian pillars. He sat behind a big ornate desk with heavy curved legs, his back to the Horse Guards. He was reading a report and did not look up to greet his visitors. He was not rude by nature, but he found the relationship with senior Civil Servants difficult. This lack of ease made him abrupt at moments of stress.

'Sir Basil Proudfoot, Secretary of State,' said the fluttering young man.

'So I see.' He got up, and waved them to a sofa at one side of the mantelpiece. 'Well, this is a fine balls-up.'

'I can only presume the IRA received advance information.'

Bernays gazed at Sir Basil, and seemed to swallow a comment.

'You presume right.'

'It would appear to be the responsibility of the Secretary of State for Defence to set in hand an enquiry as to how such precise information leaked from the Army.' Sir Basil believed that procedures were the essence of government. That was how he had become Secretary to the Cabinet.

'Mercer has already been on to me. He's started already. But I don't believe he'll find anything.'

'Might I ask why not?'

'For the simple reason that the operation was divided among four Army units. No one in those units knew the full list of wanted men. It was the full list which the IRA got. That list was known only to seven men in Northern Ireland. They are not the sort of men who go to pubs or sleep with inquisitive tarts.'

'I see.' Sir Basil took out his pipe, and the sight made Bernays snap.

'For God's sake, didn't you realize that? But at least now you do you can see the implication.'

Sir Basil spent three matches before replying.

'Yes, I do.'

'Well?'

'I shall have to speak to the Prime Minister as soon as he is available this evening. As Secretary of the Cabinet I shall ask his authority to set in hand a rigorous enquiry here as well. It should be possible to establish fairly quickly who saw the plan for Operation Roughneck.'

'That's right, that's right.' Bernays was somewhat mollified. He eased his finger round the inside of his stiff white collar. Then he spoke again less roughly. 'You're both experienced, I can speak to you frankly. I invested a good deal of faith in Roughneck, more than I can afford to lose. You know very well that I wanted a fundamental change of policy in Northern Ireland. That would have headed off the big violence we all see coming. My colleagues wouldn't agree, so I had to fall back on more orthodox means. We had a lot of intelligence information which had not been acted on for fear of precipitating trouble. Put together, that information added up to Roughneck. There was a chance that if we hauled in the top brass the second echelon wouldn't be capable of sustaining the campaign. That chance has gone now. So where does that leave me?'

It was a genuine question put to them because Bernays had no close political friends. It was not easy for either of them to answer, particularly as neither had a close interest in Bernays's career. But some answer was evidently required, and of the two Civil Servants Pershore had the more agile mind.

'The IRA may overreach themselves,' he said. 'If a new campaign of violence alienated Catholics as well as Protestants, you might be able to launch a new political initiative in the autumn with some chance of success. Nothing said in Cabinet the other morning would rule that out.'

'If we reach the autumn.' Bernays was going to say more, but checked himself.

Sir Basil Proudfoot levered himself to his feet. 'Well, I'd better get started.'

'I hope you'll be ruthless and quick,' said Bernays, also getting up. 'Above all quick.'

'These enquiries always take time. As you know, there are certain set procedures.'

Once again Bernays looked astonished. Once again he held himself back, with an effort.

'I said quick, because you can hardly expect the Army to do its job effectively if before it even receives its orders someone is already signalling them to the IRA.'

'Quite so, quite so.'

They beat an orderly retreat. On the stairs Pershore said :

'He has a certain ability. And determination.'

'A crude intellect, I should say.' Sir Basil was nettled at having been twice caught out.

'At least you didn't tell him the truth.'

'What do you mean?'

'Whenever there's a serious leak at Cabinet level it almost always turns out to be a Minister who has talked out of turn to an unreliable journalist.'

'Very true, very true.'

Hugging to themselves this slice of traditional wisdom the two men stepped blinking into the sunshine.

# CHAPTER TWENTY-FOUR

Extract from Linda Sweetey's *Window on the World, Daily Express*, 21 August:

> As you bend over the typewriter hammering out the firm's letters and dreaming of the foreign holiday you can't afford, how would you like the boss's handsome son to come up from behind, put his hands over your face, and say, 'Guess what, sweetheart, we're going on a Mediterranean cruise in a luxury millionaire-style yacht!' That's what's happened to Clarissa Strong, 29, one of the most enterprising secretaries at No. 10 Downing Street. The PM's dark good-looking son Antony Percival, erstwhile playboy turned banker, has asked her to join him for a week on Lord Cloyne's yacht *Medusa*. The lucky pair will join the *Medusa* at Nice, and from then on the voyage is a secret one. I bet the other girls at Number 10 are green with you-know-what this morning . . . as they learn of Clarissa's luck. Let's hope it's all plain sailing, Clarissa!'

'It is without doubt the most patronizing, obscene and untrue story I have ever read.'

Clarissa dumped the tray in Antony's lap. She always made his breakfast, a boiled egg and two slices of toast, but as a matter of principle refused to come back to bed and eat hers alongside.

Antony took the paper, read the piece, and laughed. The

tray tipped away from his knees, and the coffee began to spill before he grabbed it. Then he saw she was genuinely cross.

'Don't look so stuffy, it was that old harridan I was cornered by the night before last. I didn't know she had it in her to write it up that way.'

'I don't know where to begin.' Clarissa stood. 'First of all, she writes as if I was a typist.'

Antony crowed again. 'I knew that would annoy you most.'

'Second, the word enterprising as used here can only mean one thing.'

'And that's a compliment in her book – and in mine.' Antony still hoped to mock Clarissa out of her bad mood. 'After all, here you are in bed with me.'

'I am not in bed with you. I am up and dressed and going to the office. And I am not coming with you on the boat.'

Antony sat up in bed, throwing back the blankets. Below the waist he wore white pyjamas, a purple fleur de lys on each thigh.

'You must. I told Mary Cloyne you would.'

'You had no right to. I told you I would think about it.'

Antony groped for the right argument.

'We can't let her down. It's the cabin meant for my father and Helena.'

'You can go alone.'

'I don't want to go alone. I want to make love to you in one of the lifeboats on deck. For hours and hours, with a bottle of brandy under the stars. I'm told they're having a very warm summer.'

'And I want to go to No. 10 and work.'

'I'll buy you a new bikini.'

'Look, I thought you understood. Sometimes you seem to, sometimes you don't.' Clarissa sat on the bed. He tried to pull her towards him, but she edged out of reach. 'When Pershore found out about us, you did just right. You let me have it both ways. I can stay at No. 10, I can sleep with you in Ennismore Gardens. It was you that made the sacrifice.'

'No sacrifice. I'd exhausted Helena's cooking. The laundry she uses is lousy.'

'For God's sake, listen. The sacrifice you made was leaving your father. You were moving closer to him. You were getting interested in politics.'

'Crap. They bore me stiff. Even banking is better.'

'That's not true. You don't know much about politics, but they fascinate you. You gave all that up so I didn't have to choose. Because you knew I wouldn't choose you.'

'I must get up.' Antony rolled out of bed. 'It's the wrong time of day for undressing our souls. The right place for thrashing all this out is Mary Cloyne's yacht.'

'Just let me finish. I don't like Lady Cloyne. I'd hate the yacht. Nothing worse than going to beautiful places with silly people. But I'd go, just once, to be with you. That is, if things were quiet. But you know they're not.'

'Things are never quiet at No. 10. If by accident there's a moment's hush someone rushes to invent a new crisis. You haven't run my bath.'

'You can run your own. I told you about Operation Roughneck.'

'Only after it was all over. I resented that.'

'Now it's failed there'll be trouble, steady trouble, getting worse. It's my job to cope with it so far as No. 10 is concerned. I simply can't go to William Pershore and ask for leave just when I'm most needed.'

He bounced on to the bed, his chest naked against her blue dress, and his arms round her shoulders. She sat very still.

'You're dull this morning,' he said. 'Prossy and dull. As bad as John.'

She twisted away from him. He got up quickly, ran into the bathroom and turned on the taps. He heard her leave the flat and close the outside door.

Antony got into his bath. He did not have to be at the bank before ten. He looked at his stomach and thought about middle age.

# CHAPTER TWENTY-FIVE

John had brought his umbrella to Blenheim in the hope that it would rain. Alas, it was a gorgeous evening. The oaks and elms of the park stood resplendent against the fading light. It was intolerable that the majesty of English history and the incomparable beauty of England in September should lend their help to this occasion.

Jeremy Cornwall was not due till eight o'clock, but by seven the car park by the stables was crowded with buses, and the vast slope of grass between the terrace and the lake was already filled with thousands of people. They sat comfortably on rugs, munching and drinking, gathered over hundreds of miles from the cities and counties and from London itself, waiting for a great occasion. John could hear the quiet expectant buzz of their conversation as he parked his Mini under the direction of a teenage boy with a Cornwall button.

He picked his way down the slope and found a patch of grass big enough for him to spread his mackintosh. Why the hell had he come all the way from Notting Hill Gate for this? True, his weekends were sad empty things now that Clarissa was no longer his companion. But mainly he had come forth to see a prophet and his sign.

On the near bank of the lake he could see an enclosure inside which about thirty rows of chairs were set for the people who had paid £5 each. The Press had discovered that the money would go straight to Cornwall's Sinews of Britain Fund, founded recently for patriotic purposes which were far from clear. Everyone else had paid £1 per car, and John guessed there would be a collection on top of that before they were through.

There was a raft on the lake, and a companionway had been built connecting it to the ornamental bridge. Twenty minutes before Cornwall was due they switched on the lights sunk in the water around the raft. The natural light had faded completely now, except for a band of soft yellow in the west, behind the far ridge on which the first Duke's monument stood. In the dark the raft was a glittering fortress, empty except for a range of microphones on the side facing the crowd. On the slope people began to tidy up paper and put corks back in bottles.

Then it was the turn of the Red White and Blue. They were near the top of the charts week after week, but no one had linked the group with Cornwall before. So there was a gasp of pleased surprise when a searchlight picked out the five agile figures and helped them down the companionway from the bridge to the raft. Three young men and two girls, all in white, short black hair and pretty faces in the modern manner, which at John's distance were identical. There was no compère, no build-up, they were not dominating an audience of fans but setting the scene for something more important. John was sure that Cornwall handled his own publicity. The Red White and Blue, lords of many pop festivals, were here as his acolytes, humbling themselves before his coming. It was a masterstroke. They began with their own latest hit 'Bless Baby Bless'. Then as the applause began to die the eldest of them, known in the four corners of the kingdom as Red Jackson, stepped forward to the central microphone.

'That was just a warm up. But that's not why we are here. We think this is a special evening for England, and it's England that we're all thinking about tonight.'

And then, very simply in unison, without frills, or fanfares, they sang the songs of the two wars, 'Tipperary, Roses of Picardy, Pack up your troubles, There's a long long trail awinding, There'll be bluebirds over the White Cliffs of Dover'. Without stopping for applause they switched into the most sugary of them all. As they began 'There'll always be an England', the black mass of Blenheim Palace sprang into a formidable blaze of light. The five figures on the raft suddenly stretched out their arms to point up the slope as they sang. Television cameras swung and the crowd turned their heads. They saw Jeremy Cornwall standing in a Land-Rover at the top of the slope, dressed in white from head to foot like his acolytes. There was a great burst of clapping and cheering. He stood motionless as the truck drove slowly down a path cleared through the crowd, taking no notice of the applause, gazing ahead at the bridge, the floodlit raft, the Duke on his monument and the darkness of Oxfordshire beyond.

John, despite himself, on his feet with everyone else, wondered what the Press men down in front were making of this. He knew the answer. They would be giggling among themselves, but when it came to the point their stories would be enthusiastic. Why had everyone left the patriotic card for a charlatan like Cornwall to play?

The Red White and Blue stepped back from the microphones and clapped enthusiastically as Jeremy Cornwall took his place in front of them. He was taller than any of the five, and though he was certainly older by at least ten years he seemed the most glamorous of them all. Perhaps this was because they treated him as their leader. Certainly, John thought, he had made up his face for the occasion. He wondered if the Press would pick up the same impression. But he knew they would only pass it on to their readers if the evening, against expectation, turned out a flop. It was a Fleet Street instinct to be rude only about failure.

Cornwall acknowledged the cheers for half a minute, his black forelock falling boyishly across his face, then held up both hands abruptly to cut it short. Everyone expected him to begin to speak. Instead he stood to one side, as the pop group had done a minute before, and began to beckon a new figure on to the stage. There was a puzzled murmur in the crowd at this improbable sight. A thin ordinary middle-aged woman, bespectacled and dressed in black, stepped awkwardly out of the shadows and allowed Jeremy Cornwall to grasp her hand and coax her forward. John was close enough to see that she had a beaked nose. For a moment John wondered if she was a mistake, an intruder with whom Cornwall was coping as best he could. Then Cornwall spoke, and John recognized again the slight Irish inflexion of voice which heralded a speech about Ireland.

'My friends, my friends, welcome to you tonight, men and women, young and old. Because you have come here you're all my friends. I know that many of you have come many miles, and all the more I bid you welcome. Before I say anything to you, I want to introduce my friend, Mrs Spencer. My new friend Mrs Spencer, I should say. How long have we known each other?'

The woman spoke in a high artificial voice as if advertising a detergent on a television commercial.

'Two days, Jeremy.'

'Two days it is, Mrs Spencer.' His voice turned suddenly from the cheerful to the savage. 'And two weeks ago where was your husband?'

'In Belfast,' said the same high rehearsed voice.

'Yes, two weeks ago he was in Belfast, far from his family in Northampton. Two weeks ago Sergeant Spencer was doing his duty by his country. And two weeks ago Sergeant Spencer was murdered in an Irish school by an Irish bomb. Why was he sent to Ulster, Mrs Spencer?'

'I don't know.'

'Mrs Spencer does not know. Sergeant Spencer did not know. His comrades massacred in the Falls Road did not know. His eight thousand other comrades still alive in Ulster do not know. All they know is that they have been sent to Ulster by the politicians to do a job in which no army in the world could succeed.'

The first round of applause, muted as yet because people were embarrassed by Mrs Spencer and her widow's weeds. They need not have worried. She had served her purpose as a prologue and she shuffled off into the darkness. As reward for the evening's work her memoirs were to be ghosted in the *Sunday Messenger*.


And so Jeremy did his stuff. The Sunningdale Agreement, the failure of the Rees initiative, the wasted years that followed, the massacre in the Falls Road, the Matheson Report, the fiasco of Operation Roughneck – mercilessly he dragged his audience through them all. In one way John felt relieved. Cornwall was not as good an orator as he had supposed. The voice was harsh, and he kept it at the level of a high-pitched bark, which became monotonous. There was no sense of language. The adjectives came thick and fast, and because they were always strong they began to lose effect. Everything done by others was contemptible, cynical, unprincipled, and stupid beyond belief. A second-rate mind was wrestling with the English language and coming off second-best.

But he could draw no comfort from this, for Cornwall was

carrying the audience with him. Partly it was the showmanship of it all, the blazing palace, the shimmer of the water, the white suits, the sentimental music, the stars and the soft evening. Partly it was his reputation feeding on itself. Partly it was the spell cast by his dark face and slim body. He was a young man denouncing old men in a country weary of its past. Those who heard him despaired in their hearts for Ireland, and wanted to hear that it was brave and patriotic to bring the soldiers home. Whatever the reasons, whatever the defects, the message was getting home. The applause grew louder as each false peroration reached its close.

'And so in Belfast night by night there is death and failure as our English Army moves further and further into the Irish trap. In Whitehall there is bumbling deceit, lavish extravagance and unspeakable incompetence. And across that valley in the hills beyond our sight, not far from here, sleeps the old man who is supposed to be in charge. The Prime Minister is resting at Chequers. I have seen him there with my own eyes. He is sick, he is tired, he is cut off by his cronies and his family from what is happening to our country. We look for leadership and he offers us a dreary defeated silence. We look for inspiration, he potters among his roses.

'Well, we have had enough. There behind you, in the palace of Blenheim, Winston Churchill was born. Would to God that he were living at this hour! Can anyone doubt that he would have brought the Army home from Ireland long ago? Can anyone doubt that he would have seen this as the first essential to restore our self-respect? But we are his heirs, his followers, his children. Beyond those trees in the little churchyard at Bladon he lies in his grave. Let us go from this place determined to respect his memory, my friends. It is time for the lion to roar again. It is time, my friends, for us, the people of England, to find our voice.'

The clapping and cheers rang in John's ears. He ran up the slope to get his Mini free before the crowd dispersed. As he drove out along the road which leads from the Palace to the Woodstock Gate he could see on his left the white figure on the raft, now caught in a single searchlight, still bowing and waving to his huge audience. They were on their feet, shouting their loyalty. No doubt the music and the crude singing would begin again soon, and five thousand Englishmen would start for home glowing and surfeited, convinced for the moment that the cowardice which Cornwall preached would be an act of courage and salvation.

John pulled up for a minute alongside the Bear at Woodstock and picked up a copy of the *Oxford Mail* from a deserted news stand. As he put his fivepence in the tin slot he realized that his hands were trembling. He had never been so angry in his life. Thunder was gathering in his brain. To calm himself he sat in the stationary car thumbing through the paper. Nothing there yet about the speech of course, but a good deal about the preparations for the rally, and a big picture of Cornwall on the front page. And on the centre page opposite the leader, a tiny story which he noticed only because his eye was trained to catch anything to do with politics.

'*Wide Choice for Swindon Tories.* The selection committee set up last month by Swindon East Conservative Association will meet on September 14 as the first step in choosing a candidate for the next General Election. It is understood that more than a hundred aspirants have so far applied, and that the committee will interview fifteen of these. They are expected to choose six names to go before a full meeting of the executive committee at the end of next month. Swindon East is at present held by Mr Brian Crawley (Labour) who had a majority of 3,416 at the last Election in a three-cornered fight.'

He started the engine and began to drive towards London. The Bladon roundabout was festooned with posters of Cornwall and signposts pointing to the rally. The park wall was still on his right, and as he slowed his engine he could just hear through the trees that the music had started again.

Seventy-five miles to go – at that time of night it would take him an hour and a half. Not long to sort out a new life. He was determined not to let his feelings cool until he had done this. They were a fire he could see by, but he knew that the fire would not last.

When people criticized politics in front of him he usually said :

'Oh, they aren't all as bad as that.'

Then people said :

'Of course you have to say that. But you're not a dull ordinary MP. You have a fascinating job behind the scenes.'

And he would smile and change the subject. That would have to change. No more secrets, no more influence behind the green baize door, no more of the fun which comes to an unknown man who is constantly in the company of the famous. If he did what he was thinking of he would not even be an ordinary dull MP. He would be much lower in the pecking order, in the lowest position of all, a not-so-young man trying to be selected to fight a Labour seat.

Why? He was at Headington now, and the M40 opened before him. The Mini was four years old and not happy above 65 miles an hour, but he drove till she rattled. Why plunge? Because politics wasn't a merry-go-round of meetings and meals, though many politicians thought it was. It was a vocation, and he had been called.

Called in the first instance against Cornwall. Cornwall was a prostitute, using his gifts to deceive and destroy.

There was not a single person in the world to whom he could explain all this. He was lonely. Although he had taken no drink, he felt drunk. For once he was certain of himself. That was unusual. It could not be wrong. As he pulled up the escarpment of the Chilterns he doubted whether the certainty would last even till morning. It might dissolve before he reached his flat in Notting Hill Gate.

He turned off the motorway at Stokenchurch. There was a transport cafe on the edge of the village and through the bleary window he could see that it was full of truck drivers. He ordered sausage and chips from a large blonde. This was a world he would have to discover.

'I'm very sorry, there's a bit of an emergency, is there a phone I could use?'

She looked hard, sizing him up.

'In the back. There's a box for the money.'

There was a little office without a door. The desk was piled high with bills. The noise of talk and clattering dishes came loudly across the counter behind him. He dialled telegrams, and with the help of his credit card applied to the Chairman of the Swindon East Conservative Association for consideration as their candidate.

# CHAPTER TWENTY-SIX

Although Lord Cloyne had been a director of the Hesperian Bank for ten years he did not come to the Bank's offices in Gresham Street except for board meetings or for lunch. His particular responsibility was to entertain foreign clients of the Bank in the way to which they believed the English were accustomed. His fellow directors, none of whom had been to a public school, judged that he earned his keep. They knew that for him the Bank was not so much a source of income as a means of escape from Lady Cloyne, her charities, her political lunch parties, her voice.

So Antony was surprised when the trim little receptionist on the fourteenth floor of Wrangel House told him when he arrived at ten past ten one morning in September that Lord Cloyne wanted to see him. He assumed that it must be something to do with his six days on the Cloyne yacht, even though Lord Cloyne had been shooting in Scotland at the time. He felt a small twinge of guilt about the tall American blonde. He had spent half an hour one night with her in the lifeboat which he had offered to Clarissa. The night had been warm, the stars bright, the brandy sound. He had thought hard about Clarissa, about Trisha, about other and earlier blondes, but it had been no good. That particular blonde rose up intact and cross, with marks on her back from the planks which forced her to wear a silk shirt for two days. The rest of the cruise had been equally uneventful, and he had been glad to get back to London.

'How are you getting on then?' Lord Cloyne had no room of his own at the Bank and only half a secretary, so they were talking in the board-room itself, with five Canaletto copies let into the light oak panelling.

'Not too badly.' Antony was damned if he was going to thank Lord Cloyne yet again for getting him the job.

'How did it go on the boat?' Here it came.

'Fine. Lady Cloyne is a great hostess. And she had the sun on her side.'

'More than we had in Scotland.' A pause. 'But grouse don't like sun.'

Antony felt unable to comment on this. There was another and longer pause.

'I've been looking at the morning papers.' So it appeared. The lectern in one corner of the room was dishevelled and two or three papers were on the floor. Antony was reminded of his father and the sea of newsprint in which he bathed during breakfast. He himself took the *Express* and the *Sun* in bed, to Clarissa's disgust, and the *Financial Times* to read in the tube. People who read too many newspapers began to confuse them with the real world.

'That fellow Cornwall is making a bit of a splash.' And indeed he was.

### FOR ENGLAND'S SAKE
Jeremy's appeal

---

As thousands weep and cheer
### ARMY BACK BY CHRISTMAS
says Jeremy

---

Mr Cornwall resumes crusade

---

### THE NEW CHURCHILL?
Dramatic voice in Winston's home

---

Cornwall breaks summer silence
### OLD MAN AMONG THE ROSES
Sharpest attack yet on Premier

---

'A lot in what he says,' said Lord Cloyne. 'He goes too far, of course. Shouldn't have said all that about your father. But he's right about Ireland. Hopeless place, always has been.'

Antony said nothing. He could not see where this was leading. Lord Cloyne hadn't offered him a seat, and they were both standing.

'He's upstairs as a matter of fact.'

131

'Who's upstairs?'

'Jeremy Cornwall, of course.' Lord Cloyne was testy. He was not one of nature's go-betweens. 'He wanted a word with you, asked me to arrange it. This seemed the easiest way. In the penthouse flat, I expect you know it. Seventeenth floor. Then on the right at the top of the stairs.'

It was only a minute's walk up the staircase from the board-room to the penthouse flat, but Lord Cloyne had evidently tele-phoned to say that Antony was on his way. Jeremy Cornwall sat in an upright chair, his long legs folded. He wore a vivid shirt of red and blue alternating stripes under a dark blue blazer. He looked like the star of a musical of the 1920's except for the smooth sweep of black hair across his forehead. Antony, who constantly exploited his own good looks, was quick to spot others plying the same trade. Cornwall's physical appeal was cruder but better organized. But then he was not aiming at a girl but at thirty million electors.

Jeremy Cornwall leaped to his feet as if surprised.

'Antony Percival? How very good of you to come. Do you smoke? We've never met properly before. Have a seat. I've heard a lot about you.'

Antony sat and took a cigarette. He was only six years younger than Cornwall, but he felt like a child.

'Look, I want you to have a word with your father. I'm very worried about his position.'

'So I noticed from what you said yesterday.'

'Oh that, I hope he won't take any notice of that. The truth is I got carried away last night. You can't imagine what it was like at Blenheim – thousands of people cheering their heads off, the biggest audience I've ever had. Quite frankly, I was over-excited. When I have as much experience as your father I shan't drop bricks. Tell him that, will you, just as I've explained it to you now?'

He stood up and bent over to light Antony's cigarette Antony learned with distaste that they shared the same after-shave lotion. Cornwall was radiating charm as best he could but his appeal was a public not a private one, and his voice was too coarse for a small room.

'Is that why you wanted me to come?'

'Not entirely, not entirely.' Cornwall stood in front of the mock Adam mantelpiece above the grate with the mock logs

'I wanted to talk to you frankly about my own position. I tried to speak to your father at Chequers before the recess, but quite honestly I don't think I got the point across. Now I know you have a great deal of influence over him.'

'None whatever. Perhaps I am here under false pretences. I really take no interest in politics.' Antony still felt about seventeen.

'That's not what I hear. What about that evening in Rajnaya?'

'That wasn't politics, that was my father's health.'

'Well, then, let's talk about your father's health.' Cornwall settled his legs further astride, and began to use his hands. 'We were all delighted that the check-up the other day went well.'

He paused for Antony to comment, but nothing came, and he went on.

'Quite frankly, your father is indispensable. I have a great personal regard for him, though we've never been close. I would like to see him carry on as Prime Minister with the least possible strain. I know the burden he carries. And after all he's not as young as he was.'

'Who is?' Antony knew this to be feeble as soon as he said it.

'Quite so. Now my difficulty is that I feel passionately about this Irish business. My whole life is swallowed up in this campaign. Nothing else, my family, my friends, my Party loyalties, my own career — I ask you to believe that these weigh as nothing in the balance against the cause of bringing our troops home.' He slammed his fist into the palm of his hand. 'Shall I tell you how far this conviction has carried me?'

'I expect so,' said Antony.

'It has carried me to the point of discussing it all with Wellcome and the rest of the Socialist leaders. Does that surprise you?'

'Not at all,' said Antony.

'That's because you have a lot to learn about politics. I tell you, it surprised me. No one is a stronger Tory than I am. It went right against the grain to look for allies among our political opponents. But I had to do it. I had to do it.'

'Do you want me to tell my father that?'

'May I call you Antony?' Cornwall switched back to his

133

more intimate tone. 'I leave it to your judgement. I know you're shrewd in anything to do with personal relations. The point is this. The Labour Party is on the move over this. Their motives aren't the same as mine. But Wellcome as good as said they would back my crusade. There's a motion down at their Party Conference next month. I believe Wellcome will answer the debate himself and come out for troop withdrawal. And that means of course there'll be no majority for Government policy when the House meets again.'

'And so?'

'Look, Antony, the point is this. That's not what I want to happen. I want *our* Party to change its mind. I want your father to get the credit. Our Conference is before theirs. Think of the cheers if that Saturday afternoon your father announced the troops would be home by Christmas. Think of the relief through the country. Your father could dissolve and sweep back with a huge majority if he wanted to . . .'

'And if he thought it was right.'

'Of course it's right, of course it's right.' There was a glare now in Cornwall's prominent black eyes. 'We've had four hundred years of Ireland now. We've done them wrong, they've done us wrong. We're quits. It's time to go home.'

'What would you do then?'

Jeremy Cornwall laughed.

'I could go back to being a simple back bencher with a few business interests. Time for my family, time to read books, time to take a holiday. Do you know I haven't had a day's holiday this year? . . . There's nothing I would like better than some proper rest. Then if your father wanted me for anything of course I'd be available.'

Antony found the strength he had been looking for.

'Do you know, I don't believe a word of that. I think you want to destroy my father. I can bloody well see the knife in your hand. You want his place.'

Jeremy Cornwall stared, and then laughed.

'That's theatrical. But in that case why have I taken the trouble to come here today?'

'Because you're afraid of the charge of disloyalty. You know it sticks, particularly among Tories. You wanted to be able to say you'd made my father a fair offer.'

Jeremy Cornwall was not put out.

'And haven't I? I'm offering him a way out. I want him to have the facts before he decides. He's an old man, as I said last night. He's entitled to know how things really are.'

Antony got up.

'I think I'd better go.'

'I think you had. Will you tell him what I said?' For a moment Cornwall talked to Antony as to a message boy.

'Yes, I've no choice.'

'Good.' They shook hands. 'I'll see you again, no doubt,' said Cornwall. 'I'll give you one bit of advice meanwhile. You've shown your own hand. There was no need to. It was a mistake. Goodbye, then.' He sat down and picked up the phone as if Antony was no longer there.

Antony went down the stairs, not knowing if he had done badly or well. But he knew now about Jeremy Cornwall. Lord Cloyne was waiting anxiously in the board-room.

'All right?'

'Fine.'

'That's excellent. I always think it's better to have these things out. Nothing's worse in politics or business than misunderstanding.' He paused.

'There's just one other thing.'

'What's that?'

'Don't let anyone tell my wife that Cornwall's been here. She's taken against him for some reason. They had a bit of a dust-up the other day at Chequers. As much her fault as his, I thought, but there it is. You know what women are.'

'I'll keep your name out of it.'

'That's it.' Lord Cloyne, buoyed up by the apparent success of his mediation, expanded. 'You know, I keep pretty quiet when my wife's around. Doesn't do to argue in public. Would you like a cigar? I daresay a lot of people think I go along with all her opinions. But I don't, you know, I don't, I'm glad to say. You've seen that today. I've got a mind of my own.'

Returning to his office, cigar in hand, Antony thought that on the whole this was a pity.

# CHAPTER TWENTY-SEVEN

It was teatime, and at No. 10 the calm September sun slanted through the windows of John's office. The leaves on the plane trees were beginning to crinkle and turn yellow at the edges. Sunshine was always important to John, and autumn sun was the best.

Usually he liked teatime too. He could either take a cup and a gossip with the Private Secretaries in the bigger of their two rooms, or he could ask for a pot for himself, and it would come to his office on a tray, white and gold, with its cup and plate of ginger biscuits. He and the messengers preferred Indian, whereas after a good deal of minuting and a referendum the Private Secretaries had plumped for China. It was a pleasant relaxed time, a short pause from hubbub.

But not today. Today was a hurricane such as blew only once or twice a year. John had realized long ago that difficulties, small and great, hunted in packs. If you couldn't get through with your first telephone call of the morning, the rest of the day was at risk. If the first file you asked for was temporarily missing, batten down the hatches for trouble till evening.

When the tea came, the storm was still blowing. John was talking to the Duty Clerks.

'You still don't know when the PM's coming back to No. 10? Surely Lady Percival must have given some indication when you talked to her . . . the point is, if he's not coming back tonight after all, I shall have to go down to Chequers myself. There's a hell of a lot going on that can't wait. I'm sure others are in the same position, we really must know . . . hold on.'

The buzzer from the Political Office upstairs had sounded. He picked up the grey phone, and put the black one down on his blotter.

'Yes, yes . . . OK, get him transferred, will you? I'll free the line.'

Then to the Duty Clerk.

'Please, please ring Lady Percival again and try and get a decision.'

Then the grey phone. It was the Yorkshire Area Agent from Leeds. The northern branch of Jeremy Cornwall's crusade was marching through Leeds on its way to London. Jeremy Cornwall had personally telephoned the chairman of each of the four Leeds Conservative Associations asking them to send a contingent to join him. Two of them had rung the Area Agent for advice.

'No, I am sure the answer is no . . . No, I haven't been able to talk to the Prime Minister, he's at Chequers – Yes, I'll mention it to him as soon as I can . . . I hope he'll be back tonight. But meanwhile I'm sure . . . Yes, I know the pressures are strong . . . Ring the Chairman of the Party direct if you want to, I think he'll give the same advice . . . Yes, I saw the poll, but it really doesn't make any difference . . .' then suddenly and uncharacteristically, John lost his temper. 'Either your bloody Associations want to support the Government or they don't. Jeremy Cornwall is out to destroy us. It's as simple as that.' Then, as quickly as possible, he recovered it. 'I'm sure you'll do your best. You're the best judge of how to handle them. I think it really is important, you know.' He saw the Duty Clerk hovering in the doorway. 'Thank you very much for ringing. Let me know how you get on.'

The Duty Clerk had ginger hair and a large Adam's apple. Today it was bobbing fast.

'I can't get hold of Lady Percival, she's gone out for a walk.'

'She never goes out for a walk. She hates walking. When they say that it means she's asleep, or deliberately dodging the phone.'

The Duty Clerk grimaced. 'I can hardly tell them that, can I? Well, anyway, that's not why I came. William Pershore wondered if you can spare him a few minutes. He's in the Cabinet Room. Rather urgent, I think.'

'OK. I'll go in.'

The black telephone rang again.

'Is that John Cruickshank? It's the Secretary of State's office, Northern Ireland Office, here. The Secretary of State would like a word with you . . . I'll just put him on.' A messenger appeared.

'Finished your tea?'

'Yes, yes, take it away.'

'John Cruickshank?' Paul Bernays's voice always sounded fruity on the telephone. 'Look, could you slip across and have a word? It's rather important.'

'I'll come right away.' He waited till Bernays had cleared the line. 'Push all calls up to the Political Office, will you, for the time being? I've got to go across to the Irish Office.'

For a moment there was silence. The sun was lower now, and filled the room with that special intense warmth which comes at the end of summer. John glanced at the letter propped up against the glass inkwell. He had read it once. He had wanted to read it again peacefully in the afternoon. He would have to reply quickly. But he couldn't reply until he had spoken to the PM. He snatched up the letter and read it again as he walked quickly across to the Private Office.

Swindon East Conservative
Association,
5 Station Road, Swindon.

12 September.

Dear Mr Cruickshank,

I am writing to inform you that following your interview here last week the Selection Committe has forwarded your name, together with two others, for consideration by the full Executive Committee of the Association. The three candidates for selection will be interviewed by the Executive Committee in alphabetical order at a meeting to be held at 7.30 p.m. on Thursday, September 22 in the Swindon Conservative Club. Each candidate will be invited to address the meeting for approximately 15 minutes on 'What our country needs today' after which they will be asked to answer questions. I should be grateful if you would confirm acceptance by return of post.

Yours sincerely,
David Mabane,
Chairman, Swindon East Conservative Association.

There was a sentence typed in just before the signature

and then crossed out in ink. It was not difficult for John to decipher : 'The Executive Committee hope to have an opportunity to meet Mrs Cruickshank on this occasion.' Someone had done some homework just in time.

Clarissa and Ian Hanning were fiddling with the news tapes, and Hanning's broad bottom blocked John's path.

'Nothing here, at any rate,' he heard Hanning say.

'Not yet,' said Clarissa.

They saw John.

'Ian's being asked about a report that a fresh battalion is being flown to Ulster tonight to deal with an IRA attack on Newry.'

'Have they attacked Newry?'

'Of course not. The report says we had an intelligence warning that it's due at the weekend.'

'Anything in it?'

'Well, I'm not sure.' Clarissa was usually very sure about such things, as befits a woman in a man's world.

'Not sure?'

She hesitated. 'The NIO are playing it very close. They simply say they understand their Secretary of State plans to raise the matter orally at Cabinet tomorrow.'

'I'm on my way to see Bernays now. Important, he says.'

'He'd better talk to the PM.'

'Easier said than done.'

'How the hell am I to hold the Press?' asked Hanning.

'Put them on to the NIO.'

'They put them on to me.'

'It is not usual practice to disclose details of troop movements to Northern Ireland.'

'But it is.'

'Oh, for God's sake, Ian, stop it. You've smothered many better stories in your time.'

'With no bloody help from you lot.' Hanning shambled back to his office. They all knew he would deal with the Press adequately. Once a day he needed to blow off steam.

'I'd better go.' John would have liked to stay. Mrs Cruickshank would have been just right for the Swindon East Executive Committee if Mrs Cruickshank had been Clarissa.

'William's after you, you know.'

'I know. What's it about?'

'God knows. But it's pursed lips and a furrowed brow.'

'I must have left my safe open again when I went to the loo. Tell him I'll come up as soon as I've seen Bernays.'

'OK.'

John walked fast down the corridor, out into an empty Downing Street, and left up Whitehall. Damn Swindon East. For the last twenty-four hours he had been hoping they would turn him down. Now he would have to tell the Prime Minister. If he were selected it would mean that at the next Election he would not be able to help the old man. Of course the old man would almost certainly have retired by then. But John could hardly tell him that. He should have asked permission before putting his name in. He would have asked permission but for the old man being away, and his own passionate uncharacteristic hurry in reaction to Cornwall at Blenheim. Damn, damn. It looked disloyal, it was disloyal. But John knew that he wasn't disloyal.

Bernays launched straight in. He was standing in front of his mantelpiece.

'I can't get hold of the PM.'

'None of us can. He's well protected.'

'Either he's ill, in which case someone else should take over. Or he's not ill, in which case he shouldn't let his wife stop his colleagues from talking to him.'

John waited.

'We're in a mess over troop movements. The Army want to send 600 more men straight away. Half from Germany, half from Catterick. They're pressing me hard. But it's all nonsense.'

'I'm told there's an intelligence report about an attack on Newry.'

Bernays stared at him.

'Can you name one day in the last six weeks when there hasn't been an intelligence report about an attack on Newry? Or the Maze Prison. Or Harland and Wolff. Or the Bogside. Too many intelligence reports, and too little intelligence, that's been our Irish problem for years now.'

'I hear you're going to raise the question of troop movements in Cabinet tomorrow.'

'Will the PM be there?'

'So far as we know. I can't find out exactly when he . . .'

140

Bernays lost his temper. The veins in his pink neck struggled against the stiff white collar.

'It's your business to know. So far as I can see No. 10 has gone completely to the dogs. No system, no certainty, nothing. The place leaks like a sieve, and has the morals of a bawdy-house.'

John could make little of this. But he did not see why he should be shouted at, even by a Secretary of State.

'If you have any particular message you want me to pass on . . .' he said stiffly.

'The message is that the whole Irish policy is wrong, and that I won't stand it any longer. And I'll deliver the message myself.' He crossed to his desk, moving fast for so plump a man, and pressed the buzzer. 'Tell Pat to bring the car round at once. I'm going to Chequers.'

'Would you like me to ring through to warn them?' asked John.

'What the hell's the use of that? I'll simply be told that the PM is not to be disturbed and Lady Percival has gone for a walk.' Bernays recovered his temper, and swallowed hard. 'I apologize for what I said just now. I know you are doing your best. There's a big strain on all of us at present. Thank you for coming round.' He began to fiddle with an evening paper to show that the interview was over.

On his way back John found a street barrier placed across the entrance to Downing Street. He was asked for his pass by a police sergeant.

'What's up?'

'Cornwall's crusade. Due here in an hour or two.'

'I thought they were still in Leeds.'

'That's the northern lot, they'll be here tomorrow. It's the London and Wessex contingents today. Got some sympathy for them myself. Hope they don't overdo it, though.'

John hated it when Downing Street was closed. It was somehow important that people should be able to walk and chatter and hang around outside the Prime Minister's house. At the far end of the street the gate at the top of the steps down to the park past the Foreign Office had been shut and pad-locked.

Upstairs in the Prime Minister's study Pershore was putting down the telephone when John came in.

'The PM's just left Chequers. He'll be here by seven.'

'Bernays has just left *for* Chequers.' John explained what had happened.

'We ought to get a message to Bernays.'

'There's no radio in his car,' said Pershore.

'The police could intercept him and turn him round.'

'I wonder if that would be justified. They dislike that sort of thing very much.' Pershore took off his glasses and polished them while he wondered. He looked thirty instead of forty-five. John was not sure if this was because he was without glasses or because he enjoyed days like this.

'If what you say is right, then three hours in a car might be just what the Secretary of State needs to calm down.'

'Or it might make him madder still.'

'But at least he can't spend the time ringing round his colleagues in advance of tomorrow's Cabinet. I think on the whole we'll let matters take their own course.'

The glasses were back on Pershore's handsome classical nose. He frowned to indicate the weight of his worries. John noticed that he was wearing a new suit, cut tight round the thighs. He was much the smartest dresser in No. 10.

'There's one question I must discuss with you before the PM arrives. I've tried to get hold of Antony Percival too, but the Bank don't seem to know where he is. I'm afraid it's rather a delicate matter, or rather the old matter all over again.' He cleared his throat, but did not persuade John that he was really embarrassed.

'You remember that we set in hand a security investigation after it appeared that the IRA had received advance information about Operation Roughneck in Belfast?'

'Of course.'

'Well this naturally involved a check on the security clearances of all those who knew of the operation. Including eight members of the staff at No. 10.'

'So I understand. One of my referees told me he had been contacted.'

'Well, I should make it clear at this stage that there is no direct evidence connecting anyone here with the leakage. But one awkward fact has come to light. It appears that at Oxford ten years ago Clarissa Strong formed a liaison with a young man called Barry Barran, which lasted over a year. She did not mention this when she was originally vetted. Nor did her referees.'

Pershore paused, but John said nothing.

'Did you know anything of this?'

'Not from Clarissa. Her father mentioned to me that there had been something of the kind.'

'He mentioned Barran by name?'

'I believe he did.'

'You didn't pay particular attention?'

'It seemed a long time ago.'

John felt no inclination to explain that there had been too little sex in his own relationship with Clarissa to give him any rights over her past. He remembered what Bernays had just said about No. 10 having the morals of a bawdy-house.

'You see how difficult it is,' said Pershore.

'Not really.'

'Barran is now a Professor of Poetry at Cork University. He is not an active member of Sinn Fein, but the authorities in the Republic have no doubt that he is in close touch with them. And through them with the IRA in the North.'

'Have you any evidence that Barran and Clarissa are still in touch?'

'None. I have not yet spoken to Clarissa. I thought it right first of all . . .'

Antony came into the room fast, and went straight up to Pershore's desk.

'I had a message that you wanted me. What's happened?' He wore a pale blue pullover and slacks. His dark hair was untidy.

'It's rather a delicate matter . . .' Pershore wound himself to start the story over again.

'You've got some news about my father?'

'Only that he's on his way back from Chequers. He'll be here in an hour.'

'On his way back?' Antony had obviously expected something else, and was relieved.

Pershore noticed. 'What did you think, if I may ask?'

'Nothing. What does it matter what I think? I'm only his son.'

Pershore did not know how to take this. He paused and then began again.

143

'I'm afraid this is rather a delicate matter. I hesitate to intrude on your private affairs. I only do so because . . .' And so on.

Antony listened in silence, then grinned.

'OK, we're busy men, no time to waste. I'll tell you what you want to know. Clarissa was not a virgin when I took her that last night in Rajnaya.'

'That wasn't in the least what I wanted to . . .'

'And she didn't tell me where, when or who. And I didn't ask her. I'm a burglar, you see. When I see a door open I walk in. I don't worry about who rang the bell first.'

'That is really quite unnecessary . . .' Pershore was for a moment shaken out of his natural self-assurance.

'And now if you don't mind I'll go and cook Clarissa's supper. Fish in the bag. Delicious. Have either of you tried it?' He turned at the door. 'Can I ask you just one question in return? Would it have occurred to either of you to let me know that my father was coming back? No, of course it wouldn't. You'd have left it to Clarissa – if she knew. Or I could have read it in the papers. As I said, I'm only his son.' The door banged behind him.

'I think we deserve a glass of sherry,' said Pershore, opening a cabinet beside the window seat. 'I'm not sure where that young man got his strong streak of vulgarity.' He spoke as if he were sixty.

'I don't think you know him well,' said John. 'He's genuinely concerned about his father. No sherry for me, thank you.'

'I noticed that,' said Pershore. 'I noticed that with interest.' He switched quickly to the immediate future. 'If Whitehall is going to be full of the crusaders, the PM will have to be dropped on the Horse Guards and let in through the Garden Room door. We can't risk a mix-up. I'll ask the Duty Clerk to radio a message to the Inspector in the PM's car . . .'

'What are you going to do about Clarissa? You can hardly sack her on that evidence.'

'Sack her?' The idea of dismissing an established Civil Servant obviously startled Pershore. 'Good heavens, no. Though I suspect there will have to be action of a less drastic kind. Perhaps I was too lenient over the last matter. The next step must obviously be to interview Clarissa herself. If time allows I shall do that before the PM returns. Even if that involves some delay for the – what was it? – for the fish in the bag.' He lifted his telephone. 'Duty Clerk, please.'

Back in his own room John poured himself an inch of whisky. It was past six. Ordinary mortals were travelling home, grumbling about politicians as they read the evening papers on their way to peace and comfort. For the politicians and their staffs this was the worst time of the day. Peace and comfort were a long way off. Their natural supply of energy was running out. They had to draw fresh reserves from somewhere to get through the evening.

John looked at his in-tray, stacked with letters, minutes and messages. He would have to stay until the PM got back, but he did not feel in the least like tackling the paperwork. His mind was at a dead stop. He took out the letter from Swindon and read it again. The first gulp of whisky did its job. He pulled a sheet of No. 10 notepaper from his top drawer. He would not have a chance to talk to the PM alone that night, but with luck the old man would flip through the papers in his political box before Cabinet.

'PM.

I attach a self-explanatory letter from the Swindon East Conservative Association. I apologize for not consulting you about this at an earlier stage. Subject to your views, I would like to go for interview. If I happen to be selected as candidate I could of course continue working here up to the edge of a General Election. I would have to find a replacement to help you during the campaign itself, but there will be time to work out a proposal on this for your approval. May I proceed?'                    JC. 21.9.

It was bald, of course. Nothing about Cornwall and the Blenheim rally. Nothing about why he was fed up with Pershore and the sherry and Clarissa and the news tape machine and the whole business of living behind a green baize door. Nothing about the conflict between all this and his loyalty to the old man.

It was bald, but it would have to do. Even if he had been able to talk to the PM he would not have found the right words. He pinned the minute to the Swindon letter and dropped them into the open black box on the chair by his side.

The oldest messenger appeared in a frock coat through the half-open door. Like Pershore, he was in a state of pleasurable excitement.

'Head Housekeeper's compliments, sir, and he'd be grateful if you'd shut all windows and draw your curtains.' He hobbled across the room and began to tug at the curtain-rope. John got up to help him.

'What's up, then?'

'It's the crusaders, sir, can't you hear them?'

Though the crowd was on the other side of the building in Whitehall, John could just catch the noise, sharper and less regular than the usual murmur of traffic.

'Quiet they are so far, I'll say that for 'em. Waiting for Jeremy Cornwall, they say. Thousands and thousands of 'em, all the way up to Trafalgar Square. Down the Strand too, the wireless said. And these are just the ones from London and those parts. Wait till they come from the north tomorrow. Rough lot, the Geordies. I know, I served in Newcastle during the war.'

'Why the fuss about the windows?'

'Security, sir, security. They're likely to find their way round this side before long. Never know what they might be carrying. Stones, grenades, anything. Mr Pershore's given strict instructions – Look over there, sir, there they come.'

The last glimmer of day had faded behind the park. But by the street lights they could see the flow of dark figures coming towards the garden wall of No. 10. They must have been allowed by the police to stream through the Horse Guards gateway when Whitehall became dangerously full. They stopped at the wall, and began to form ranks along its whole length, two deep, then five, then ten. Some carried banners, a hand carrying a flaming torch, the emblem of the crusade. They were very quiet. Although John was separated from them only by the width of the garden, he heard only the shuffle of their feet.

'Spooky, isn't it, sir? Not like that Vietnam lot when I first started here.'

Clarissa appeared in the doorway.

'Thank you very much, Mr Hawkins, that's fine. I feel much safer now.'

'Better safe than sorry, sir. If they saw you through the window here with that whisky they might come and have a go. Thirsty work, all that marching. Good evening, Miss Strong, didn't see you there. Quite a do, isn't it?'

The old man shuffled out, chuckling so hard that he did not notice the tears pouring down Clarissa's face. She flopped into John's arms. He did not know what to do. He stood awkwardly, holding her tight enough to stop her falling, pressing his cheek against her hair. When she pulled her face away his coat was streaked with wet powder at the left shoulder. He felt no emotion stronger than embarrassment.

She took the handkerchief from his breast pocket and began to dab.

'Sorry. I've had a bit of a shock.'

'Pershore?'

'You know, then. I thought he might talk to you. Bloody little man. To think I once liked him. Consulting people about my private life. I'm not, I'm really not an inter-departmental committee.'

'That's better. Sit down, have a drink, tell me all about it.'

'There's nothing to tell.' A brief, final sob, ending in a sip of whisky. 'I went to bed with Barry Barran at Oxford in my last year. Twice, three times. He was very good looking. He wrote poems. He had never watched television in his life. His body was even better than his face.'

This was the first physical remark he had ever heard from Clarissa. Perhaps she was not an inter-departmental committee after all. John thought for a moment about Antony and the bedroom in Rajnaya.

'Then he left me. I didn't chase him. It had all worn off quite quickly. He didn't take many baths. I had my Finals to think of.'

'And that was it?'

'Of course that was it.' She took a cigarette from a cheap enamel box which a Chinese millionaire had given John during the PM's visit to Hong Kong. 'I didn't tell the security people this when they vetted me. Why should I? It had nothing to do with my job.'

'They asked you about . . . that sort of thing?'

'I can't remember. I suppose so.'

'Was he very Irish then? Politically, I mean.'

'Yes. It went with the rest of the scenery. A strange and terrible beauty, that sort of thing. It meant nothing to me.'

'I could never stand Yeats.'

'I've never read him since.' She stood up, puffing fiercely at the cigarette. 'Tell me one thing. Am I going to lose my job because of this?' Her voice quavered despite herself.

'What does Antony say?' He could not resist it. She had a lover. He was just a rejected suitor. There was no reason why he should be wheeled into action as a sort of ombudsman.

'Don't be unkind.' The quaver was there again. His mood changed back to the friendly and matter-of-fact.

'No, I don't think you'll be thrown out of the Civil Service. But it'll be hard for you to stay on here at No. 10. First Antony, now this.'

Clarissa stood up, and stubbed out the hardly-smoked cigarette. She surprised him again with her sudden fierceness.

'I *must* stay on here. It's the only thing I care for. If I ask Antony, he'll simply laugh and say I'm lucky to be out of it. You understand, you're much the same yourself. You've got to help me.'

John thought of the Blenheim rally and the letter from Swindon East lying in the open box beside him. She did not really know him at all. Nor Antony, if it came to that. For the first time he felt superior to her.

'I'll try,' he said. 'I'll speak to William again, and to the PM, if necessary.'

Clarissa pulled herself together.

'Thank you, John. Thank you.' She came forward and kissed him on the forehead. I'd better go.' Now she, too, was matter-of-fact.

'Yes. Antony's cooking your dinner.'

'Not now. He's coming back to see his father. I suppose the PM will be here any minute.'

'Have you looked out of the window? He'll have trouble getting in.'

The police must have closed the Horse Guards archway, for demonstrators were no longer pouring across the gravel of the parade-ground towards the garden wall of No. 10. But the old-fashioned street lights were strong enough to show John and Clarissa the crowd which had formed. They seemed to be mostly women, standing silent in regular ranks seven or eight deep. The odd thing was that they had their backs to No. 10 and were facing the road which runs between the parade ground and the park.

'Waiting for Cornwall,' said Clarissa.

They heard the sound of engines, quickly drowned by the burst of cheering. Twelve motorcyclists rode in formation, white helmets and white jackets blazoned with the crusader's torch. Then Cornwall standing beside the driver in an old-fashioned open car, wearing a white suit as at Blenheim. There were small searchlights fixed on the bonnet pointing upwards and backwards, and two others on the back of the car facing forwards. In the back of the car stood two women with black veils and long black dresses, holding between them a huge white scroll of paper. The whole impression was that of an illuminated float at the funeral pageant of some defunct emperor. Cornwall stood rigid in the glare of light, not acknowledging in any way the cheers of his supporters. Another group of motorcyclists followed him.

John shivered.

'Vulgar beyond belief,' said Clarissa.

'Particularly the widows,' said John. 'But frightening.'

'Illegal too. I'm sure those searchlights are contrary to the Road Traffic Acts. And the escort, Public Order Act 1936, wearing of uniforms.'

The car moved slowly up to the junction with the Mall, then turned right towards Admiralty Arch and Trafalgar Square.

'I suppose he'll come down Whitehall, and hand in that petition. He's driven all the way from Plymouth, I gather.'

'Standing like that all the time?'

'Of course not. Only through the towns.'

'May I come in?' Pershore knocked on the open door. He was always punctilious in small matters.

'The police have just radioed that the PM is coming down Constitution Hill. He'll be here in two minutes.'

'Lucky you're bringing him in by the garden gate.'

'I knew Cornwall was expected about now. The police at the entrance to Downing Street have instructions to let him

149

through on foot to present his petition, with not more than two companions.'

'Who'll receive the petition?' asked Clarissa.

'The Duty Clerk, as usual,' said Pershore.

'He won't like that. Shouldn't a Private Secretary do it?'

'Don't be silly,' said John. 'Cornwall hasn't the faintest notion of the difference between a Duty Clerk and a Private Secretary.'

'However that may be,' said Pershore, 'I see no reason to depart from established practice. Now I suggest that we go downstairs and wait for the PM.'

And so the Prime Minister was smuggled back into his own house by the back door while Cornwall's cohorts besieged the entrance to the street. The operation went smoothly, for the crowd on the Horse Guards had flowed back into Whitehall once they had seen Cornwall's cortège pass, and the two black government cars cruised quietly over empty gravel. Seeing the PM silhouetted in the garden doorway John could not help feeling disappointed. Still old, still bent, still slow-moving. The weeks of rest had worked no miracle, and a miracle might be needed. But Sir James was brisk and matter-of-fact: He brushed aside Helena who tried to steer him at once to the upstairs flat.

'No, no, there's work to be done first. We'll go to the Cabinet Room, and sort out the agenda for tomorrow morning.'

'Shall I ask the Secretary of the Cabinet to join us?' Pershore was always punctilious in matters of consultation. After all, he had his future to consider. Nothing wrecked a Private Secretary more surely than a reputation for cavalier behaviour towards other Civil Servants.

'No, no, just family. Hello, there's Antony. What a surprise.' The old man was pleased.

'More surprises outside,' said Antony. His black eyebrows were drawn together as happened when he was angry.

'What do you mean?'

'Cornwall and ten thousand Englishmen, and a petition nearly a mile long. Plus a score of howling widows.'

'I briefed you, Prime Minister,' said Pershore. 'The Police Commissioner did not feel they could ban it. There's another tomorrow from the North.'

150

Sir James did not seem to hear any of this. He was on his way to the front door.

'Prime Minister, you said you wanted . . .'

'Yes, quite right, the Cabinet Room can wait just a moment . . .' The Inspector, concern written large across his face, overtook the Prime Minister on his way down the corridor. At that moment the policeman outside knocked on the front door, the doorkeeper opened the door, and Cornwall stepped over the threshold.

'Shut the door,' said the PM sharply to the doorkeeper. John, following fast, could see the cluster of television cameras outside, and admired the old man's quick responses. The last thing they wanted was a shot of the two men together, decrepit age and ardent youth.

'Well, Jeremy,' said the PM, smiling.

Cornwall was too surprised to react. He carried under one arm the petition, now folded into a tight scroll.

'I thought you were still . . .'

'No, I came back. This evening, in fact. I'm so much better, you see. We were just going to have a little talk in the Cabinet Room. Review the situation, as they say. Would you care to join us? There's malt whisky, I believe.'

Cornwall looked round him. He saw grey able men whom he did not know, watching him from a world he did not understand. Through the closed door down the street came the sound of the other world which he had conjured up and made his own – shouts, cheers, songs.

'I must go back to my own people,' he said, raising his voice. 'The time has gone for compromises – Here is their petition. They ask for the total and unconditional withdrawal of all the troops by Christmas. Take it or leave it.'

He thrust the petition towards the PM, who did not move. Cornwall was trapped in a theatrical gesture which after a few seconds even he felt was ridiculous. He turned on his heel, threw the scroll on to the chair by the door and flung open the door. The cameras whirred, and he was gone.

'He's going mad,' said the PM. His step back to the Cabinet Room was slow and dragging. 'He's going mad. Poor Jeremy.'

'You didn't ever like that poisonous creep?' said Antony.

'Like, like, what is like? I admired him. When he first

came into the House I tried to be nice to him. He could have led the Party one day.'

'He thinks he's leading something bigger than the Party,' said Clarissa.

'Ah, but he's wrong,' said the Prime Minister. 'No one can lead the British people. Not any longer. A mob or two here and there, yes, but not the whole people. It's annoying of course, for a Prime Minister, who thinks he could do it right. But it's very reassuring to know it can't be done by Cornwall.'

'And you're sure of that?' asked John, thinking of Blenheim.

The PM stopped and looked at him. They had reached the ante-room.

'Quite sure,' he said. 'Quite sure.'

At that moment John heard the telephone pealing in his office. He left the group as they entered the Cabinet Room and grabbed the receiver in time.

'Is that John Cruickshank? It's Paul Bernays here.' John had forgotten all about him. How awful. He felt guilty. Not because he liked Bernays but because he believed in an orderly world. In an orderly world Secretaries of State were not left to career about the countryside.

'Where are you?'

'At Chequers, of course. Mrs Jennings is about to give me a good dinner.'

Bernays sounded remarkably relaxed. John could not understand why.

'I'm so sorry about that misunderstanding. As soon as I got back here I heard the PM had left. There didn't seem any way . . .'

'Not to worry, not to worry. It may all have turned out for the best.' Bernays became more formal. 'I should be grateful if you would give the Prime Minister two messages. The first is the more urgent. Is Mrs Jennings entitled to open one of the '57 clarets on my behalf?'

'I'm sure . . .'

'Tell him he has five minutes to object before the cork is drawn. The second message is that I shall not be able to attend Cabinet tomorrow. I have already arranged with the Cabinet Office for Jock Sinclair as my senior Minister of State to take my place.'

John was astounded.

'But you know they're likely to discuss . . .'

'Precisely, John, precisely.' Bernays had never called him by his Christian name before.

'I think the PM will be very surprised. After all . . .'

He could not think how to end the sentence. If the world was orderly then the place for Bernays tomorrow morning was in the Cabinet Room. Why didn't the man see it?

He realized from the silence at the other end of the line that he had overstepped some mark. Eventually Bernays said:

'I should be grateful if you would simply pass on those messages.'

When he did so, having found a chair beside Pershore in the Cabinet Room, there was a pause. John felt bound to add: 'The Secretary of State sounded rather strange. Not at all like himself.'

'You mean he was tight?' asked Antony. John saw Pershore frown. It was a sign of the times, of an increasingly disorderly scene, that Antony was in the Cabinet Room at all, for all the world as if he were a genuine member of the No. 10 staff.

'No, not drunk,' said the Prime Minister. 'It's something else. The Secretary of State has a hard head.'

'He's decided to go to bed with Mrs Jennings,' said Antony.

'He's been under considerable strain,' said Pershore.

'He's a conscientious man. Intelligent, a bit slow, dependent on advisers,' said the Prime Minister slowly. 'For such men in politics there's one experience which doesn't come often.'

'What's that?'

'I think that the Secretary of State for Northern Ireland has just experienced the supreme pleasure of making up his own mind.'

# CHAPTER TWENTY-EIGHT

11.30 p.m. Prime Minister.

I understand you are already aware that the Secretary of State for Northern Ireland is unable to be present at tomorrow's Cabinet, and that Mr Sinclair will take his place. As you know, the Secretary of State had agreed to raise orally the question of the despatch of further troops to Northern Ireland. The Secretary of State for Defence spoke urgently to me about this tonight. He regards it as essential that the Cabinet should discuss and decide this matter tomorrow if anticipated moves by the IRA are to be forestalled. I have not been able to consult you at this late hour and have therefore exercised my discretion and inserted this as the first item for discussion. A revised agenda is attached. The Secretary of State for Defence offered to circulate a paper, but in all the circumstances I thought you might prefer to lead the discussion yourself.

> Basil Proudfoot,
> Secretary to the Cabinet.
> September 16, 19—

9 a.m.

Quite right. Next time come up to the bedroom and knock hard.                                                        J.P. 17/9

11.15 a.m. PM

Many thanks. That was superb. I never know if one is allowed to pass notes in Cabinet. The troops can be flown from Brize Norton tonight. But what's happened to P.B.? Is it true you've locked him in the dungeons at Chequers?

> Joe Mercer 17/9

11.22 a.m. S/State Defence.

Nowadays even dungeons have notepaper. The attached

was handed to me just before we started. There may be worse to come. There'll be a long argument on the Concorde item. We won't get through it before 1. Are you free for lunch?

J.P. 17/9

Midnight. September 16, 19—                                  Chequers
Dear Prime Minister,

I am writing to inform you that after long reflection I have decided to offer my resignation as Secretary of State for Northern Ireland.

I have come to this decision with great reluctance. You have my full confidence as Prime Minister, and with one exception I am in enthusiastic agreement with the policies which your Government has been pursuing. But as you know I have come over recent weeks to the conclusion that our response to the increased tension in Northern Ireland is fundamentally misconceived. You and the majority of our colleagues believe that we should maintain and indeed increase the presence of the Army in the province as a back-up to the fresh political initiative on which with your approval I had been working. I have come to believe on the other hand that only by withdrawing the bulk of the Army from Northern Ireland can we create the conditions in which a political initiative can succeed. I will not weary you with the reasoning behind this belief, for you are already familiar with it. Certainly withdrawals would be a gamble, but it would be preferable on all counts to a rapid return to the terrible conditions of violence and terrorism which characterized the period 1969-76.

This is a fundamental difference of opinion in the area of policy over which you gave me direct charge. It would clearly not be right for me to continue as Secretary of State for Northern Ireland or indeed as a member of a Cabinet following an Irish policy with which I deeply disagree.

I am most grateful for the friendship which you have shown me over the years, and above all for the privilege of serving under you in what I am sure will prove to be a distinguished and successful administration.

Yours sincerely,
Paul Bernays.

11.25 a.m. W.P

Please ask J.C. to get the usual private room at the Carlton for lunch. The one with Lord North over the mantelpiece. Six people at 1.15. Mercer and some others. I'll ask them.

J.P. 17/9

11.27 a.m. PM

A bad letter. He owes you more than that. What a bore. Yes, to lunch. I've cancelled my other engagement. Why oh why do our colleagues rabbit on so long over unimportant matters?

J.M. 17/9

11.45 a.m. PM

John Cruickshank has secured the room for lunch at the Carlton Club as you asked. I am not quite clear who you wished to attend. Sir Basil Proudfoot can make himself free if you so wish; so of course can I.

William Pershore. 17 September.

P.S. I attach a letter from the Leader of the Opposition. He was told that you were in Cabinet, but asked that it be brought in to you. As it is marked 'Strictly Personal' it has not been opened.

W.P.

11.53 a.m. W.P.

No, lunch is political. Mercer, Bross, Newings, John. Antony too, if John can get hold of him. Ask John to make sure there's smoked salmon. I am not allowed it upstairs.

J.P. 17/9

From the Rt. Hon. J. Wellcome, OBE, MP. House of Commons, London SW1A 0AA.

September 16, 19—

Dear James,

We have kept in close touch about Northern Ireland and stayed in general agreement. I must let you know that this is not going to be possible any longer. You will have noticed the mounting pressure in the Parliamentary Labour Party in favour of withdrawal. It is now reflected in the Shadow

Cabinet and, more important, in the National Executive of the Labour Party. I myself believe that the time has come for a change of policy. Even if I continued to agree with you (which I do not) I could not hold the line at the Party Conference next month.

Yours ever,
James Wellcome.

P.S. Nevertheless I hope we can continue to keep in confidential touch.

P.P.S. Cornwall has a lot to answer for.

Extract from Cabinet meeting, September 17, 19—.

*The Prime Minister,* summing up, said there was a fairly even division of opinion between those who believed that the British Aircraft Corporation should be allowed to retain its profits from the sales of Concorde III in order to finance the development of Concorde V, and those who insisted that 75 per cent of these profits should be repaid to the Exchequer in accordance with the 1978 Agreement. The general view was that a compromise should be sought, providing for an immediate payment of a portion of the due profits to the Exchequer combined with the possibility of a waiver on further payments if after discussion with the French Government and further market research agreement could be reached on a work programme for Concorde V.

*The Cabinet*
    (a)   agreed with the Prime Minister's summing-up;
    (b)   instructed the Aerospace Committee to be guided accordingly.

The Cabinet adjourned at 12.50 p.m.

# CHAPTER TWENTY-NINE

'What's happened to Clarissa? She wasn't around this morning.'

John and Antony were sitting next to each other. Two

waiters were clearing away the smoked salmon plates and conversation was general.

'She's sick.'

'What d'you mean?' For a moment John thought she might be pregnant.

'On sick leave, anyway,' said Antony. He looked exhausted himself, and John noticed for the first time lines cutting upwards and inwards above the corners of his mouth. 'The Blessed William Pershore said this was best. It was all the Blessed William could think of. Thank God he's not bidden to this feast.'

'How did she take it?'

'She sat up all night telling me the answer to that. I can't remember what it was.'

'She's passionately attached to the job.'

'I don't understand why. It's not as if she's got any convictions.'

'She loves the work.'

'You've got it in one. Not surprising, you're the same. She doesn't want to achieve anything. But she'd be lost without the framework of it all. The wheels have to go round. It doesn't matter if they don't engage with anything. The people at the Bank are the same. That's why each year we do less business.'

'You'll stick with her?'

Antony shrugged his shoulders.

'Not if every night's like last night. No supper, no sex, and worst of all, no sleep.'

'You must.'

'Must?' Antony emptied in two gulps the glass of claret which had just been poured for him.

'We'd better talk,' said the Prime Minister at the far end of the table. 'There's not much time.'

The waiters had served the saddle of lamb, the roast potatoes, the brussels sprouts, the mint sauce, the redcurrant jelly, the claret, and were finally out of the room.

'You've all read both letters? Better give them to John for safe keeping. I must reply to Bernays before tonight. Well, then, David, what's the arithmetic?'

David Bross, the Chief Whip, understood at once what he

meant. He put on his spectacles and consulted a piece of paper in front of him. His voice was soft, and went well with the white fingers and the dark oval face. He knew his job and rarely spoke unless spoken to.

'We have an overall majority of 33 including the Ulster Unionists. If Labour turn against the Irish policy we obviously can't rely on the Liberals or the Scots or Welsh. Cornwall has ten certain supporters in the House, four occasionals. If all those voted against us and the rest stayed firm we'd still win by five votes.'

'But?' asked the Prime Minister. They all, even Antony, knew there was a but.

'But I estimate that Bernays would carry at least twenty votes on top of Cornwall's. Perhaps thirty.

'So you would say that with Bernays gone we have no chance of holding the Irish policy in the House of Commons?'

'As things stand, no.'

'Then we must get Bernays back,' said Mercer briskly. 'Offer him another job. He can have Defence for a bit, and I'll carry on as Chairman of the Party without a Cabinet post. Or you could give him the Exchequer.'

'He rules out that approach in his letter.'

'You could try.'

'I think he's made up his mind. Unless of course you change the Irish policy.'

'We can't do that,' Mercer snapped. They realized that Mercer would resign if the policy was abandoned. The Government without Bernays would be at risk in the Commons. The Government without Mercer would be at risk within the Conservative Party. The Party Conference was only five weeks away.

'Is it not possible to compromise?' David Bross was studying his fingernails. He had taken only a light helping of the main course, and had already finished. 'I gather the new political initiative is almost ready. Paul Bernays must want to present it himself. It's his brainchild. Could we not experiment with withdrawal, say a third of the troops out by Christmas? We could judge the result in the New Year before going any further. That might be enough to bring Paul back.'

'It would certainly be enough to clobber the Army,' said Mercer. 'You can't make political calculations over troop strengths. Either there are enough troops to do the job, or you don't do the job. Nothing in between makes sense.'

'But there are things you could do,' said John. In this small circle of men he knew well he talked much more freely than with other Ministers such as Bernays. 'You could publicly link the level of violence with the rate of withdrawal. The fewer incidents, the fewer troops. This might have a useful effect if it . . .'

'Too complicated,' said Newings.

The door opened and a fat man in a morning coat wandered in.

'Is this the Bellairs wedding lunch?' he said, the words fading as he saw that it wasn't.

'I'm afraid not,' said John. 'I'm sure one of the waiters could tell you . . .'

'Not a waiter in sight,' said the fat man, still focusing. 'Damn silly idea to have weddings in the morning, anyway.' Finally he realized what he had stumbled upon.

'Sorry to disturb,' he said, backing towards the door, Then, gathering courage as he retreated. 'While I'm here, I'd better give you a word of advice. A good Tory, I am, anyone in Sevenoaks will tell you. Paid up member for thirty years. Make it up with Jeremy Cornwall, that's my advice. The country's behind him, any fool can see that. Those Irish, never any good.'

'Thank you very much,' said the Prime Minister evenly. 'I hope you have a pleasant luncheon.' Then to John. 'Go and find someone to bring us some cheese, will you? Coffee at the same time. No one wants brandy or port? Good.'

Back in his seat John wondered whether to pursue Antony about Clarissa. He looked at the portraits round the room – Lord North pop-eyed and straining at his waistcoat, Neville Chamberlain stiff and platitudinous, Lord Eldon grey and tired. Not a very auspicious set of spectators. Only Disraeli had a gleam about him.

'Why am I here?' asked Antony. A waiter was in the room and conversation was general again.

'No idea,' said John.

Antony lit a Gauloise.

'What's stilboestrol?' he asked.

'Never heard of it.'

160

'I'll find out. My father's got some of it in his room. He spent twenty-five minutes in the lavatory this morning before Cabinet. And ten minutes again just now.'

'Nothing particularly sinister about that.'

'Perhaps not. Ellerman's coming this evening. He was at Chequers yesterday.'

John looked hard down the table. The Prime Minister looked better than he had before his holiday at Chequers. Old certainly, but stronger-voiced, more definite. He had walked up the stairs instead of taking the lift.

'You're imagining things.'

'Now I shall tell you what I think.' The Prime Minister broke through the hum of voices, and stopped it.

'The basic equation in Ireland is what it's been for twenty years now. No military solution is possible. No political solution can be imposed from here. Both Protestants and Catholics have the power to destroy any solution which they dislike. Therefore only a solution which they both agree can work. The new initiative is designed to help them agree among themselves. It picks up where Whitelaw and Rees left off. It may not work. It certainly won't work without the Army. Without the Army the two communities won't talk to each other, they'll kill each other. So the Army must stay.'

'Exactly,' said Mercer.

'If we can keep it there,' said Bross. 'It's a big if.'

'We can't get Paul Bernays back without a compromise which will give us the worst of both worlds.' The Prime Minister went on. 'But without him the arithmetic in the House is against us. So we must change the arithmetic.'

John saw what he meant. The others did not. There was a pause.

'I believe we should dissolve Parliament and hold an Election. Next month, cancelling the Party Conference.'

There was a long pause. Newings had been almost silent through the meal, concentrating on his food. He put down a sliver of cheese which he was carrying to his mouth. His thin lawyer's face registered amazement.

'You can't do it. Elections are always unpopular. It's only seven months since we got in.'

'Wilson managed it in '74. What d'you say, David?'

David Bross was polishing his spectacles.

'The opinion polls are reasonably favourable,' he said in a quiet analytical voice. 'So far as I know there are no bad surprises coming in the next few weeks. Prices, unemployment, not too good, but people remember that under Labour they were worse. We've kept the unions quiet without giving them anything new . . .' he paused, still wiping. 'But Ireland's the problem. The latest trouble is new, it doesn't show yet in our standing in the polls. But all the evidence is that Cornwall has judged it right. If the main Election issue was troop withdrawal, we would lose. Perhaps heavily.'

'Not if we put it across right.' Mercer was eager. 'Courage against cowardice, responsibility against betrayal, honour against shame. It could be a splendid campaign.' Mercer had never been at home with economics.

'Is that your considered view as Chairman of the Party?'

'No, I suppose not.' Mercer clenched his hands as he thought and the freckles stood out. 'The experts in Smith Square will be horrified by the risk. But it is my view as Joe Mercer.'

'And it is my view as Prime Minister. Indeed, that is the only basis on which I carry on. I shall put it to the colleagues tomorrow, and if they won't have it they must look for a new leader. Now then, will you two back me?' The old man leant forward in his chair. He meant Mercer and Bross. The rest were audience.

'Of course,' said Mercer.

David Bross looked at his clean plate. He had taken no cheese. He hesitated for a second.

'Yes, I will back you,' he said, so low that it was hard to catch.

'Right, then, there is a great deal of work to be done. Cabinet tomorrow, then the Queen, a broadcast, the 1922 Committee. John, I expect you have some contingency planning for my own campaign.'

'Yes.' John tried hard to remember what was in the bundle marked 'Election Arrangements' at the back of the filing cabinet.

'Of course you may not be here yourself. With luck, you'll be fighting in Swindon. Antony, will you do John's job for me if John is selected? He'll tell you what it's all about.'

John had never seen Antony blush before. But then he had never seen his father give Antony such pleasure before. He himself had forgotten all about Swindon. He felt affection for the cold old man at the end of the table. He had read John's Minute in the black box, he had understood the worry, he had taken the trouble to put him at ease.

The waiter came in with a note. 'Mr Cruickshank?'

'Here,' said John, stretching out a hand. Then 'It's Paul Bernays. He's here. He wants to see me.'

'We will wait,' said the Prime Minister quietly.

'You have no message for him?'

'I think not.'

Paul Bernays was standing by the window in the big drawing-room, also on the first floor, looking out over St James's Street. There was no one else in the room. His suit was beautifully pressed, his black shoes polished, his collar starched, but in spite of all this he seemed in disarray. He was clutching a copy of the *Evening Standard*.

'How did you know we were here?' asked John.

'I didn't. I came here for lunch. A fat man told me. I don't know his name. What the hell does it matter?' He pointed at the *Standard*.

Bernays and Jeremy in shock threat.

The TERRIBLE TWINS

Resignation blow to Tories.

'This is rubbish,' said Bernays. 'Absolute rubbish. There's no connection between me and Cornwall at all.'

'It's inevitable people should make one.'

'Why is it inevitable?' Bernays twisted the paper in his hand. 'Cornwall is a charlatan. He's saying exactly the opposite now of what he said six months ago. I've been Secretary of State, I know how desperately difficult it all is. It's an entirely different approach.'

John felt that this was a special day, on which ordinary rules of deference did not apply.

'But you would not take another place in the Cabinet? And you would not vote against the Irish policy? In the same lobby as Cornwall?'

Bernays glared at him. Then he climbed back where he felt safest, on to his high horse.

'Please tell the Prime Minister that I shall issue an immediate

163

statement denying that there is any connection or collusion between me and Jeremy Cornwall.'

'You'll get no coverage. The Press don't like grey areas.'

Bernays turned on his heel and left the room. Back in the little dining-room John told them what had happened. At first there was a gleam of hope in David Bross's eyes. It faded, but the Prime Minister had noticed it.

'What do you say, David?'

'He used to know what politics were about. It's sad. Since he became a Minister he's lost touch.'

'He was a good Minister.'

'That makes it even sadder. The two skills are not the same.'

'No, indeed. Antony, have you got all that down?' While John was away they had gone through what needed to be done and Antony had filled the back of the menu with notes.

'The Blessed William will throw a fit,' he said to John.

'We must go,' said the Prime Minister.

In the Carlton it had been warm and bright. After the first shock they had been buoyed up with the excitement of planning an Election.

Outside in the street they walked thirty yards to the waiting cars. The Inspector had joined them in the hall. A cold wind blew up the street, bringing scraps of paper and the sound of a newsvendor's voice. The sun had gone in.

To the west, across St James's Square and the Haymarket, they could just hear the first of the massed bands escorting Cornwall's crusaders from the North of England as they entered Trafalgar Square.

'Turned chilly, sir,' said the Inspector.

## CHAPTER THIRTY

The lunch at the Carlton Club was the last leisurely event for a month in the lives of those who ate it. The pace of their days quickened, their minds contracted. Horizons closed

They skipped the foreign news in the papers. They stopped thinking about their wives and children. They ate sandwiches without knowing what was in them. They did not notice if it was wet or fine. They went to bed late, slept badly, rose early. They met hundreds of people and were seen by millions. They cursed the day when they chose politics as a profession. Their suits turned shiny and their shoes wore out. They fought an Election campaign.

Downing Street was full of wires. At the end of every wire was a BBC technician. It took between twenty and thirty of them to set up the Prime Minister's ten-minute broadcast announcing the Election. They wandered round amiably supervising each other, and drove Pershore to despair. He took it out on John.

'You realize of course that we shall have to take back tonight the typewriters we lent the Political Office in the spring?'

'Yes, you told me.'

'And of course your girls won't be able to use No. 10 notepaper. Or crested envelopes. Or the photocopying machine. No official facilities of any kind for campaign purposes. We'll have to charge you for telephone calls.'

'You made all that quite clear. I told you, the Political Office will move over to Smith Square tomorrow. I'll keep this room here myself, but do all my dictating over in Smith Square.'

'If you're not selected tonight at Swindon.' Pershore began to relax.

'I won't be.' John tried to sound definite rather than bashful.

'Why not?'

'Too closely associated with the PM. They don't like that. They've got absolutely free choice, but they don't really believe it. So they'll prove it by choosing someone Central Office has never heard of.'

'Such as?' Like many Civil Servants, Pershore was fascinated by the minutiae of party politics.

'There's a dentist from Chipping Camden. In the last three, and highly fancied.'

'Well, good luck, anyway.'

There was a pause, and John realized that Pershore had nothing to do. Government business had almost dried up. Foreign governments had stopped communicating. Even in Ireland there was a check in the killings.

The telephone rang. John listened and answered in monosyllables. Then 'I'm sorry. I'll have to go up to the study.'

'The PM said he wasn't to be disturbed. He's still not happy about the text, I gather.'

'*I* said he was not to be disturbed.' John could not resist showing Pershore that the Civil Service were no longer sovereign of the PM's hours and minutes. 'But this is urgent. The BBC want to give Cornwall TV time.'

He sprinted up the stairs to the study, brushing aside eight wandering technicians and the messenger on duty outside the door. Inside the PM was at his desk, resting his head rather heavily on his hand. In the room was the Director of Publicity from Central Office, a brisk young man from the Research Department, and an even younger man with a wispy fair beard from an advertising agency. John could see at once what the argument had been about. Both young men were flushed in the face. Research Department liked long words and lots of statistics. The agency preferred monosyllables and not a figure in sight.

The PM used John's arrival to break it up. 'That's enough, I think. I'll do it as it stands now.'

'Can they put it on the autocue?' asked the Director of Publicity quickly. He had been silent for ten minutes, praying for a decision, any decision, so that they could get on.

'Yes.' They shuffled out, the two young men glaring at each other. 'John, I must go upstairs and have a bath and a drink. Otherwise I won't see the day out.'

The day, fine, but what about the month? The old man looked tired already.

'I know, I'm sorry,' said John. 'It was Joe Mercer on from Smith Square. He's just heard the BBC and ITA want to give Cornwall three party political broadcasts. On TV that is, and another three on radio. It's right against the rules of course, the crusade's not a recognized party, he hasn't even said he's going to put up candidates . . .'

'But he's asked for time?'

'Yes, and there's an emergency meeting of the Broadcasting Committee tonight to settle it. Mercer will represent us.'

'What do Labour think?'

'They're torn, Joe Mercer says. They don't want the rules bent, but they know Cornwall would do us harm and them good. Mercer thinks he can win them round.'

'Win them round?'

'To saying no. That should clinch it. The broadcasting authorities wouldn't proceed if both the big Parties objected.'

'But we mustn't say no. Of course people will want to hear Jeremy put his case. There'd be great resentment if he was refused.'

'But . . .'

'And tell Joe Mercer as well that what J. Cornwall is good at is oratory. He can capture thousands of people at a go, provided they're all in one place. But millions, scattered in millions of different little rooms – that's a different thing. Let him try, by all means let him try.'

'He did well last time.'

'This time is a different ball-park.'

The old man moved to the door. John would have argued if there had been time.

'When's your train?' asked the Prime Minister, turning as he went out.

'My train?' Once again John had forgotten Swindon.

'Or are you driving?'

'Yes, yes, I'm driving. I'll just have time to ring Mercer back before I have to leave. The M4 should be pretty clear by now.'

'How many in the final?'

'Just three.'

'Well, good luck.'

Outside on the landing John watched as the Prime Minister slowly climbed the steep flight of stairs to his own flat.

# CHAPTER THIRTY-ONE

There was a single-bar electric fire, but it had fused. There was a small outside window against which squalls of rain lashed. There had been weak white coffee in dark green mugs. There were five people in the room, and they had already been there for an hour. John guessed that this was normally the cloak-room where members of the Swindon Conservative Club left the coats before enjoying themselves at the bar, in front of the fruit machines, and on the dance floor. It was now the room in which the three finalists for selection as the candidate for Swindon East, two of them accompanied by wives, awaited the verdict.

The door was not quite closed. Through it they could occasionally hear a voice from the crowded room across the corridor, though not what it said. They had no idea whether any ballots had been held, or whether this was still preliminary discussion. Their own small talk had long since evaporated. The two women had kept on their coats.

John was in the least comfortable chair in the room. He was the youngest person present, except possibly for the wife of the dentist from Chipping Campden. He sat silently, wanting to be back at No. 10. He wanted to help run the Prime Minister's campaign. He did not want Antony to take over his job as he had taken over Clarissa. In short, he wanted to lose.

This had suddenly come to him as he parked his car outside after the two-hour run from London. But he had not acted on it, he hardly knew why. He had given them the speech he had worked out days ago on why he wanted to be their candidate. He had done his best and they had liked him. The questions had been easy, except for a brisk tough lady with a crusade badge. She had badgered him about Ireland and he had lashed out. What had they made of that?

The dentist was whispering to his wife. The other man,

grey and pink-faced, took no notice of his, but sat staring at the floor. A nasty clock on the wall gave a hiccup as it approached ten o'clock. This jerked the grey man, who stood up and walked to the door. As he did so he crooked a finger to John, who followed him for want of anything better to do.

From where they now stood in the corridor they could be certain that discussion in the main club room had stopped. The ninety-six members of the Executive Committee behind those closed doors were unnaturally silent, not a shuffle, not a cough. Presumably they were filling in the voting forms.

The grey man, whose name was Hooker, took out a small silver flask from his hip pocket and offered it to John.

'Not enough for the dentist as well,' he said. It was whisky, and welcome.

'You'll win,' said Hooker. 'Tonight, I mean. Of course we shan't beat Labour here, barring a landslide.'

'I don't think I'll get it,' said John. 'I'm too close to headquarters.'

'They won't take me,' said Hooker. 'A bit of a hack, fought too often too unsuccessfully. On the old side, too.'

'I hear they want a local chap.'

'My dear fellow, they always say that. Indeed that is what they do want for a week or two, until it comes down to actual names. They take one look at the list and forget it.'

'But the dentist is a sound man.'

'He may be fit to be Prime Minister for all I know,' said Hooker. 'But you can be sure there's someone in there had a tiff with his receptionist. Or granny's filling fell into the Christmas pudding fifteen years back. They'll all know about it by now.'

'I'm not married.'

'You're young enough for that not to matter. And thin as well. More than half of them are women. Feed him up, straighten his tie, and he'd be quite nice-looking. That's what they're saying.'

John wondered whether to tell Hooker he didn't want it. At that moment the silence in the big room was broken. It sounded as if someone was making an announcement from the platform at the far end.

'Quick. Back to the condemned cell,' said Hooker. 'They're breaking.'

'Thanks for the drink.'

'Any time.'

A minute later the Chairman of the Association entered the room where they were waiting. He was a pleasant-looking curly-haired old man in a high state of nerves. He held a piece of paper.

'I've been asked by the Executive Committee to thank you all for coming,' he said. 'Some of you, I know, have come a long way. We're grateful. Most grateful. We're happy to pay travelling expenses.' A pause. 'I'm also asked to say that we had a most difficult choice. A very difficult choice indeed. We decided that you all have great talents. We think you will all have distinguished political careers. With your charming wives, of course.' He smiled unhappily at the corner of the room where the two ladies sat gripping their chairs. 'But of course we had to make a choice. After all, that's what we are here for, I suppose. Not everyone can win on these occasions. The more's the pity, but there it is. I think you probably all recognize that, as old hands at the game.' There was another and longer pause, while he consulted his bit of paper. Hooker winked at John. The dentist looked desperate. John did not know how he looked.

'But actually it's . . .' a final glance at the paper . . . 'it's Cruickshank.' In a final spasm of nerves he advanced firmly with outstretched hand towards the dentist.

He veered sharply just in time and found John. Hooker shook John's hand next.

'Sorry I didn't lay you odds.'

The dentist also shook hands, fiercely and in silence. The defeated quartet escaped quickly into the darkness. John was ushered towards the door by a sudden swarm of well-wishers. He glanced back at the room, the mugs, the spattered curtainless window, the useless fire. He felt as if he had lived there all his life.

Two local photographers flashed at him in the dark corridor. Somebody flung open the main door. Inside there was a friendly light, heads turned to greet him, and a buzz of pleased anticipation. John had many times entered a room full of cheering people. He found it was quite a different sensation when the person they were cheering was himself.

# CHAPTER THIRTY-TWO

Antony and Helena sat at each end of the sofa in the centre of the three drawing-rooms at No. 10. The sofa had been tilted round so that they could see the Prime Minister through the doorway. He was bathed in bright lights, and assailed by an army of gadgets, like a patient in an operating theatre, now advancing, now retiring. Behind the gadgets, half-lit and sinister, worked the technicians who directed the attack.

'For four hundred years Ireland has blighted and plagued our country. The temptation to cut the link, to abandon the effort, is great indeed.'

The Prime Minister leant forward, both elbows on the desk in front of him, and gazed at the people of Britain.

'It is a temptation we must resist if we are to respect ourselves and if others are to respect us. Rather we must make a new effort, find a new way to stop the killing and bring together the two communities. That is the purpose of the initiative which I have outlined to you this evening. Many people have had a hand in preparing it; but I would like in particular to pay tribute to Paul Bernays for the sterling part which he played.'

Helena snorted. 'Pompous little man. Why waste words on him?'

'We want to keep him quiet,' said Antony.

'You're beginning to sound just like John.'

'If we are to succeed with our plan we shall need the co-operation of the leaders of opinion in Northern Ireland. We shall need the continued devotion and courage of our troops. We shall need a more decisive assurance of support in the House of Commons than we have today. Above all we shall need your support, your understanding, your determination. That is the reason why I yesterday asked Her Majesty the Queen to dissolve Parliament. That is why we are holding an Election on October 17.

'It is always easy to find brave arguments for an act of cowardice. It is always easy to dress up surrender in shining words. That is what Jeremy Cornwall has been doing in recent weeks when he calls on us to pull the Army out of Northern Ireland. He has now dragged the Labour Party behind him down this dishonourable path.

'We have chosen a different path. Patience, determination, courage – these are not always dramatic virtues. But they are the qualities we need in Ireland, in Britain today. We offer leadership and practical policies based on those qualities. Because these are the typical qualities of the British people I am confident in asking for your support.'

'Terrible ending,' said Helena. 'People aren't interested in that stuff any more.'

'What the hell happened to my poem?' said Antony.

'Poem?'

'It was in the first draft. By Larkin. Got smaller and smaller with each redraft. Now sunk without trace.'

'You're out of your mind. Pray God John doesn't get his seat. At least he sticks to prose.'

'A sonnet a day keeps Labour at bay.'

The Prime Minister crooked a finger from his circle of light, now less fierce. Antony went over.

'I'll have to do it again. I stumbled quite badly just before the last para. There's plenty of time before it goes out.'

The BBC producer looked appealingly at Antony. He was thirty-five and almost bald. He had a fierce jutting beard and weak eyes.

'I was explaining to the Prime Minister that though he did stumble at that point it didn't really matter. Made it sound more natural, I think. If we run the whole thing again, it'll be much less spontaneous. Less effective, I should guess.'

'I agree.' Antony found himself sounding brisk. No one had ever asked his view on a thing like this before. 'It sounded perfectly all right.'

'Very well, very well, if you want me to sound like a stuttering fool.' The PM did not need much persuading. 'Sorry about the poem,' he said, standing up from his chair. 'In the end it didn't fit.'

'Helena and I want to talk about your Election programme.'

'Any news from Swindon yet?'

'The Area Agent will ring as soon as they know, or Central Office.' Antony could feel his father's eyes upon him.

'Very well.' The Prime Minister walked through the steel circle of gadgets as if breaking a spell. Their lights and noise quenched, they were no longer formidable. He wandered among the army of acolytes. 'Good-night, thank you so much. Thank you so much, good-night. You'll all stay and have a glass of whisky before you go, won't you? You'll excuse me if I don't stay, I've got a good deal to sort out before tomorrow. I'm most grateful, good-night. Good-night, I'm most grateful.'

Upstairs, it was cold consommé and a fish so smothered in sauce as to be incomprehensible. Antony opened the Vouvray. He had put copies of the draft programme beside all three plates. The points on which decisions were needed were underlined in red.

D−17 Adoption meeting.

D−16 Birmingham.

D−15 Plymouth *or* Bristol.

D−14 ⎫ Scotland. Press conference Glasgow, rally Usher
D−13 ⎬ Hall, Edinburgh *or* Press conference, Edinburgh,
     ⎭ rally, Apollo Centre, Glasgow.

and so on down to D−1, the eve of poll.

Helena served the fish, and launched her attack.

'It's settled then that I should come round with you − as well as John or Antony?'

Antony sat silent. The Prime Minister chewed slowly.

'You'd hate it,' he said at length.

'Of course I'd hate it.' Her long pale face came alight, under the flaming hair. 'I can imagine nothing worse. Noise, shouting, overheated trains, wet cold streets, bloody people. But you know I've got to.'

'Ellerman can come.' The words came slowly.

Helena looked hard at her husband. Antony looked at his plate.

'You'd rather I didn't?' she said slowly.

'I'd really rather you didn't.'

Helena had not touched her fish. She got up and left the room. As she reached the door she pressed the napkin to her face and burst into tears.

The Prime Minister sat very still. His son did not know

him well, but he knew loneliness when he saw it. The telephone rang and Antony went to the study to take it, pausing to let Helena push into her bedroom.

When he came back his father was eating salad.

'Well?'

'That was Central Office. Good news and bad. John has got Swindon East. By two votes, I gather . . . There's an ORC poll in the *Express* tomorrow. Labour five points ahead. And 68% say they want the troops home from Ireland.'

'What was that figure last time?' Helena was forgotten.

'I didn't ask.'

'Fifty-three, I think. They should have told you. It's always the trend that counts, not the figure.'

'I should have asked.'

'Yes, you should. You will next time.'

Antony sat and drank his wine. It was too warm. He thought of Helena, red hair piled on her head, desolate with the napkin against her face.

'Now you're going to be with me, you'd better know about it all.' His father's tone was bleak. 'I have a disease called carcinoma of the prostate gland. At least that's what they think.'

'Cancer?'

'Of course.'

Antony felt useless. Money, sex, drugs, the law – these were troubles well known to him and his friends. Disease was a distant acquaintance, death from disease almost unknown.

'I thought the hospital check was OK.'

'The swelling in the leg went down. I felt better. That was rest, and a drug called stilboestrol. It holds the cancer in check. Tablets, three times a day.'

'And now?'

'The leg hurts again. In the mornings I have difficulty in passing water. This is another symptom they expected. But they can step up the dose. It is still at a very early stage. Even Ellerman can cope. I can carry on without difficulty. The pain only comes occasionally. But you understand why Helena was upset.'

Antony was so shocked by his father's matter-of-fact tone that he forgot to keep his usual distance.

'You ought to be in bed. You ought to be out of here, out

of all this.' He pointed at the papers on the table. 'And yet you've deliberately gone out of your way to call a General Election.' He paused, then added with a tone he had never used to his father before: 'You must resign at once.'

'Resign?' The Prime Minister had found a pear. 'You talk as if I called the Election for fun. It is necessary, and an old man's illness couldn't stand in the way.'

'But the old man needn't fight it himself.'

'That depends if he wants to win it.' He peeled the pear with exact symmetry. 'If I resigned, Mercer would be elected Leader. He would lose the Election because he would lose his head. I shall keep mine and win.'

'Even if you do, you . . .'

'Yes, of course, I shall give up. Within six months at the latest. But that should be enough.'

'And if we lose?'

'Then I go at once. Everyone can then say it's all my faullt. The Party, having got rid of me, will quickly recover.' He finished his glass. 'You see, I have tried to think these things through. That is one advantage of not sleeping well.'

He reverted to his usual matter-of-fact manner. 'And now, if you've had enough to eat, we ought to finish the draft programme. I would like to switch round D – 4 and D – 2, so that the last big rally is at Oxford. Two marginal seats there now after redistribution, and the Town Hall is magnificent for a rally . . .'

Half an hour later they had finished. Despite himself, Antony had enjoyed it.

'Well, off you go, Antony. William Pershore's gone to bed, so I think I can get a car to take you home without running into trouble. Earls Court, isn't it, nowadays?'

As Antony put on his raincoat in the tiny landing the Prime Minister said:

'Poor Helena. But you can't see me sitting quiet with her in the country for the rest of my life. Which of us d'you suppose would hate it more?'

# CHAPTER THIRTY-THREE

Of course winning was fun – even winning the chance to fight a safe Labour seat. Waiting to lose had been a momentary loss of nerve. After the long drive back to the flat in Notting Hill Gate John was tired but still happy. The one sadness was that he had no one to tell. Loneliness was having no one waiting at the end of a telephone. He thought of Clarissa.

There she was. Not an image, but a substantial shadow leaning against the wall by the tall dark green plant outside his front door. Even in silhouette he could see that her hair was untidy. She drooped, and looked as if she had been there a long time.

'Where have you been?' There was no particular tone in her voice. She would not be interested in the answer.

'Come in.'

He felt in the darkness for the right shape of key, opened the door and turned on the light. Against the bare orange walls of the entrance passage she looked terrible. At one stage of the evening she had put on a good deal of make-up, more than he had ever seen, but it was now streaked with tears. She looked messy and middle-aged.

'Come in,' he said again, and led the way down the passage to the small room lined with prints which served as sitting-room and study. He moved a tray with unwashed plate and coffee cup from the sofa. She had often sat there talking about films and books and No. 10. It seemed a long time ago. He was about to sit in the armchair but she motioned him to sit beside her on the sofa.

'What am I to do?' she asked.

He put his arms round her shoulders. She neither flinched nor moved towards him.

'Tell me what's happened,' he said.

'Nothing's happened. William has sent me away. Take a month's leave, he said, while he sorts things out. He won' even let me set foot in No. 10.'

'You know what he's like. It'll blow over.' She said nothing.

'Where are you going to go? What does Antony say?'

She twisted away from him.

'You always ask about Antony. What's the matter with you?'

'I'm sorry.'

'Antony's hooked. I never thought it would happen – he's only interested in his father. And in the Election, for God's sake.'

'You saw that coming.'

'That doesn't make it better.'

There was a pause.

'You'd better go home, I suppose. Your father will understand.'

'They're away for a month. On a cruise.' Then she added fiercely, 'I want to go back to No. 10. That's all I want. I want to see it through – the Election, the old man, the whole business. It's my life, it's all I am.' She turned towards him. 'Will you help me?'

It was unreal. He put his hand on her knee.

'I'll talk to William in the morning.'

'Thank you, John.' She put her hand on his.

'What exactly do you want to happen?'

'I want to take my turn going round with the PM. I want to help. I want to see it through. Afterwards I don't mind. But to be thrown away now, like this, when even Antony . . .'

'I understand.'

'I don't suppose you do. But thanks, anyway.' There was another pause. John did not like to look at his watch. He knew it was between one and two in the morning. He was very tired.

'And now,' she said, 'let's go to bed.'

There seemed nothing more to say. She had never been in his bedroom before except on the way to the lavatory. She turned on the light and took off her sweater. He went into the bathroom, brushed his teeth and put on his pyjamas.

When he came back Clarissa was sitting naked on the bed, her long slim back towards him. When she turned he saw that she had washed the make-up off her face, and was fifteen years younger. She climbed into bed with him. There was

177

just room for them both if they kept close together. He leant over her and kissed her hard on the mouth. Her fingers brushed his stomach as she felt for the top button of his pyjama trousers. For a second he felt not only desire but happiness. The telephone rang in the next room.

'Leave it,' she said. But desire and happiness had gone. He had never left a telephone unanswered in his life. He rolled out of bed and buttoned up his pyjamas as he crossed the room.

'It's the Prime Minister here. Very many congratulations I am delighted. How did it go?'

They talked for a minute about Swindon East.

'You'll be round in the morning? Antony and I covered a good deal of ground tonight, but there's plenty still to discuss before you finally hand over to him.'

'Yes of course. I'll be in about ten. Thank you very much indeed for ringing.'

'Good-night, then, John.'

'Good-night.'

He went back into the bedroom. Clarissa had pulled the bedclothes right up under her chin. A wisp of fair hair had fallen across her forehead. She was fast asleep.


# CHAPTER THIRTY-FOUR


For a fortnight it rained. On elm trees, on hoardings, and in front gardens the blue, orange and red posters were sodden as soon as they were put up. The rain drove at the legs of canvassers in doorways and blotched the marks on their canvas cards. It slashed sideways under the umbrellas at tiny street corner meetings. It soaked three white suits of Jeremy Cornwall's on three successive days. It blurred the windscreen of Mr Wellcome's Ford, so that he ran over a dog in a highly marginal constituency. It drove lady pollsters to weep in high streets because no one would stop to answer their questions.

The rain made the journalists bad tempered as they crowded into the daily Press conference at Conservative Central Office. As the television lights warmed the room a few of them began visibly to steam. Antony decided the Conservatives had made a mistake in bagging the first slot. Nine o'clock was too early for successful mass communication.

Mercer in the chair was too brisk for his own good.

'First question, then. Let's make them a bit snappier today than they were yesterday.'

'Sir James, is it true that Cornwall has decided to tell his supporters to vote Labour?'

'You'd better ask him.'

'What would be your reaction if he did that?'

'That's a hypothetical question.' The old man was not at his best.

'It would do the hell of a lot of damage to Tory chances, wouldn't it?'

'It's always better to have your enemies out in the open.'

'How can you say that when you're already five points behind in the polls?'

'We've got a fortnight to go still. In 1970 Ted Heath was twelve points behind with only two days to go. And he won.'

'How many Tory candidates are paid-up members of the Cornwall crusade?'

'Off-hand I have no idea.'

'Hadn't you better find out?'

No answer. A question from another part of the room, a German, very slowly.

'Mr Prime Minister, is it still your opinion that your Party will emerge victorious from the present electoral conflict?'

'It certainly is, Herr Krag.'

Mercer cut in.

'All the reports we're getting in from the country are of great enthusiasm from our supporters, and an absolute determination to win.'

Antony saw disbelief flicker across the faces around him. He wondered how long it would be before one of them commented in print that the Prime Minister was answering questions sitting down.

179

# CHAPTER THIRTY-FIVE

'Only an hour before we eat. It hardly seems worth going ashore.'

'We must. I particularly want to see the Temple of Demeter.'

'You could go alone.' At home Brigadier Strong accepted without question on all occasions the company of his wife. On their annual cruise he liked to snooze alone in his cabin before dinner.

'There's the stadium too, but that's ten miles inland. Even if we found a taxi we could not get back in time. It really is most tiresome of the captain to bring us in so late.'

'It's not his fault that the engine failed.'

'Of course it is. The Greeks never bother about proper maintenance.'

They had been stationary for almost three hours off a rocky beach, watching the empty brightness of midday gradually refine into the colours of evening, purple on the sea, blue-grey against the rocks, green-yellow against the strips of pasture where goats grazed. The hubbub around the scowling captain had died away, none of the ship's officers would answer questions, and the desultory noises of repair work from the engine room had seemed simply an exercise in public relations. Sir John Witson, the renowned and expensive archaeologist hired for the cruise, had composed himself for a long sleep under the awning. Then to everyone's surprise the MS *Kyrenia* was under way. Life and chatter had begun again. Sir John had woken and grumbled for his tea. Within an hour they were in harbour, though the captain still scowled.

'I shall go down to the cabin and write to Clarissa. It's odd that there was nothing from her at Athens.'

'She'll be tied up all day and all night with the Election. And anyway the more you educate a girl the less trouble she takes about other people. Least of all her own family, I've always said the same, but you took no notice.'

Indeed she had, and indeed he hadn't. Brigadier Strong looked affectionately at his wife. The repetitious arguments and turns of phrase which had once so annoyed him now after forty years bound him more closely to her.

Within reason, of course. He caught sight of the archaeologist, flushed with sleep and ginger biscuits.

'Sir John, could you possibly take my wife to the Temple of Demeter? She's very keen to go, and I've got a letter I must write before we sail again.'

He watched them go down the gangway together, he fat and slow, she tall, thin and faded. Then he went down, lay on his bunk, and slept over his detective novel. There was no point in writing to Clarissa. She would know that he thought about her, and nothing else much mattered.

## CHAPTER THIRTY-SIX

'Is that Redburn 2365?'

'It is.'

'This is Number Ten Downing Street here. Is Miss Strong there to take a call from Mr William Pershore?'

'Clarissa Strong speaking.'

'Oh, Miss Strong, thank you, I didn't recognize your voice. I'll put Mr Pershore on.'

A pause and a click.

'Clarissa.'

'William.'

'Good morning. How are you feeling?'

'There's nothing whatever wrong with me.'

'No, of course not, I didn't mean that. Are you having a pleasant rest?'

'When can I come back?'

'Well, as I explained, the technical position is that you're on leave pending transfer. I'm still discussing it with Basil Proudfoot where you could be posted – taking into account, of course, as far as possible, the preferences which you expressed.'

'I didn't express any preferences.'

'Come now, Clarissa, I don't want to go over all that again. Please remember that this is an open line. You did say that if you had to . . .'

'But there's no reason why I should leave No. 10.' A pause, and then Pershore's voice went a little higher.

'That is a matter of opinion. A matter of my opinion, in fact. But that's not in the least why I am telephoning. I understand that you would like to go with the Prime Minister on one of his Election tours.'

'I want to take my turn with the other Private Secretaries. I don't want to be left out.'

'It's a strange taste.'

Silence. Pershore went on.

'Well, anyway, I have discussed the point with the Prime Minister. He has agreed that, out of old friendship as it were, and without prejudicing the decision about your transfer, he would be glad to have you on the Election roster.'

'Which meeting would I go to?'

'We thought Oxford on the 15th. That's two days before polling day. Antony Percival is of course in charge of the arrangements as Acting Political Secretary. I will get him to send you the details. Is the date convenient to you?'

'Of course.' A final pause. 'William, I'm most grateful to you. I really am.'

'My dear girl, I don't know why you want to go, but you obviously do, and whatever has happened we owe you more than that.'

'Thank you, William.'

'Not at all, not at all. Are you all right down there by yourself in the country? Your parents are abroad, I gather.'

'Yes, on a cruise. But I don't mind. I like being alone.'

'Now, there at last I agree with you. Well, good-bye.'

'Good-bye William.'

Clarissa went back to the man drinking whisky in the drawing-room.

'It's all right,' she said.

# CHAPTER THIRTY-SEVEN

'How many still to come? It's just on half-past.'

'Well, Henry said he would, and give Jill a lift. But if he's overslept or something, she'll be stranded.'

'His car's always breaking down.'

'The Devizes people said it was too early for them.'

There was still more light from the sodium street lighting than from the dawn. John took the big blue rosette from his pocket and pinned it on the lapel of his jacket. It was raw and cold for October. He had originally been promised by his acting agent a team of at least a dozen. The present count, including himself, was four.

'I'll take Gate 4, then. Mrs Davies, would you stay with me?' Mrs Davies, though a fiercely loyal Conservative was a bit muddled. He preferred to keep an eye on her.

'We'll take 5 then.'

'I should move sharpish. The night shift will be out any minute. Half-past six on the dot, I was told.'

And suddenly there they were, grey figures pouring from a dozen doors, tributaries joining a stream which flowed out of the factory with compressed force through the narrow gorge of Gate 4. Their heads were down, collars up against the cold. They moved silently and fast, few even bothering to pause and buy the *Mirror* or the *Sun* from the stand just inside the gate. Outside the gate some turned right to the car park, some pressed on towards the buses which would take them to the council estates on the edge of Swindon or farther afield through the villages of four counties. There was no question of talking to any of them.

'The housing leaflets please, Mrs Davies. And "Common Sense on Ireland". And my own local one with the photograph.'

His fingers grew clammy with cold as he handed them out.

'John Cruickshank, good morning. May I give you one of these?'

'Good morning, I'm John Cruickshank, your Conservative . . .'

John Cruickshank. May I . . .'

'John Cruickshank. Thank you.'

'John Cruickshank.'

Some recognized him from his posters, smiled, said good morning and took the leaflet. Most thrust the leaflet into a pocket and strode on without any reaction at all. Some rejected him without a word. One or two scrumpled up the leaflets and threw them to the ground. Mrs Davies, who was passionate against litter, began to retrieve them from the puddles until John stopped her.

A big man paused.

'What are you going to do about bloody Ireland, then?'

'It's all in here.' A leaflet was thrust forward and ignored.

'Don't want politician's talk. Are you for Cornwall or that bloody old Percival?'

'Percival. After all, he's . . .'

'That's enough. I'm off to my breakfast. Me and my mates will vote Labour, same as usual. If you'd have said Cornwall, some of us'd have to do some thinking.'

'Some of you would have found that hard,' said Mrs Davies to his large retreating back.

'Watch out, here comes the other lot.'

It was the morning shift, coming fast from behind them, most on foot, some on bicycles, for the bicycle shed was inside the gate.

The two opposing streams met in a maelstrom near the gate itself, then quickly sorted themselves out. John and Mrs Davies stood back to back, dishing out leaflets as fast as their numbed fingers would allow. The morning shift moved more slowly, some reading the football page as they walked. Though it was grey, the daylight had prevailed over the street lights. Gradually the movement in both directions thinned out.

'Let's go,' said John. 'It's almost an hour before the clerical workers come. There are only a few dozen of them. Not worth waiting.'

Mrs Davies was disappointed for she had thoroughly enjoyed herself.

'We're going to win,' she said, looking for her gloves. But John, finding them for her, thought different.

184

# CHAPTER THIRTY-EIGHT

'Better loved ye canna' be;
Will ye no come back again?'

A few voices were feebly raised. A mistake by the organist, thought Antony. Edinburgh audiences were most unlikely to sing at the end of a political evening in which they had partaken of no refreshment. Nor was love the emotion which his father aimed at. But otherwise, watching the audience troop out, listening to their high gossiping voices, he judged it had been a good meeting. He had stood at the back of the hall, which was the best place to gauge reactions. There had been empty seats at the back and in the gallery, but not too many. The PM's Press handout had dealt firmly but reasonably with the TUC's threat to hold a one-day strike before polling day as a demonstration in favour of pulling out the troops, with the threat of more strikes later if the Conservatives won. After that his father had gone to give them his basic speech about Ireland, and it had been well received. Not that they agreed with him. Antony could tell that. That particular audience did not want a political solution in Northern Ireland. They wanted a quick bash at the IRA, and then out. But they enjoyed the little cracks which Antony had written into the text – at Wellcome's capitulation to Jeremy Cornwall ('His name suggests he was descended from a doormat, but even in Scotland you can carry ancestor-worship too far') and at Cornwall's white suit ('I know he cannot decide whether he is a pop singer or the Archangel Gabriel, but he must stop trying to play both parts on the same night'.) They had warmed to his peroration about duty and honour, and were now trooping out into the chilly night, not convinced but partly comforted.

The young Press officer from the Scottish Central Office stood in the foyer, clutching a scrap of paper. He recognized Antony and came up to him, some relief showing on his tormented pimply face. Bad news shared is not so bad. It was his first Election campaign.

'Terrible, isn't it?'

The scrap of paper said: 'NOP poll *Daily Mirror* tomorrow. Labour $14\frac{1}{2}$ per cent lead.'

'Has my father seen this?'

'No. It was on the ITN News at Ten. He came out so fast I couldn't reach him.'

Antony grabbed the bit of paper. A lighted sign at the end of the foyer pointed to the Neptune Room up a flight of steps. His father had promised to look in there for a quick drink with the office-bearers of the Edinburgh associations.

The small room, decorated in ochre, was full of people whom he did not know.

'Can I see your ticket please?'

'Is the Prime Minister here?'

'He left a wee while back. He took just the one drink, thanked us all, and was away.'

Antony ran down the stairs. Why had he ever agreed to do this terrible job? On the pavement he saw the Prime Minister's Rover draw out in front of him. He could just see the back of his father's head, thick white hair against the cushion.

He found William Pershore standing beside him. Pershore had chosen to come himself as the Private Secretary on duty for this expedition.

'Anything the matter?'

'Can you take me to the hotel?'

'Of course.' Pershore was quick to sense trouble. The well-trained Government driver in her green uniform was only a few yards away.

The Prime Minister's car was held up going down the Mound by a group of Cornwall's crusaders carrying flaring torches. It took the police several minutes to clear a way, and by that time the car carrying Pershore and Antony had caught up. A demonstrator thrust his torch at the closed window to see who was inside.

'Out! Out! Army out! Percival out!' he chanted.

By the light of the flare Pershore read the scrap of paper.

'The worst yet?'

'Much the worst.'

'You've got another week.'

The car jumped forward, but another group of demonstrators surged shouting across the road and separated them from the Rover. They were two minutes behind the Prime Minister at the Caledonian Hotel.

'Thanks.' Antony jumped out, sprinted across the pavement cleared by the police, and hurled himself at the swing doors. Inside, the spacious entrance hall of the hotel was crowded with journalists and Party workers. He was separated from his father by about forty excited bodies and a cloud of tobacco smoke.

'Excuse me, excuse me, it's urgent.'

Shoving hard, he made good progress. In front of him his father was moving slowly to the foot of the stairs, the tall Inspector watchful to one side. Antony pushed to within earshot, still grasping the scrap of paper.

As the Prime Minister began to climb the stairs a tall man with a black moustache spoke loudly through the banisters. Antony recognized him from the Press conference as the political correspondent of the *Glasgow Herald*.

'Just before you go, Prime Minister, what comment do you have on the latest NOP poll out tomorrow?'

The Prime Minister stopped, and a silence began to spread round him.

'I have not seen it,' he said slowly.

'It gives Labour a 14½ per cent lead. What is your comment on that?'

The old man stood absolutely still, no expression on his face. Antony could see a muscle twitch at the side of his mouth. At length he said slowly: 'I never comment on polls. You should know that by now.' His face was grey, or was it just the swirling tobacco smoke?

'Doesn't it show that your campaign is a failure?'

'Has there ever been such a wide gap between the main Parties with only seven days to go?'

'What changes are you planning in your campaign strategy?'

'Is it true that you are throwing in your hand?'

'What about the TUC's threat of industrial action?'

The questions beat upwards at him as he slowly climbed the stairs, but he made no further reply.

In the sitting-room of his suite he lowered himself into the armchair.

'I tried to warn you,' said Antony. 'We were held up.'

The Prime Minister sat in silence. Outside in the street they could hear the rhythmic chanting of the demonstrators. The old man seemed to shrink into the chair, just as he had that evening in the guesthouse at Rajnaya.

Pershore joined them, for once at a loss.

'The polls have often been wrong,' he said.

'Would you like to see Ellerman?' asked Antony.

'It's late,' said the Prime Minister eventually. 'I shall go to bed.'

He tried to raise himself, failed, succeeded the second time, and shuffled into the bedroom. He closed the door sharply behind him, and they knew that he did not want their help.

'Lord Salisbury said it was an accursed profession,' said Pershore.

They looked around them at the flowers, the fruit, the telegrams, the red boxes, the autograph books of Edinburgh schoolchildren open for signature, the champagne unopened in the ice bucket, and the other meaningless trappings of power.

# CHAPTER THIRTY-NINE

'Tonight Election Parade interviews the most colourful figure in the whole Election campaign, the man the politicians love to hate. Where will he throw his influence on polling day? Is he at heart Conservative or Socialist? Or is the man they once wrote off as a glamour boy bringing a whole new dimension into British politics? Here in the Election Parade studio with Simon Searing is the leader of the famous crusade, Jeremy Cornwall.'

A grossly biased introduction, thought John, sitting in the small upstairs residents lounge of the Marquis of Granby, Swindon. He had finished his canvassing early. It had been a gloomy evening, and his shoes were wet. There was no fire, for the television set squatted where the hearth had been in the days when this was the best bedroom of a staging inn.

Simon Searing was immensely good-looking, and at thirty-three had obeyed the BBC house rule which lays down that television interviewers should not grow old. He specialized in long eyelashes and a soft voice. For once Jeremy Cornwall wore a dark suit. Alongside Searing he looked hard and virile.

'A great many people support you up and down the country, Jeremy, but they are puzzled about what you are aiming at in this Election. You yourself are of course standing again in Mid-Staffordshire, but you, or rather your crusade, are not putting up candidates anywhere else. Why is that?'

'Let's get this absolutely straight from the start. We in the crusade are not a political party, playing a game for jobs in the Cabinet, knighthoods and all the rest of it. We are working for just one purpose – to rescue the British Army from the Irish bog.'

'But how are people going to support you if you don't put candidates into the field?'

'Well, I'll tell you a secret, Mr Searing. I have had a thousand special crusade badges made in silver. I've brought one along to show you. Here it is.'

He held a badge towards the camera so that everyone could see the fist gripping the torch. Searing stretched out a hand for it.

'No, no, Mr Searing, you are not entitled to one. They cost seven pounds apiece and I've paid for them myself. These badges will be sent in the next three days by me personally to any candidate of any party who commits himself to our cause. In writing, of course. The candidates who can show the crusade badge get the crusade's support. The others had better watch out.' He scowled, and the black lock fell across his forehead.

'And you yourself? You'll be voting in London as usual?'

'I shall vote for the Labour candidate in Chelsea. I have seen his Election address. A badge is already on its way to him. Badge No. 2, in fact.'

'And badge No. 1?'

'I'm a modest man, Mr Searing, don't press me on that.'

'What do you say about the violence associated with the crusade? What about the assaults on bystanders in Edinburgh the other night?'

'I'm a man of peace and a man of law, Mr Searing. I don't condone any of that. But there's one thing you've got to understand. Our people are angry, very angry indeed, so it's not surprising . . .'

And so it went on. Searing was giving him a soft ride, keeping his claws sheathed. The Prime Minister had been wrong. Cornwall was still just as effective on television as at a rally. Tonight he was no showman or glamour boy angling for headlines, just the plain man against the politicians.

John took off his shoes, and thought of St Ethelburga's Crescent, where he had just spent an hour. They had not minded him on the doorstep with the blue rosette, indeed he was part of the accepted paraphernalia of an Election. A few had not answered the bell, though he had seen the light behind the curtains and heard the shrieks and giggles from the quiz show which had them in thrall. But most had come to the door, been glad of a word or two about nothing in particular, and accepted his bits of paper. It was an ageing council estate, one fifth Conservative, two-fifths Labour and the rest Don't Know, which usually meant Labour-but-don't-want-to-hurt-your-feelings. In the next few days the sitting Labour member would get Cornwall's badge, and with it a bonus of a thousand, maybe three thousand votes. Enough probably to turn John's defeat into disaster.

Searing did not know or care about policies. Personalities were his mainstay. He had four minutes to go. He began to purr.

'Let me put one question which I know many people are asking. What are your own personal feelings now towards the Prime Minister? After all, you still call yourself a Conservative, he is the Leader of your Party, there must be a real personal . . .'

'It's not a question of personalities . . .' In Searing's experience they always said that. It damn well would be a question of personalities by the time he'd finished with it.

'I must press you on that, Jeremy. How do you now here this evening feel towards the Prime Minister?'

John saw Cornwall hesitate. He recognized the signs. The man was thinking of saying something which he had no intention of saying when he entered the studio.

Cornwall plunged.

'Sir James Percival is a distinguished man. I admire him and I like him. But he is an old man, a tired man . . .' A final second of hesitation. 'He is also a very sick man. I am reliably told that he is suffering from a form of cancer which is bound to end his life within a year. That is not the man I want to see as Prime Minister.'

Even Searing looked scared. John guessed that the producer was gesticulating, offering him another minute beyond the set time to exploit his breakthrough. But Searing did not know what to do with it. The cat had finally found the cream, and was drowning in it. John saw him give a slight shake of the head.

'And so on that fascinating note we must say good-night from Election Parade. Thank you very much, Jeremy Cornwall. Thank you for listening. Good-night to you all.'

Jeremy Cornwall began to speak again, but there was no sound except the fragment of the *1812 Overture* which Election Parade used as its envoi.

John ran out of the room and down the stairs towards the telephone. He was halfway down the stairs when the lights failed. In his fatigue and excitement he had forgotten. the power worker's union had announced a three-hour blackout that night to demonstrate their democratic support for the Labour Party and the crusade.

\*

*A spokesman at No. 10 Downing Street categorically denied last night an allegation on a television programme by Mr Jeremy Cornwall that the Prime Minister was suffering from the advanced stage of a malignant disease. The spokesman recalled that the Prime Minister had had a thorough check-up during the summer, and pointed out that he was now engaged in an energetic Election campaign. The spokesman also denied reports that Sir James Percival would be issuing a libel writ against Mr Cornwall. 'A lot of strange things are said in an Election,' he said. 'It doesn't do to take them all too seriously.'*

# CHAPTER FORTY

The evening of Sunday October 13 was raw, and in advance of the darkness a pale mist obscured the downs and the tops of the beech trees. John parked his Mini under the tulip tree in the forecourt of Chequers. He jammed back into his pocket the security pass which he had had to show at three different police checkpoints in the last three minutes. Because he was ten minutes early for the meeting which the Prime Minister had summoned to discuss tactics he walked through the side door into the garden. There had been no frost, but the remaining roses were mildewed and battered with rain. There was a broken deck-chair half-tidied away by the wall. Because of the Government's fuel economy campaign to counter the rash of political strikes no lights had yet been turned on in the house. Both the miners and the power workers had already held twenty-four hour strikes in favour of the crusade, and had threatened to do the same again without notice. John imagined the Prime Minister, battered and ill, groping round the darkened rooms. Antony would presumably be at the meeting. He wondered whether Helena had deigned to overcome her dislike of Chequers. He wondered why everything in life was moving downhill at such speed. He wondered whether it would ever be summer again.

He heard a car scrunch on the gravel and returned to the forecourt in time to join Joe Mercer on the steps. The moment they pulled at the bell the front door was opened by the pleasant-faced housekeeper, Mrs Jennings, and they were made welcome.

Antony stood in the great hall, now dimly lit by two standard lamps. There was no fire in the hearth. John, who had not seen Antony since the Election was called, thought he had lost his poise. He looked dishevelled and shrunken in a big purple sweater with a high neck.

'Have a drink.'

'It's only half-past five.'

'My sun set long ago.'

He pulled a whisky flask from his hip pocket, and half-filled a teacup on the floor by the chair where he had been sitting. He jerked the flask invitingly at Mercer.

'No. What's the truth?' John saw that Mercer was tense.

'The truth?' Antony swayed slightly and stumbled against the huge elephant's foot presented by Theodore Roosevelt to Lord Lee of Fareham long, long ago.

'About your father's health.'

'You read what No. 10 put out last night.'

'That's why I am asking for the truth.'

Antony took a grip on himself.

'My father may have cancer of the prostate gland. They were not sure in the summer. They are pretty sure now. What they don't know is how long it will take. It's moving very slowly. It might be six months. Or two years.'

'Treatment?'

'There's a drug, tablets three times a day. That holds it up. Plus pain-killers, of course. But the pain is only intermittent. It was bad last night.'

Mercer looked round the dark hall, the minstrel's gallery, the huge pictures dim in the gilt frames. John wondered if it was the glance of an heir-apparent taking stock of his inheritance. But that was not the nature of the man; and anyway the inheritance seemed damned.

Bross and Newings came out of the shadows. They had shared a car from London, and had been quarrelling. Not that you could tell this from Bross, who was sleek and calm as ever. He wore a dark suit with a dark red shirt. But Newings, in a sports jacket and grey flannels, was tired and ruffled. Down in Devon a Liberal with a beard was said to be running him close. He would be grudging the time away from his constituency. Bross's seat in Surrey was safe.

'I'm still not persuaded. In spite of all you say, I've a mind to resign, if he doesn't quit.'

'There would be no point in either gesture,' said Bross.

'How can you say that? You were the most cautious of all at the Carlton that lunchtime. And we didn't even know then how ill he was.'

193

Bross took no notice. He advanced into the light and greeted John.

'How is it at Swindon, then?' He did not wait for an answer, but turned and shook hands with Joe Mercer. It was an odd gesture for two Englishmen who met frequently. The two men were supposed to dislike each other. John felt oddly comforted.

Newings continued to sound off. His lawyer's calm seemed gone for good. In his annoyance he knocked off the central table one of the candles left there in case the lights failed.

'He's landed us in an impossible position,' he said loudly. 'We owe it to the Party to tell him so.'

'Good evening, gentlemen. I apologize for interrupting your campaigns. I thought we ought perhaps to have a talk.' The Prime Minister's voice came from the dark of the gallery above them. He must certainly have heard Newings's last remark.

A bottle of champagne was opened for them in the White Parlour. The housekeeper turned on all the lights in that small elegant room, beech logs glowed in the grate, and for the moment it was possible to believe that all was well. The Prime Minister sat in silence in his usual chair, staring at the bubbles in his glass. Like Newings, he wore a tweed jacket and grey flannel trousers. John could see no particular change in him, but he knew why that was. An Election campaign gave a shock of energy to everyone who took part. The nearer the top you were the greater the electric urge you received. Even a sick man could carry on until it was over.

They none of them knew in the least what the Prime Minister would say. They were all in uncharted waters. Antony felt that of all the men in the room he knew his father least.

'There are always on these occasions two matters to consider.' The Prime Minister spoke in his flattest most practical voice, as if introducing a particularly minor item on the Cabinet agenda. 'There are men. There are measures.' He paused. 'Men come first. You can all guess the truth. I am ill. Not so ill that I cannot carry on for the present. But ill enough to die within a year or perhaps two. So the question arises: should I resign now?'

They sat in silence. A log fell in the grate.

'You can't,' said Mercer. 'It would kill you at once, and it wouldn't save us.'

'Very practical,' said the Prime Minister. 'David?'

'I agree,' said Bross. 'We are likely to be defeated. If you go now we shall be annihilated. People would never understand why we let you hold an Election at all in these circumstances.'

'And do you understand?'

David Bross took the glasses off his long nose, breathed on them, and wiped them with a silk handkerchief.

'I do not recall that we had much choice,' he said evenly. Newings butted in.

'Why *did* you do it, though? I've been loyal to you all my life, but I find this hard to take.'

'When people begin to talk about their loyalty I reach for my bullet-proof waistcoat,' said the Prime Minister. 'There will be time enough for explanations later. Do you think I should continue?'

'I'm tired and worried,' said Newings. 'I think I'm going to lose my seat. I can't think straight. You mustn't pay attention to me.'

Antony had slipped out of the room.

The Prime Minister did not consult John, who sat on a hard chair just behind the main circle.

'And measures?'

'Even more so,' said Mercer. 'To change the Irish policy now would be unthinkable.' He ran his hand fiercely back through his thick carroty hair.

They all agreed. This time John was asked for his opinion. He had an idea, nursed all the way from Swindon.

'Shouldn't we try to bring Paul Bernays back? He has quite a following, you know, but he's lying very low, refusing to appear on the box or speak outside his constituency. It would make a big impact.'

'Certainly not.' Mercer often spoke before he thought. His instinctive reactions were those of a grassroot Conservative. It was always useful to know them, even if he later abandoned them himself. 'It was Bernays who messed it all up. If it hadn't been for him, we would be happily coasting along.'

'That's no reason why he shouldn't be asked to clear up his own vomit.' David Bross as Chief Whip had suffered most from Bernays's defection. But he never allowed resentment (or indeed gratitude) to outweigh calculation. 'You could bring him back into the Cabinet as Minister without Portfolio for the time being. That wouldn't upset the others.'

'Tony?'

Newings swallowed.

'I suppose so. Not that he deserves it. Do you know, he wears that stiff white collar for canvassing in a cattle market. A neighbour of mine saw him at Devizes last Friday. But he carried weight, more's the pity. Bring him back, if you can.'

'You can't.' Antony stood in the doorway. 'I've been watching the news in the study. Bernays has issued a statement advising everyone to vote only for candidates who favour withdrawal from Ireland.'

'Including Labour candidates?'

'Particularly Labour candidates.'

'Just like Cornwall, then.'

'Just like Cornwall, except that Bernays argued mainly on the grounds of expense.'

'It's the blood, it's not the expense that will beat us,' said Mercer.

It was the second time someone had mentioned defeat. There is usually a rule in politics that however grim the evidence you dismiss the possibility of losing, until of course you have lost. The Prime Minister stared at the fire.

Blow on blow on blow, thought Antony. The harder they strike, the less impact they seemed to have on his father. Since Edinburgh the old man had been very silent. Even today in discussion with his intimates he was saying little. Perhaps he felt that he had no intimates any more. Perhaps he felt that he no longer had a son. He did not look particularly ill, or even particularly tired. He was simply receding from the real world. Or perhaps he was receding from the unreal world into his own reality.

For the first time for ten years Antony had been to church that morning, at Wendover. In the cold emptiness, with the rhythm of the 1662 Communion Service pouring over him, he had gone up to the rail for his father, not for himself. Back at Chequers with the scrambled egg and the terrible headlines he had felt foolish. Hence a day too full of whisky.

He broke the silence.

'You need to decide the form of the last broadcast. Are you going to let the BBC produce it, or call together our own team? They're standing by, but there's not much time to get everything together by Tuesday night.'

He succeeded in pushing them all on to something practical. For half an hour they talked. The whole Cabinet would be asked to concentrate exclusively on the Irish question in the remaining four days of speeches and broadcasts. The private in-depth surveys showed that this was the most important issue in the public mind, and the worst for the Conservatives. There was no point in talking about anything else. The Prime Minister, having recorded the final party political broadcast, would drive to Oxford for his last rally on Tuesday night, then spend Wednesday and polling day itself in his constituency.

'The meeting at Oxford's supposed to be at lunch time,' said the Prime Minister.

'We'll have to change it to the evening.'

'They won't like that. Mean a lot of telephoning.'

'I don't think we can help that. You'll need the whole day on the broadcast,' said Antony.

'Who'll be with me, then?'

'I will, of course,' said Antony. 'And remember you agreed that Clarissa should be on duty on Tuesday.'

'So I did.' But his mind was elsewhere.

'You say that Bernays concentrated on the expense?'

'Yes. It was folly to waste all that money in Ireland when there were so many uses for it here. Plenty of figures, he's always good at them.'

'That poem. Have you got it?' He turned to John.

John knew at once what he meant.

'Larkin's poem. The one you cut out of the broadcast?'

'Yes, yes. It didn't fit there. It would fit now. Do you have it with you?'

'My copy's in London.'

'Work it out with Antony. I'll use it on Tuesday.'

They talked for another half an hour, the Prime Minister much more alert and interested. The time came to go. They put on their coats in the hall. The raw wind slashed in through the front door when Mrs Jennings opened it to see if the two official cars had come round from the back.

Mercer, bold with champagne, said something which had been in all their minds.

'You'll make sure Helena looks after you, won't you? I'm sure she will if she understands it all. It's not a week a man should face alone unless he has to.' Mercer's wife was calm, pleasant and necessary.

The Prime Minister stood in the gloom. They could see no expression on his face. Certainly there was none in his voice.

'It appears that my wife has chosen this moment to go off with Lord Cloyne. To Cannes, I believe. Good-night. It has been very good of you all to come. Good-night and good luck.'

John thought of the damp mottled roses and the broken deck chair on the terrace. The wind in the forecourt was cold enough for mid-winter. He wondered again if to that house summer could ever return.

## CHAPTER FORTY-ONE

She looked pretty from a distance, dazzling white against the sea and the purple line of rock which was the arm of the harbour. At the beginning they had been fond of her. They had forgiven her first mishaps. But now it was clear that the MS *Kyrenia* would not move again this season, and affection had turned to anger.

Most of the passengers were in the small sweaty tourist office on the quay. It carried among other names the sign of Byron Tours, the cruise company, and that at least gave them someone new to complain to.

'I insist on an immediate refund.'

'Nothing but delay and deceit.'

'Hire cars' . . . 'book us on a first-class flight' . . . 'book us in a first-class hotel in Athens' . . . 'my insurance' . . . 'my luggage' . . . 'my travellers' cheques' . . . 'my wife.'

The angry English hubbub surged over the fat man behind

the counter. He had two things to say, and he said them often. There was a bus, which would take them to Athens. If necessary two, three, buses. There was a plane which would take them to London. No, he did not know when the plane would go. He did not know the answer to any of their other questions. All these matters could be resolved in Athens. For the moment the important, the essential thing was that they should collect their luggage and board the bus and go away, far far away with their angry voices and complicated problems, from his peaceful harbour.

One by one they retired. Brigadier Strong had an afterthought. He walked quickly back into the office and it was five minutes before he rejoined his wife. She had sat herself in a little cafe, spurning Coca-Cola and mourning the Temple of Demeter.

'Sorry to be so long. I made that chap promise to send a telegram to Clarissa. Better let someone know we're cutting it short.'

'Where did you send it?'

'Redburn. She might be there this weekend. God knows where she lives in London now.'

'She'll be too busy with the Election to go down and air the sheets for us.'

'I expect so. But it's better to let her know.' They set out to find the bus.

Back in the office Sir John Witson was the only Englishman left, and the only one of the fat clerk's visitors who was in good humour. His contract as lecturer and high-class guide held good for three weeks until October 31. He always made sure the contracts were drafted in this way. The collapse of the MS *Kyrenia* gave him ten days of highly-paid leisure. The clerk helped him with his hotel bookings. Athens first, then Istanbul.

Then the clerk said:

'Can you help me, Sir Witson?'

'Of course, of course, what can I do?'

'The telegraph from here is, as you English say, rather cold.'

'Rather cold?'

'Not warm.'

'Oh, not so hot.' Sir John chuckled at his own cleverness. 'Well?'

199

'There is a message . . .'

Sir John read Brigadier Strong's scribbled note.

'Very well, very well, I'll send it from Athens.'

'Thank you so much. It is most kind.'

'A pleasure, a pleasure.'

Because his other pockets were full, he put the note behind
the handkerchief in the breast pocket of his light grey suit,
and rammed it down. He did not see it again until he prepared his suit for the cleaners back in the Woodstock Road,
Oxford. That was a fortnight later.

## CHAPTER FORTY-TWO

'Telephone for you.'

The committee-room was crowded with John's supporters.
Three days from polling day, they were in good humour. On
their tweed jackets they wore blue rosettes with 'Carry on
Cruickshank' printed at the centre. The second cup of tea
quickly followed the first, and the buzz of conversation grew
thicker. It was not that the national Election news was any
better, or their own canvassing returns particularly cheerful.
But over three weeks they had become a team, they were in
a fight, and the fight was near its close. Also, they liked John.
After tea, before it got too late, he was going to visit two old
people's homes. He had just come from the mothers collecting their children outside the biggest primary school. A few
of those present were going to the Prime Minister's rally at
Oxford, but most would be out again on their rounds.

The telephone in the corner was shielded from the noise
by a glass panel, but it was not enough. John could not at first
identify the excited voice at the other end.

'Sorry. I didn't catch that, who is speaking?'

'It's Roger Strong. Strong, Strong, STRONG, blast it,
can't you make them shut up, it's Clarissa's father.'

'Oh yes, good afternoon, sir. What can I . . .?'

'Look, something very odd has happened. I can't explain

on the phone. I rang your agent, he said you'd be there. Can you come over straight away?'

John thought for a moment that the Brigadier must be calling from Greece. Certainly the crackles suggested hundreds, if not thousands of miles. Someone thrust his cup of tea round the panel. There was nowhere in the booth to put it down. He lowered it to the floor, banging his head on the coin box as he stood up again. He missed part of the next few sentences.

'. . . blasted engine broke down, had to call it off and come back here. Got here half an hour ago, and found an extraordinary thing. That fellow Barran was here. Barran, Barran, BARRAN, you know, the man Clarissa used to . . . that's right, I told you. My study is full of papers, plans, drawings, I can't make head or tail of them. No, no sign of Clarissa, not a word, though we sent a telegram. Barran ran off as soon as we appeared, through the window, blast him, must have had a car handy, I suppose. The point is, can you come over here now?'

John could make nothing of this. Clarissa seemed a long way away in time and place. He hadn't thought of her for days. This certainly wasn't the moment to start poring over her emotional affairs with her parents. Blast Barran, certainly, but later.

'I don't think I really can . . .'

'You must, man, you must. There are things Barran left I can't . . .' The line blurred. 'No good going to the police. I'm not a scaremonger. I wouldn't ask unless . . .' They were cut off.

John was sweating from the tea and the enclosed atmosphere. Damn the telephone service. Damn the Brigadier. Damn, damn, damn. The Brigadier would ring back, he supposed. It was the convention that the person who started the call restarted it when the connection was lost. But he couldn't hang around, he had a full evening ahead.

He fumbled for coins, kicking over the tea at his feet. Then he found the Redburn number in his black pocket diary, and dialled it. Engaged. He put down the receiver. The Brigadier must be trying to reconnect. But no call came.

He waited half a minute, then rang the operator. A helpful girl, and she promised to check.

'No, no speech on that line. They must have left the receiver off. It's always happening. I'll try again in half an hour and if it's still engaged I'll ask the Godalming office to send round an engineer.'

Back in the room John munched a biscuit, appetite gone

'Nothing the matter . . . ?'

'No, no, nothing.'

'There's no more news of the PM's health?'

'No, no, he's at Oxford tonight of course.'

'Say what you like, that man's got guts . . . We ought to be going, oughtn't we? I promised you'd be at the Abbeyfield Home by 5.15.'

Watches were looked at, cups drained.

'Just a minute.'

Back in the booth, he dialled again.

It was Mrs Strong's voice, high and fraught, all affectation gone.

'Who, who, who? Oh, John Cruickshank. How on earth did you know?'

'Know what?'

'I've rung the police, they're coming round at once. thought that was best. Where's Clarissa? Is she with you?'

'No . . .'

'I must get hold of her. You must get hold of her for me. can't . . .' She was sobbing.

'Why? Mrs Strong, what has happened?'

His brisk voice pulled her together. After all, she had been married to the Army for thirty years.

'My husband chased that man Barran away. Then he started to telephone someone. As he was on the telephone Barran came back with two other men. They stole my jewel case.' She faltered.

'What happened then?'

'They fired at Roger. Three times, I think. I was in the kitchen. Making scrambled egg. We'd had no lunch, you see and eggs were all there was in the house. The daily lady brought them.' Formality returned. 'Mr Cruickshank, would you please find Clarissa for me, and tell her that her father is dead?'

# CHAPTER FORTY-THREE

Good God, how many more? We're only away for one afternoon.'

Antony and Clarissa were watching the messenger pile red
boxes into the two Government cars, the Prime Minister's
specially built Rover, and the Ford which would follow with
the Garden Room girl.

'More than that. He's decided to go to Chequers tonight
and come up early for tomorrow's Press conference.'

'There hasn't been any Government work for days. The
moment you come back the boxes fill by magic.'

'William's been holding a lot back. Trying to spare the PM.
He doesn't think he can hold back any longer.'

'That's because he doesn't know who his boss will be by
Friday afternoon. Awkward to have a lot of unsigned letters
about the place if the wrong man wins.'

'Why did no one tell me you'd changed the time of the
rally? I turned up ready to set out before lunch.'

'You've had a lovely afternoon setting No. 10 to rights.'

Clarissa did not smile. Antony thought she had lost weight.
He looked forward to the drive to Oxford in her company, if
only she would keep her mouth shut. He did not feel in the
least guilty at having left her alone with her troubles. She
valued her independence, and this was part of it. He wondered
if she would let him into her bed at Chequers. Probably not,
but he would try. It would take his mind off the rest of the
mess. He watched the cloth tighten across her back and thighs
as she bent to check that the right boxes were in the front car.

The traffic thinned as they passed Northolt, and the Rover
picked up speed. Antony, sitting on the jump seat in front
of Clarissa, began to feel alarmed. His father had read the
evening papers between No. 10 and the entrance to the
Westway. Then he had read more thoroughly the morning

papers which he had skimmed through at breakfast before the Press conference.

'Polls no worse this morning.' They had in fact converged to give Labour a 10% lead. This could not be considered good news. But it was something that no more would be published before polling day.

'You really must clear the speech,' said Antony. 'You've hardly looked at it.'

The draft lay in a buff folder on top of the pile of red boxes which separated the Prime Minister from Clarissa on the back seat. The Press Department in Central Office had a copy. As soon as they reached Oxford Antony would have to ring through the changes which his father had made. Then he would have to get a fair copy typed at the local Conservative offices and rolled off in sufficient numbers for the journalists who actually came to the rally. But the Central Office operation was the essential one. Unless they could get their handout to the London mornings and the agencies within the next three hours Press coverage tomorrow would suffer. Time was already short.

The Prime Minister flipped open the folder.

'Plenty of time,' he said.

Antony knew that his father would make a good many changes once he turned his mind to it. He had only sketched out the theme for the speech to the writing team. Luckily his handwriting, even in a car, was very clear; the girls at Oxford would not have too much trouble.

'Plenty of time,' the Prime Minister said again.

'Any letters to be signed, Clarissa?'

Antony saw that his father was deliberately provoking him. If this meant that he was feeling better, he was glad. But he was provoked all the same.

'For heaven's sake, we're on the motorway already. You can sign the letters on the road to Chequers tonight if they're urgent. Most of them have sat around in those boxes for days already.'

'You're beginning to sound just like John,' said the Prime Minister.

Clarissa laughed. The pitch of her laughter was higher than usual. With relief he saw his father take out his pen and set to work on the draft.

# CHAPTER FORTY-FOUR

There was a queue of cars at the temporary traffic lights where they were constructing the Faringdon bypass. Artificial mountains of wet grey chalk loomed to the right of the old road along which John was driving towards Oxford.

He wondered if he was doing the right thing. He had rung No. 10 at once, but Clarissa had just left with the others. He could have got them to radio a message to the Inspector sitting in the front of the Rover. But that did not seem the right way for a girl, even a career Civil Servant, to learn of her father's death. He had spoken to William Pershore, and Pershore said he would get on to the local police at once and find out what was happening. Pershore had offered to drive to Oxford and tell Clarissa, but John had decided he should do this himself. So he had cancelled his evening meeting and sent off his canvassers, muttering with disappointment, to visit the Abbeyfield Home without him.

The traffic jerked forward. The rain had begun again, and the surface of the road was shiny with the trail of the construction lorries. The car immediately in front of John stalled, and in the time needed to restart the engine the lights turned red again. Through the dusk cars and lorries began to lumber towards John from the other end of the one-way stretch.

He thought about Clarissa. How would she react to this? Almost against his will, he began to analyse Clarissa. She was certainly fond of her father, and would be shattered by his death. But Barran? An old boy-friend of hers, who had been to Redburn years ago with her. Fallen on hard times, he had remembered the house and its possessions. It was easy to find out by local enquiry when the Strongs would be on holiday, and a burglary had been planned. Surprised in the act, Barran had fled. Gathering courage, or being bullied by his colleagues, he had returned with them. They had hoped to overpower

Brigadier Strong but found him armed. In panic they shot him and made off with the jewel case.

It was a possible scenario. John did not believe it for a moment. Nagging at his mind was a question to which he could not find an answer. Why had Clarissa concealed her affair with Barran from the security officers at her first vetting? Pershore had assumed she was ashamed of the past. This was certainly untrue. Clarissa was ashamed of nothing. If she had admitted the affair and if it was all past and over, the story would have done no harm to her prospects. In concealing the story she had taken a considerable risk. Why should she take such a risk, unless there was some life and importance still left in the affair?

And then another nagging thought, quite unconnected with the first. Why had she insisted so hard on taking part in the Election campaign? She had explained it to him. Because of her pride, her passionate feeling about her career, she hated the thought of being excluded. But it did not ring true. Her pride and her desire to keep her career would have held her back once she had met with a first refusal. She knew the ways of Whitehall. If she pressed Pershore too hard, he might give way to the immediate irrational request for the sake of a quiet life, but he would be the less likely to mend her career for her afterwards. She must have seen that. It did not make sense, unless there was some special reason for wishing to be with the Prime Minister. Antony, perhaps. Perhaps it was the only way she could see of fighting her way back into his company. But that didn't fit either.

The lights changed just as another possibility entered John's mind. Terrible, absurd, unlikely. He tried to dismiss it. It stayed. The car behind him hooted crossly. John jerked into gear, drew out from behind the light into the main roadway, and drove to Oxford faster than he had ever driven in his life.

# CHAPTER FORTY-FIVE

'This then is our policy for Ireland, this is our political initiative, this is our hope for the future. But have no doubt about it, this policy, this initiative, this hope will surely fail without the continued presence of the British Army in Ulster.'

There were shouts from several parts of the hall, drowned in a groundswell of applause. The vast majority of the audience had bought tickets in advance for a nominal sum, but two hundred seats had been left unbooked so that some of the crowd outside could be admitted. The stewards had had instructions to keep out those wearing crusade badges, but this precaution had obviously not worked well.

As usual Antony was right at the back of the hall. Clarissa had interpreted her role as an impartial Civil Servant very strictly, and was not in the hall at all. She had retired with the Garden Room girl to a scruffy little dressing-room which had been rigged up as an office for the occasion, with a telephone link to No. 10.

A stout middle-aged woman a dozen rows in front of Antony hoisted herself on to her seat and pulled out a placard from inside her coat. Antony saw only the back of the placard, but the woman shouted 'Bring the Troops Home Now.' There was a scattered clap. Two stewards began to move towards her, but she climbed down and put away the placard. They let her be, but her neighbours on either side began to argue with her.

The Prime Minister took her up. Antony could feel his father dragging out the last reserves of his voice.

'Bring the Troops home, the lady says. What an easy cry. What a tempting prospect. Bring the Troops home, so say I, so say we all. But bring them home when their job is done. To bring them home now would be a disgrace and a disaster.'

He abandoned the rest of the handout. Antony saw the director of the BBC television crew throw aside his copy and order the lights on again. This was going to be news.

'It is not for such an ending that I have spent thirty years in public life. It is not my purpose to preside over the disintegration of the United Kingdom. If that is the will of the British people, so be it. But the Conservative Party cannot sail with that wind, cannot be swept along with that current. We are not time-servers, we are the anchor. We must hold the ship steady till the storm has blown itself out. And so this evening we call to our aid against those who march and shout the stubbornness, the good sense, the steadiness of the British people.'

It was ragged stuff, suddenly improvised from scraps of the past. It was poorly delivered, the old man bending too close to the microphones. It was interrupted by a growing medley of shouts. But it was enough.

For the first time in the Election campaign an audience warmed to the Prime Minister. They had come fifty miles or more, having spent three weeks in rain and cold, on doorsteps, in draughty halls, at street corners, clobbered at regular intervals by bad news, working for the success of the man who now stood behind the massed blue hydrangeas on the stage before them. He was ill, they knew that despite the denials. He was courageous, that was clear enough. Above all he was there with them, not a head on a poster, not an image on a screen, but a human body and a real voice. He had quoted from a poem they had never heard before. He had touched a theme in which they desperately wished to believe. For if the British people were not at heart sensible and steady, of what use were all those tense hours of uncomfortable effort, that work which most of them found embarrassing?

And so with imperfect words and poor delivery Sir James Percival scored a triumph. The audience rose, in ones or twos at first, then the candidates and functionaries on the stage, then the mass. They drowned with their applause the continuing shouts of the opposition. The journalists at the Press tables immediately below the rostrum did not join in. A few looked bored in a professional manner, others began to scribble. The Prime Minister raised his hand in greeting, then for a moment seemed to lose his balance and gripped the lectern with both hands to steady himself. No one seemed to notice. The sweat on his forehead was natural enough, for the Town Hall, which had been dank and cold an hour before, was now warm. The

Prime Minister smiled and waved again. The organist, obeying a signal, cut short the applause with the opening chord of the National Anthem.

As the audience sang and the television lights dimmed the Detective Sergeant from No. 10 pushed his way round the back and found Antony. He was a stout friendly young man who was never ruffled.

'Thank God I spotted you. The reception afterwards has been cancelled. We're going straight back to Chequers.'

'What's happened?'

'Inspector Jones has whistled up the cars. They're on the way round to the side entrance. The PM's not coming out through the hall. You'd better follow me.'

'But what the hell's happened?'

The Sergeant spoke sideways, twisting his head round as he jostled expertly against the outward flow of the crowd.

'Don't really know. May not amount to much. But the Inspector's in one of his flusters. Been an IRA incident in Surrey today, a man got killed, the locals found something which suggested there might be an attempt on the PM at Oxford tonight. So we're getting him away quick. Probably nothing in it.'

'Have you warned Clarissa Strong? She'll need a minute or two to pack up the Government Office.'

'Yes, I told her before I found you. I imagine she'll travel in the second car with me and the girl. That'll leave more room in the Rover.'

'My father will want to sleep.'

'Not much sleeping time between here and Chequers.'

'You'd be surprised.'

They were about to leave the main hall and plunge into the maze of corridors and little rooms which led to the side door. Antony looked back across the disorderly lines of empty chairs. The last of the audience were straggling out in the direction of the main exit. Suddenly he saw a familiar figure.

'There's John Cruickshank.'

He shouted to catch John's attention, but it was too late. John, finding the hall almost empty, turned round and began to push his way back to the main entrance. He looked harassed and dishevelled.

'What on earth is he doing here?'

209

'Oh, there are people from all over, farther even than Swindon.'

'Typical not to get himself a place on the platform. He should have told us he was coming. Have I got time to go and find him?'

'Not really, if you don't mind. I promised the Inspector I'd keep you at the side door till the PM came. He doesn't want to hang about.'

Antony did not press it. John had obviously been looking for someone and would not want to be interrupted. If he had wished to make contact with the No. 10 party he would have done so at the start of the evening.

They did not have long to wait by the side door. Within a minute Clarissa arrived. She carried a red box in each hand. The secretary behind her was struggling with the weight of a typewriter, and quantities of unused paper. Antony and the Sergeant went to help them with their burdens.

Clarissa looked exalted.

'Dramatic, wasn't it?' said Antony.

'Oh, the speech. Did it go well? I didn't hear it. We were busy.'

The Inspector appeared from another passageway. The Sergeant had not exaggerated in saying that he was in a fluster.

'The PM won't be long now. Saying good-bye to the notables behind the stage. They persuaded him to have a quick drink.'

He wrestled with the side door and wrenched it open to see if the cars were there. Two black bonnets gleamed reassuringly through the rain. Two police motorcyclists were revving up in front of the Rover.

'Could I have a minute with you?' The Inspector drew Antony into a dusty black corner, stumbling against a fire extinguisher. He was a cadaverous and normally silent man with whom Antony was not yet quite on Christian name terms. But this, he thought, was the moment.

'Calm down, Eric. You've faced worse alarms before.'

The Inspector, taken aback, laughed.

'It's not that. At least, it's not only that.'

'What is it, then?'

'Sergeant Davies told you something. But there's something you don't know, nor does Clarissa. The dead man is her father.'

This made no sense to Antony.

'It's still sketchy,' said the Inspector. 'The IRA were using an empty house in Surrey as a headquarters. The Strongs' house, in fact. The old Brigadier and his wife came back unexpectedly. I don't quite know what happened, the story's confused, but they killed the old man and escaped, taking some jewels as a cover. The locals were quicker than usual. They caught them at a roadblock. It came out in interrogation, God knows how, that they believed the PM had been killed. Here, this afternoon, at Oxford. Then they shut up like clams. Wouldn't say how, when, by whom.'

'Grief.'

'Grief indeed.'

'This meeting was supposed to be at lunchtime.'

'It was.'

'Christ.'

There was a sound of opening doors and approaching voices.

'Look,' said the Inspector. 'You and Davies go with the PM. I'll take Clarissa in the back car and break the news to her.'

'OK.'

The PM was with them, repeating farewells and thanks to the still pursuing dignitaries.

'Many thanks, a great success, thank you indeed, good-bye, good luck, good luck, good-bye.'

'You'll want to rest on the way home,' said Antony. 'I'll come with you, and Clarissa will follow in the second car.'

'I'm awfully sorry,' said Clarissa. 'Some urgent messages came through during the meeting. I really ought to discuss them with the PM before he gets to Chequers.'

Antony glared at her. 'Messages? He's dead beat, can't you see? He damn near fell over a few minutes ago in front of two thousand people.'

But the Prime Minister had overheard.

'What sort of messages?'

'One Northern Ireland, one Middle East. Both really need a decision within an hour.'

'I'm not as tired as all that. Clarissa, you come with me. Don't let's hang about, Inspector. I thought you wanted us to get going before we're all blown up.'

He was out of the door and into the car, Clarissa following closely with the boxes. The engine started, Antony and the

211

Inspector sprinted, side by side, down the pavement to the second car.

'We'll have to tell her at Chequers, then,' said Antony, as they ran.

'It doesn't really make much difference.'

'I suppose not. But you do it, not me. You've got the facts.'

'Very well.'

Antony collided with a figure in a raincoat just as he reached the second car. It was John.

'What the hell are you up to?'

John was half-winded.

'Clarissa . . .'

'Yes, yes, I know, her father's dead. We've got to go. We'll tell her.'

'Hang on . . .' John had pre-packed the necessary words into two or three sentences, knowing that he might not have long.

One of the police outriders had trouble with his clutch and when John had finished the Rover was still stationary.

Antony ran back towards it. The Inspector and John followed, but more slowly. Antony flung open the door, jerked the jumpseat back into position and pushed his way in. As the Rover drew away, he slammed the door.

'What on earth is happening?' said the Prime Minister.

Antony twisted round to face Clarissa sitting behind him. 'Your handbag,' he said. He had tried to think hard.

'My handbag?'

'Where is it?'

'What are you talking about? I couldn't carry it with all these boxes. It's with Mary in the second car.' The Rover was moving fast down the dark shiny High Street towards Magdalen Bridge. Antony glared around him, baffled.

'What in God's name persuaded you to jump in like that?' said his father. 'You might have been killed.'

Antony gave a shout.

'The boxes!' Four of them were neatly stacked on the seat between Clarissa and the Prime Minister. Clarissa jerked herself upright.

'It's all right,' she said. 'They're all here. I've checked.'

'Open them.'

'You're mad. I can't possibly. There isn't room.'

'Open them up!'

'Antony, you really must behave . . .' said the Prime Minister. 'If you're drunk or . . .'

She must have the box keys on her somewhere. Antony slipped out of his seat and threw himself on Clarissa, feeling for the pockets of her trousers. She twisted sideways and fiddled for a second with the lock of one of the boxes.

'Stop the car,' said Sergeant Davies from the front seat. The pile of boxes began to slither forward as the driver braked. The car skidded into the middle of the road.

There was a crack and the sound of splintering wood, from the Prime Minister's side of the car. On her side Clarissa had the door open. She grabbed Antony's wrist and bit it hard as he tried to hold her. The door swung, and she fell heavily into the road. The following car, trying to brake in turn, struck her on the head.

Antony turned to his father. The old man had fainted. Six inches in front of his slumped figure a heavy arrow with a thick metal tip was embedded in the car's upholstery. The boxes were tipped on to the floor, and the one at the bottom of the original pile had sprung open. Antony could see the crossbow which it contained, the trigger Clarissa had activated through the lock, and the mock red cardboard panel on his father's side through which the arrow had so easily passed.

During the next minute Clarissa Strong died, in silence, half-way up Headington Hill, under the dripping beeches.

CHAPTER FORTY-SIX

Flowers and telegrams, telegrams and flowers. Outside it was yet again a damp overcast morning, the soft greys, greens and browns of the landscape composing together the colour of England. Inside the bedroom there was warmth and light and chatter, centred round an old man in bed with a radio.

'Meriden – Conservative elected. Conservative gain from Labour.

'Southampton, Test – Conservative elected. Conservative gain from Labour.

'Oxford – Conservative gain from Labour.'

'So that speech at Oxford did some good after all.'

'It was far from the best, but it went down well.'

There was a silence. They all knew that it was not the Oxford speech which had caused the Conservative landslide, the greatest since 1931. It was that arrow sticking in the upholstery of the car.

They had brought the old man unconscious to Chequers, put him to bed, cancelled his final engagements in his own constituency, and waited. On Wednesday Helena appeared, and without explanation took control of the domestic arrangements. That afternoon he revived. Prayers, support, enthusiasm were flooding in from all over the country. All through Thursday he improved, and fretted because he could not vote. Now on Friday morning he was cheerful, but somehow distant. He looked small against the pillows. The edge had gone from his voice.

'It was a crib from the Kray Brothers,' said Antony. 'They had a crossbow like that in the 'sixties. In a suitcase.'

'How the hell did you guess?' asked Helena.

'John guessed. Not the box, but Clarissa. If he hadn't appeared I'd have sat tamely in the second car. She'd have scored her bullseye.'

'Why not use a gun?'

'Davies in front might have seen her draw. This way was invisible.'

'But she'd have been caught. Even if she got away from the car.'

'Oh, yes, she'd have been caught.'

'Swindon East, recount still in progress, result expected shortly.'

'Good God, John's doing well. It's always been safe Labour.'

Antony wished John were in the room. He wanted to talk about Clarissa to someone who knew her. He could still feel her warm skin under the silk blouse when he had thrown himself on her in the car. That moment was more real to him than the nights they had spent together. Why had she done it? Not sex, Antony was sure of that. He had never met Barran

214

But no man's face or body or personality would lead Clarissa as far as that. The newspapers were already saying different, but that was their trade.

'She caught a fire,' said his father unexpectedly.

'Like a cold?'

'Like a fever. The Irish fever, the worst variety known to man. It destroys all gentleness, truth, sensible calculation. When Englishmen catch it they get it worst of all. And Englishwomen. She's not the first.'

Again Antony thought of John. He himself was not sentimental. He had desired and liked a girl who was dead. She had let him down with the rest. He would shed no tears. John was different.

'Swindon East. Conservative elected after recount. Conservative gain from Labour.'

The don on duty on the BBC broke in. He was even fatter than in March. 'That really is a most amazing result, a swing, let me see, a swing I make it 12.75 per cent, the clearest illustration we've had yet . . .'

'I'm glad,' said the Prime Minister. 'He'll need a change.'

Pershore and Mercer came into the room, having driven down from London together.

'May I be among the first, Prime Minister . . .' said Pershore. Mercer said nothing, but looked hard at the face on the pillows.

'The champagne is warm,' said Helena. 'This really is a most intolerable house.' She and Mrs Jennings had already quarrelled.

'What's the news from Ulster?' asked the Prime Minister.

'Quiet,' said Mercer. 'The Unionists are piling in big majorities. The Provos are said to be much shaken by what they did. Or rather, failed to do.'

'They always make the same mistake. Violence doesn't scare people when they come to the crunch.'

There was silence, broken by Pershore.

'Prime Minister, you ought to consider the main ministerial appointments, any changes you want to make. The Chief Whip is still at his own count, but he asked me to say . . .'

'No, William, no, quite wrong.'

'But the Queen . . .'

'I shall ask for an audience in a day or two. But meanwhile

I shall advise her to send for the Secretary of State for Defence and ask him to form a government.'

Joe Mercer stood still in the middle of the room.

'You can't resign now. You've won.'

'That's why I can resign.'

'I don't think I can do the job.' Mercer seemed unaware of the other people in the room. He was very tired, and the freckles stood out on his forehead.

'No sensible man is sure of that in advance. No sensible man refuses to try. The Party will elect you without trouble.'

'I shall need help,' said Mercer slowly. 'All the help in the world.

'You for example.' Mercer pointed suddenly at Antony.

'I'll stay as long as you need me.' Antony was amazed at what he found himself saying.

A secretary pushed into the room with a pile of telephone messages. She was asked who they were from. Lord Cloyne, the Lord Mayor of London, the German Chancellor, Mr Jeremy Cornwall . . .

'What does he say?'

'Very many congratulations on a splendid triumph.'

'A first priority,' said Mercer, 'is to find an Attorney General who can get that man behind bars.' Pershore and several others gathered round him to comment. Sir James was left alone, in the bed that was too big for him.

The Prime Minister is dying, thought Antony, long live the Prime Minister. He caught his father's eye and found a sardonic glint reflecting the same thought. Then the old man turned away towards the window. He seemed absorbed in the square of light, the shape of a beech tree, and the sparrows chattering to each other in the creeper.